NIGHT CAME WITH MANY STARS

ALSO BY SIMON VAN BOOY

FICTION

The Secret Lives of People in Love: Stories
Love Begins in Winter: Stories
Everything Beautiful Began After
The Illusion of Separateness
Tales of Accidental Genius: Stories
Father's Day
The Sadness of Beautiful Things: Stories

NONFICTION

Why We Need Love
Why Our Decisions Don't Matter
Why We Fight

CHILDREN'S FICTION

Gertie Milk & the Keeper of Lost Things
Gertie Milk & the Great Keeper Rescue

NIGHT CAME WITH MANY STARS

 A NOVEL

Simon Van Booy

GODINE

BOSTON | 2021

Published in 2021 by
Godine, Publisher
Boston, Massachusetts

LIBRARY OF CONGRESS CATALOGING-IN-PUBLICATION DATA
Names: Van Booy, Simon, author.
Title: Night came with many stars : a novel / Simon Van Booy.
Description: Boston : Godine, 2021.
Identifiers: LCCN 2020050053
ISBN 9781567927030 (hardback)
ISBN 9781567927047 (ebook)
Classification: LCC PR6122.A36 N54 2021 | DDC 823/.92--dc23
LC record available at https://lccn.loc.gov/2020050053

First Printing, 2021
Printed in the United States of America

This book is dedicated to
Alfredia, Samuel, Sam, and Uncle Rusty

AUTHOR'S NOTE

This work would not have been possible without the love, friendship, and family stories entrusted to me over three decades by the members of one family from rural Kentucky.

NIGHT CAME WITH MANY STARS

CAROL

1933

AFTER CHECKING FOR his truck in the front yard, Carol hurried downstairs to scour the cupboards for some breakfast. She sang because the house was empty. Her voice filled each room like invisible writing. Finally, under the stairs, in a crate hidden by some Model T tires, she discovered flour in a round tin the government had given them last year. She carried it to the kitchen table, then went outside to the well, still barefoot and moving quickly through the wet, nodding grass and green weeds. Carol knew the water was cold from how the rope smelled in her hands. The bucket glugged from a black pool fed by a slow river that was even deeper than the bones of her grandpa, who had died in a plowed field with no sound, just a quick folding up into the brown waves. Carol could hardly speak then. But she remembered the body being brought to the house with his face the color of winter.

Her father sold the land after that. Put down the old man's tools and picked up a bottle. A deck of cards. A gun when necessary.

Carol hauled the full bucket inside, trying not to spill. Her daddy would return soon, and like a dark spirit see through every fallen drop, as if each were an eye and her life a succession of small, glaring mistakes. She had woken up hungry with the desire for an egg. But the chickens were long gone; a scar on her back proved it. Sometimes Carol reached around and fingered the scar, pushed on the memory knitted beneath. The henhouse door had been left open and coyotes got in. The morning her father had found it empty, he yanked and ripped at the coop until it rose like a stiff net. There was spit whipping from his mouth as he pulled at the frame, snapping thin ribs of wood. Carol had squeezed into a kitchen cupboard where she could smell the sweat from behind her knees. She thought about crawling under the porch, but the darkness there, the rotting planks and those limp, eyeless creatures roaming the damp soil was terror of a different kind. When her daddy came to a wood slat that wouldn't break, his rage changed course and he followed it into the house, eyes churning with fury.

That was years ago now, though Carol still liked to imagine the coyotes' eyes glowing with careful intent as they carried her father's birds, wet in their mouths, to a place more smell than touch.

When Carol outgrew the cupboards she made for the deep woods, where she could be lost without being lost from herself. They were a refuge, an exhalation—except when snow lay thick and drifted and the cold tore at anything it could touch. Then, Carol waited for spring the way a person waits for some beloved friend who has already begun the long journey home. At the end of winter, with the cold still loose but weak, Carol would enter the woods, wade through currents of dead leaves, watching for a single eye of color that meant it was close. She wondered where those early flowers came from, how they knew the moment to blink their eyes in the soil.

A small clearing in the forest was Carol's favorite place. She could lie on her back beneath the blank canvas of sky. When her mother was alive they would spread a yellow cloth, then sit and eat apples. Carol cannot remember anything her mother said, only the sound of her voice, and that she sometimes took off her shoes and unfastened her hair so that it tumbled like ribbon upon her shoulders and neck.

6

. . .

Carol found some dry branches near the back door and broke the wood into pieces. Then she lit a fire in the stove and mixed flour, baking powder, and the remnants of butter lifted from the dish with her finger. When the fire was really going, Carol used a rag to drop open the stove's heavy door. Heat flooded the room as she slid in the greasy pan. There was nothing to do after that but sit and wait with her cotton doll, Mary Bright, hoping her father would not return before her biscuits were ready. He said she was too old for the doll, but Mary Bright disagreed and would not be put away. Carol also had to hide the fairy picture she had pinned up by her bed—the one that came alive when the moon breathed on it.

Fire cracked the bones of sticks. Carol imagined her doll's bones tucked safely into plump, cotton flesh.

Then she waited. Staring at flames that flickered on the surface of her eyes. The grease in the pan was melting quickly. The biscuits would rise up from the heat and light. Like Jesus, Carol thought, our savior. She tried to remember his eyes from the Bible pictures at school. But years had passed since she'd sat in the classroom, her feet resting on dusty floor planks.

The smell of cooking biscuits soon filled the kitchen. Carol imagined hammering, and the reluctant hands of carpenters putting his cross together. The wood had once been just an innocent tree, she thought. Before that, a seed in the earth like a tiny eye about to open.

Carol stroked her doll's hair. Jesus had flowing locks, she thought. He loved ever'body, but that wasn't enough. They killed him anyway. People watched it happen, as though they had something to gain. She thought about those people, wondered where they went after. Home to meals they ate with bare hands? Could they sleep that night after what they had seen? Or did they lay awake in their straw beds, suspended over sleep, crucified themselves by pity for those ebbing bodies on the hill?

The look on Jesus's face in the darkness, thought Carol, with no one watching, would have been the pain of disappointment. She knew it well. Maybe all fathers needed forgiving for what they did, or what they didn't do. Even the good ones, like her granddaddy, whose death, her mother once said, set free the pain he had fought to save them from.

Carol folded Mary Bright's apron two times, then three. Tried to feel the numb hands and numb feet that Jesus himself must have felt on that day of his crucifixion. Once they had been children's feet, small and warm like baking biscuits. It was his momma Carol felt most sorry for. She had promised to keep him safe. He was her little baby. Her pain was the worst of all because it was for someone else. She would just learn to live with it, like a shadow no one else could see.

Carol's mother had sewn Mary Bright on the yellow tablecloth with her Singer machine. It was black and heavy, a cannon that spat thread. The yellow tablecloth still covered the hall table. It had stayed the same while everything else in her life slowly unraveled.

Sometimes Carol lay her cheek upon the surface of the yellow tablecloth, between the ghost of her mother's elbows.

She had been gone a long time.

Carol did not remember much, and so it was not a woman she missed, but a bare foot on the sewing pedal; a voice at the side of her bed; the smell and softness of hair; the spreading of that yellow tablecloth in the woods. Carol's mother was no longer a person at all, but a collection of moments. A bag of precious stones with different weights and colors gently knocking against her life without breaking.

After her mother died, Carol felt more like Mary Bright, with eyes to look but never see and arms to reach but never touch. That was when she believed you could talk to spirits, that the dead were webbed into the corners of our lives.

Carol remembered watching her mother sew Mary Bright through the banisters. It was late at night while her daddy was out playing cards with the money from selling the fields.

She was so young then. A tangle of bony limbs on stairs. Just staring. Waiting. A moth drawn to the light of her mother's sewing lamp.

When the biscuits were ready, Carol pulled out the pan and fumbled with it. Then she carried a cooling biscuit in her dress to the porch. She sat down on a broken chair, tearing pieces of hot dough and slipping them into her mouth.

It must have been close to noon because nothing had much shadow. Then she heard a faint rumbling and her daddy's truck appeared in the distance. Once he stayed away for several days. She thought he was dead. The happiness she felt must surely have been a sin.

Her daddy's truck was a faded green. It crawled over the dirt like a giant beetle. She could feel her heart beating quickly now, and finished the biscuit in her hands. They'd had a horse before the truck. But he always beat it. She could hear it being beaten from her room. Once, it fell down and wouldn't get up, so he put a knife in its mouth.

She watched him stop his truck, then sit with his hands on the wheel.

There were holes in the porch where the wood was rotten. Carol dreamed he would step through one and just keep going. He'd be with the devil then, and her mother would be safe in heaven. If that happened? Her father going to hell through a hole in the porch? Carol knew she'd be just fine, selling fists of foxglove and bluebells for a nickel to people on their way to church. Just sitting there barefoot at the side of the road on a bucket in an old dress with Mary Bright at her side. A flower girl, living on biscuits and well water.

If her daddy couldn't walk straight from the liquor, she'd go through the kitchen, grab a biscuit, and run to the woods.

But his climb down from the cab seemed deliberate. He looked at the house for a moment, then put his hat on. When he got to the

9

porch steps, he came up slowly, then passed his daughter without even a look. Carol wondered if he had died in the night and this was his spirit returning to linger like the taste of something after it's swallowed.

Then he came back out, his overalls and boots still on, clutching a biscuit. He sat down on a crate and took a bite. Carol turned her body toward him but knew not to look up—not to look at his mouth kneading the food into a paste.

Lost bad last night, he said finally, staring out at the rusting machines and tall weeds. Lost so bad that Travis Curt gonna come by in a while to collect his winnuns.

Carol had both hands on Mary Bright. What he win? The truck?

Her father ripped at the biscuit with the teeth he had left.

Not the truck.

Carol moved her bare feet on the dusty wood. Flattened them. Felt the dirt push on her skin.

What then?

Well, what he win was my daughter.

Carol felt dizzy and sick, as though her soul were trying to pull free of her body. Her father got up. His shadow was small and weak in the noon light.

Quit your cryin' and get your stuff together, it's all been settled, he's comin' out today.

Carol had dreamed of the day she might leave home, get away from her daddy even though she'd drag him like a stone through the rest of her life. She pictured herself working in a store, toiling in a flower patch, or sewing things the way her mother had when she was still alive.

Her daddy's mouth stretched, but it was not a smile. I done lost the bet. You know how that works, Carol, and besides, I got plans for your room. I was going over it in the truck—I'm gonna git boarders who can pay me a lil' bit.

Carol tucked Mary Bright under her legs.

Truth be told, you ain't hardly worth nothin' to me just sittin' around. Not like the truck, or the house, or even that barn I'm gonna fix up someday. Those things got uses, Carol, they pay their way, whereas you jus' take. To be honest, you bin takin' your whole life. Why, you even took your mother from me—weared her out with all that stretchin' and kickin' when you was inside o'her.

Carol stared at the dumb porch planks. White crumbs had fallen from her biscuit and watched her like tiny eyes.

She heard him laughing then. Why, you're too stupid to know when you is better off. Listen, Carol, he's got hogs, chickens, tobacco, what else—corn! You can eat your fill of corn. Get nice and round. I'll come visit from time to time—don't worry about that. You'll see me, I promise.

Carol kept her head low as she wept, waiting for the blows that always came as small, bright flashes behind her closed eyes, like the murdering of stars.

But for some reason he backed away. Carol heard the clunk of his boots and looked. Her father's head was bowed like a hook.

It's me what should be cryin', Carol, I'm the one who lost something. Take a look around. I don't see no other daughter but you.

When Carol's daddy had made the bet, the four other men at the table fell silent and he felt he'd already won. From that moment, he sensed he would always be above them in some way. Prepared to do things they were not.

So, when a few moments later his cards fell short, he just couldn't understand it. His head buzzed with more confusion than anger. The victor, Travis Curt, was sitting there like nothing had happened.

Carol's daddy peeled the man with his eyes. Look at him jus' sittin' there like a jackass. He's a winner and don't even know it. What does that tell you?

Travis Curt forced a smile and pushed himself away from the table. I jus' didn't expect it, is all.

That ain't no good prize, Travis, said Old Man Walker, a Cherokee from the hills east of town. Some kid on your property, runnin' her mouth and takin' the best of your bacon. I bet she eat like a mule.

Carol's daddy spat out some tobacco and said calmly. Well, you're wrong about that. She hardly eat nothing. You ol' bastard. You jus' want her for yourself.

Old Man Walker claimed he was a child in the Civil War. Had seen men swinging from the covered bridges like ornaments. Bodies black with flies.

Travis looked at the cards in his meaty hands. Unable to grasp how a person's life could be decided by the faded drawings of kings and queens.

He arrived a short time later, as her father had promised.

His face was red and cologne stung his cheeks where the razor had nicked. There were hornets swarming over a hole in the roof of the house. Travis stood and watched them flit in and out, black dots that from a distance made no sound. Then he listened for voices inside the home but heard nothing. He seemed unsure now how the transaction would take place. He'd only ever traded animals. All he'd needed then was a length of rope and some water.

When he got up on the porch, the front door was open. Inside he saw a yellow tablecloth spread over a wood table. A pair of bare feet stuck out from beneath. They were young feet, with dirty nails and hairs so soft they were almost invisible.

Anyone home?

The table shook as the feet pulled in.

Hullo there? Travis said.

When the figure beneath the table didn't move, Travis went back to his rusted 1929 Model A and honked the horn. Then he stood on the running board, one hand on the wheel for balance.

After a few moments, there was shouting, and Carol's daddy appeared on the porch pulling his daughter by her arm. She was sobbing and letting her legs go limp so she'd fall. Her father thought that was funny.

She actin' like a trapped 'coon, Travis, but I swear she's a lady!

Travis seemed suddenly afraid of what was happening, and was going to call off the bet, when the girl broke free and ran to the barn. Carol's daddy spat tobacco juice and swung his head with irritation.

Come on in the house, Travis! So we can discuss this like genl'men.

They both agreed that at thirteen, she was too young to be married. There weren't many preachers who'd do it unless she was pregnant, and folks in the town would talk, maybe even tattle to someone from the county seat about their card games.

It was decided they would tell people she was going to Travis's farm to cook and clean. Thirteen, they agreed, with a year of schooling was enough for anybody, especially a girl, and so it was acceptable for her to commence this kind of work.

The two men tried explaining this through the barn door to Carol. It took some effort, but eventually the girl inside believed them and came out.

There was nothing on her feet but that didn't matter. Travis lifted her basket of things from the porch—but Carol wouldn't let him touch Mary Bright.

Her daddy sat on a crate and watched his barefoot daughter walk slowly toward Travis's truck. It was so warm you could smell the trees and hear the insects rattling from green pockets.

At the last moment, Carol's daddy jumped up. Carol was already in the truck and Travis was starting the engine, but he flew down the rotten porch steps, flung open the door, and pulled his child out. Travis sat with his hands on the wheel and the basket of girl's clothes beside him as Carol's daddy dragged her back to the house.

Weekends, he hollered at the man who'd beaten him at cards. She'll come by on weekends. You'll get her then!

SAMUEL

1986

STUDENTS FILED INTO shop class and stood looking at lathes and baskets of tools. The smell of metal and sawdust was something they knew, having fathers who worked with their hands.

Shop class was final period on Friday for eighth graders, so everyone seemed lively and the teacher was in a good mood. They put on worn shop coats, then took from a bucket of scratched safety glasses.

Eddie Walker motioned for Samuel Roberts to follow him to a workbench at the back of the shop. They could be alone to discuss skateboarding in the Dollar Store parking lot, or what kind of pizza had the most cheese, things that were important because they were both thirteen years old.

Samuel had known Eddie since second grade, when his friend's family moved up to Kentucky from Tennessee. Eddie lived with his mother, but she was not around much now that Eddie could use a microwave and get himself up for school. Samuel had met her a few times. She was always in a hurry, and her face made-up, as though at any moment the life she had imagined for herself would suddenly begin. Eddie's father had spent the last two years of his life on the run through Alabama and Florida. He was wanted in three, maybe four states. One night he got drunk in a bar, then driving to a motel, stopped to piss in the arc of his headlights. A state trooper came around the corner and hit the car, which slammed into Eddie's father, killing him outright.

Eddie often got in trouble at school. Once when someone called Samuel a dumb-fuck, Eddie emptied the boy's backpack in the middle of the playground and stomped on his things until they were in tatters. He was suspended for a day, and his mother had to pay the boy's parents fourteen dollars. Another time, a high schooler called Mitchell Riggs kicked Samuel's radio-controlled car when they were playing with it on the BMX track. Eddie laughed like it didn't matter, then picked up a rock and drove it into the older boy's lips. The police found Eddie at Samuel's house. There were two officers, and they marched him out to the cruiser, one on either side. Over dinner that night, Samuel's father said that Eddie was cursed from day one. It hurt Samuel to hear that, to know some people could be singled out for pain.

After Eddie and Samuel found their blocks of wood at the back of the shop room, it was time to pick tools. They lined up with the other students, then chose from an assortment of files, hammers, and chisels that were in metal baskets. Some of the tools were broken and sat at the bottom of the baskets in pieces. Eddie was trying to figure out a way to make his mother a jewelry box, a place to keep the things she felt were most precious.

Right now she's using a shoebox, Eddie said.

Sometimes when she was away, Eddie would go into the box and touch those things.

When they heard the teacher shouting, they switched to whispers.

Let's ride our bikes to the dump tomorrow, Samuel said. We ain't been there in a while.

Eddie kept his eyes on the wood. Imagine if we found a motorcycle or a car nobody wanted. It would be ours right?

Yeah. My dad would help fix it up.

Eddie's eyes sparkled. I could live in it.

I have to be home by three tomorrow, so let's meet there after breakfast.

Why you got to be home?

Guess.

Eddie shrugged. Family stuff?

Knight Rider.

Oh. I love that show.

Want to watch it at my house?

Eddie blushed. I was hoping you'd say that because my momma sold the TV.

Why?

Actually, she took it to her boyfriend's house because he sold his.

At the front of the shop, the teacher was now screaming at a boy with long hair. A moment later, he grabbed the student by the arm and dragged him into the hallway.

What an asshole, Eddie said.

Yeah. If he did that to me, Samuel said, my mom would have it out with the principal.

Eddie laughed. Yeah, mine too. I wish your mom was our teacher, Samuel.

She only teaches second grade.

She could teach any grade I bet.

Well I wish you could live with us. I'm sure Mom and Dad wouldn't care.

What about Uncle Rusty?

He's your uncle too, Eddie.

The boy looked down at the wood block he wanted to transform into something for his mother, some beautiful object that for a moment might hold her attention.

I wish he was. Uncle Rusty loves ever'body, Samuel. He's like Mister Rogers.

I ain't seen that show in a while.

Do you still watch it?

No, do you?

I guess not, said Eddie. Though I would if you wanted to. For ol' times' sake.

If you lived at my house, we could watch *Knight Rider*, *Dukes of Hazzard*, and *Airwolf*—that's Uncle Rusty's favorite.

And anything with Coca-Cola written on it, right? Don't forget about that.

The teacher must have still been in the hallway because some of the girls were screaming and tossing nuggets of dried glue. Samuel felt carried away by the swell of excitement and grabbed some wood, which he flung impulsively at Eddie, hitting him square in the chin. His best friend was shocked at first, then grinned.

I'll get you back, you son of a bitch.

Call me Michael, Samuel said. Michael Knight.

Eddie laughed. I'll be K.I.T.T.

But that's a machine.

Ok, Eddie shrugged. Devon Miles then.

Later on, near the end of class, in the clamor of everyone cleaning their work spaces, Eddie snatched a bent nail off the counter and flung it at Samuel just as he looked up.

It was a quick, fierce pain. His instinct was to cup his eye with one hand until the burning stopped. He could hear Eddie's voice, asking if he was okay, and if he was faking, to please stop.

Samuel lowered his hand. Am I bleeding?

Eddie looked closely. It's just a lot of white stuff and water. Looks like you got slimed, Egon.

It hurts like hell.

I didn't mean to get your eye, Eddie said. I was just messin' around.

Then the bell rang for the end of school.

Help me to the bathroom, Samuel told him, 'cause I don't know if I can walk straight.

Eddie's face was ashen as he steadied his best friend down the corridor to the boys' bathroom. They shut themselves in a stall. A thick, white syrup was now oozing from the center of Samuel's eye. Eddie started to cry. Mucus streamed out of his nostrils.

Call my mom, Samuel said, his voice shaking. Tell her to come get us.

Alfredia had just walked in from the elementary school when she got the call. A couple of her students missed their buses home and she'd waited with them.

When she arrived at the middle school parking lot and saw the state of her son, she tried to conceal her shock and concentrate on getting him home. Back at the house, she and Eddie took one arm each and helped Samuel inside. Working quickly, she taped tissue over the oozing eye, then wrapped an ice pack in a paper towel and told Eddie to press it lightly against Samuel's head. Then she called and left a message with the doctor's office. Uncle Rusty, who lived with them, was at Walmart, greeting people with yellow smiley stickers. He wouldn't be home until the evening but had a key he wore around his neck on a red string.

While they waited for the phone to ring, Samuel peeled the tissue away from his face and said he couldn't see anything but a red mist through the damaged eye.

Alfredia telephoned the doctor again, then dialed the number of her husband's work. Randy was called from the production floor to the factory office. In the background, cars were being bolted together. Alfredia wrote down what he said to do on a pad, which included covering the other eye, as eyes always move together.

When she got off the phone, Eddie was crying again. Alfredia touched his hair, trying to detach herself from a prickling anger that threatened to electrify her words. When she spoke, it was in the voice she used for her second-grade students.

It was just innocent horseplay, she said. You didn't mean it, and you're not to blame. It could very well have been your eye that was in the accident.

I wish it was.

That's because you're his best friend.

I'm his best friend, but I hurt him real bad.

Samuel will be fine. You'll see, Eddie. Now fix yourself a glass of juice, then go on home. I'll call when we get back and give you an update.

The moment he left, Alfredia telephoned the doctor a third time but he was still out on a call. The receptionist asked what it was about, then said there was an eye clinic in Elizabethtown with an emergency room. Alfredia wrote down the address on her pad, then bundled Samuel into their brown Ford Granada.

She was nervous about getting lost but drove quickly anyway. The tissue over her son's stricken eye was leaking fluid.

When they arrived at the clinic, Samuel said he felt faint, and needed help getting up.

The worst will soon be over, his mother told him, trying to believe it herself. The doctor is going to make you feel better.

There were a few people in the waiting area, but when they saw Samuel, a woman took him to an exam room right away. The physician wore a clean white coat and striped bow tie. He was very skinny with a hooked nose like an eagle. He peered into Samuel's eye with a special light, then looked at his watch.

I think I can save it, but I'll have to operate.

Alfredia had her pad and pen ready. Her hands were shaking, but she managed to write, SAVE IT, which she underlined.

Samuel was in a daze. The burning had stopped, but he could feel a fizzing at the center of his eyeball. He wondered if he'd have to wear a patch for the rest of his life. What would everyone at school say? Then he wanted his father, and pictured him changing out of the blue shop overalls at the Ford plant in Louisville. He saw his father's face, calm and stony, hardened to suffering by tours in Vietnam before Samuel was born.

Could you be ready in an hour, Mrs. Roberts?

For what?

For your son to be prepped for surgery.

Oh dear, Alfredia said, wiping her nose with a tissue. I still can't believe this has happened.

It's not uncommon, the doctor explained, with thirteen-year-old boys. Are you calm enough to drive your son and meet me at the hospital?

I think I should call my husband again.

Where is he?

Ford.

The Louisville plant? Give me the number. I'll tell him where to meet us. Then I'll call and have an ambulance take you both over there. I think that would be best. Now, Samuel, you just keep breathing, young man, and look after your mother.

The hospital was full of telephones ringing and people rushing about with clipboards. Samuel could tell the floors were very smooth and he imagined skateboarding on them with Eddie, dodging gurneys and pools of blood. Then, for a moment he wondered if he would die. If it could really happen like that, so quickly, without any time to prepare or say the things he had never said, but felt. Then Samuel heard a voice and a man was suddenly helping him into a wheelchair.

Your mother is staying at the desk to fill out some papers, the man said. I'll let her know where you are.

Samuel nodded his head.

He was pushed down a long corridor and then into a room, where the orderly left him alone. After several minutes the door swung open.

Sorry to barge in. I'm Nurse Lori and you're...Samuel. That right?

Yes, ma'am.

A cupboard door opened. What color gown would you like? We have white, pink, blue, and green.

The pink one.

That'd be a first. How's green?

She took it off the hanger and put it on Samuel's lap.

It ties in the back, I'll leave you alone once I finish this paperwork.

Samuel sat with the green gown, listening to her pen scratch the paper. He wondered what she looked like. If she was as pretty as her voice.

The doctor thinks I might lose it, he said. My eye.

They'll do their best, they always do.

If they can't it's okay because I got another one right next to it.

Samuel heard the pen stop on the paper. She must have been looking at him. How old are you?

Thirteen, ma'am.

Well you sound like a man already, making jokes when you're in pain.

There was a knock at the door and it opened.

Your folks are here, Samuel, so I'm going to leave you for now.

Samuel tried to stand then, but his father rushed forward and lowered him back into the seat. He was still in his overalls. Samuel could smell the oil and feel rough fabric still cold from outside.

You alright, boy?

Samuel held out the green hospital gown he was supposed to put on but couldn't speak. He had been fine with his mother, but the voice of his father gave him the confidence to be afraid.

CAROL

1933

FINALLY, THE WEEKEND came and it was time to go. They didn't speak much in the truck. The basket of things that sat between them trembled with the motion of their journey. Carol had wanted to bring Mary Bright, but her father said it was time to give up childish things.

When they pulled up to the white farmhouse, an old sheepdog rose from his place in the shade. The yard had some patches of yellow grass, but it was mostly dirt dotted with chickens and a few mossy trees.

That's Russ, Travis Curt said. Good ol' dog. He won't hurt you.

The animal followed them inside the house, its tail sweeping back and forth.

I usually got chores on a Friday, Carol. But I took the day off workin' so's we could spend time together.

There was furniture, but it seemed very old and the sofa was losing its insides. In the main room was a fireplace with soot stains up the wall and logs left over from a cold spring. The whole place was dusty and smelled like old shoes.

Travis stood in the hallway, looking from room to room, holding the basket of girl's clothes.

Why don't you go out on the porch with Russ. I'll put this down somewhere and bring you sweet tea.

Without speaking, Carol turned and went back outside, choosing to sit in the very middle of the bench seat. The dog rushed forward and began shouldering his body into her legs. Carol reached down and stroked one of his ears. But it wasn't enough, and he kept moving his head around under her hand.

When Travis appeared, Carol took the glass and drank the sugary liquid in a few gulps.

I can get more if you'd like.

I'm fine.

When she didn't slide over, he leaned back against the wooden rail.

Carol was now moving her hand up and down the dog's coat, even letting it disappear into the fur where she could feel the shape of his bones.

Travis watched the whole thing, sipping on his drink.

You lived with your daddy a long time? he asked, finally.

My whole life. Where *your* folks at?

They out back... he said, pointing with his glass. Buried under the peach tree.

Travis put his drink down and pinched some tobacco from a round tin, which he stuffed into his gum. When you're ready to start cooking I'll show you the kitchen. I'll bet it's more'n what you got now with your daddy.

Carol spent Friday afternoon preparing things for a meal. There were so many cans she couldn't decide what would go best with the animal Travis intended to slaughter. And it was hard to move around the kitchen with Russ under her the whole time, his tail swinging wildly.

In the end, Carol made biscuits, beans, and corn to go with the chicken.

At the table, she chewed her portion slowly and looked at the green and white tile floor. Everything was different at Travis Curt's. Even the white supper plates were painted with green grapes and vines, as though somebody had planned for everything in the house to have something in common.

When Travis cut into his chicken it was raw on the inside. He picked it off the plate with his fingers and gave it to Russ, who chomped the meat hurriedly with his mouth open. Travis had killed and plucked the bird that afternoon on the porch. Carol watched through a screen door, wearing an apron Travis said once belonged to his mother.

I can't believe how good these biscuits are, Carol. He held one up. Russ's eyes widened and he made a noise. How'd you make 'em?

My momma taught me.

Where she at?

Carol glared at him. In heaven with your folks I expect, lookin' down on us this very minute.

Travis coughed and put the biscuit down. Russ made a noise too, then slumped back under the table.

Your daddy said you could hardly do nothing, but this food ain't half bad. I'm much obliged.

After the meal, they sat on the porch as the sun lingered low on the horizon, not realizing it was already night under the trees. Travis went inside and came back with two peaches he had rinsed in a bucket.

We're about like my own parents was, sitting out here, Carol. Ain't that something? How's your room? I made it pink, which as you know is a woman's color. When Travis laughed, the flesh under his chin moved up and down, reminding Carol of the chicken that had sat in his arms like a small cushion, turning and tilting its head moments before he wrung its neck.

That bed I give you was the one I got borned in—if you can believe that. And the one Momma died in, too.

Carol's mouth twisted with disgust. I can't sleep in no dead person's bed.

It's clean, Travis insisted. No one's slept in it for goin' on twenty years.

I ain't never slept where someone died, Carol said. That's all.

You afraid of ghosts or something?

Carol didn't answer.

Russ was on the top porch step, his head down on two front paws.

Well now, Travis said, tossing his peach pit into the darkness. You could always sleep somewhere else if you're afraid.

I ain't afraid, Carol said sharply. It's just somethin' I'm not used to is all.

But that first night she slept on the floor, not wanting to touch any of the dead woman's things.

Carol kept busy on Saturday, moving from room to room sweeping, mopping, and wiping away the dirt from years of silence. She wanted to sing but wouldn't allow herself. Travis came in from time to time for glasses of water, and would praise how good a job she was doing. It was very hot, even with the windows open, and whenever Carol sat down to catch her breath, she would hear little steps and then from around the open door a small face would appear.

That night Carol was so tired she slept in the bed, but stayed in her clothes, watching the door as long as she could—waiting for the handle to turn by itself.

On Sunday morning they were back on the porch with mugs of black coffee, watching the chickens peck and raise dust with their sharp feet. When Travis spat tobacco juice into the yard, some of them jumped back.

That was where Momma used to sit, Carol. Right where you are now.

Carol shuffled around, as if to dislodge the image balanced in Travis Curt's mind.

Beyond the porch, a honeysuckle bush roped up one side of the house. Carol could taste its flowers in her nose and mouth like tiny, melted secrets. There were no holes in Travis's porch, no wet wood that had been left to rot.

He told Carol that his parents had died a few weeks apart in the flu epidemic when he was thirteen himself. He asked if it was flu what killed Carol's momma, but she didn't know.

By the time my folks passed, he went on, I knew all there was to know about cropping. Never went to school like some kids now 'cause I never had no use for book learning.

When he drove her back Sunday night in his pickup, her clothes smelled like cooked food and her hands were dried out from the soap powder she'd used to scrub his underwear and socks on a wooden board. They didn't talk and passed only a few other cars. When they hit a hole in the road, Travis's knee knocked into Carol's leg and she jerked back like one of the chickens in his yard. Then she opened her window and spat into the rushing air.

When she got home, it was completely dark. Her father was just a shadow on the porch, but she could smell the liquor like a heavy, dumb perfume.

I bet you had yerself a good ol' time, he said. If you're anything like your mother was.

Carol passed without a word. All she cared about was getting upstairs to where Mary Bright had been waiting, unable to see or touch or feel without Carol. Now they would stay up, as Carol told her everything there was to know about dogs.

Early next morning Carol dressed in the wash of dawn light. Then she took her doll and the yellow tablecloth out to that clearing in the woods, where memories of her mother gave her hope that life would not go on forever in the same way. In that green place on the special cloth, ringed by trees and loose ribbons of birdsong, Carol imagined herself and Mary Bright escaping on Russ's shaggy back, guided by fairies and sprites from the picture she kept in her pillow.

She stayed there until the day's color began to fade. Then she returned to her daddy's house with hunger clawing at her insides.

The next weekend, Travis was proud to show her a radio he'd bought. Now, he promised, she could listen to country music any time she pleased. But all Carol wanted was to pull Russ up into her arms. For the rest of the day he followed her everywhere, as if attached by a length of invisible cord.

In the evening Carol served dinner on the plates with green grapes and vines. Travis sat at the table studying his hands, which were sore and swollen from digging trenches in the dry field.

I'm not surprised that apron fits you so well, he said without looking up. Not surprised one bit.

Carol smoothed the front where his mother, long ago, had stitched a strawberry into the fabric. After supper, Travis told her to sit out on the porch while he wiped the dishes clean. Carol said no, but he insisted. It's what my own papa would do sometimes, when Mama was t'ard from cookin'.

When he had finished, Carol heard the screen door open and there he was, red in the face and with sweat running down his neck. He sat next to Carol, but they hardly spoke. Light was draining quickly from the world they shared.

Sometime later, Carol left the porch and went up to bed without saying anything. Russ tried to follow, but Travis held him back, listening as she disappeared through the screen door and then trudged barefoot up the stairs.

An hour later, Carol was in bed when she heard a creak and saw the handle turning. He was whispering her name over and over from the doorway. She was so afraid that all she could do was pretend to be annoyed.

What is it? she hissed. I'm sleeping.

Do you need anything?

No, I do not.

Glass of water?

I'm fine.

Then she heard him creep closer. You mind if I stay awhile? I'll just sit on the end of the bed if it don't bother you.

Carol pulled the blanket up to her chin.

It's your house, she said. Sit where you want.

Earlier that day, Carol had wondered if she might come to Travis Curt's house more often. The look on Russ's face when she left was too much.

Now the shame of that wish was cutting her small heart into pieces, as if to devour it.

The bed tilted with his weight. Carol thought about the dog outside in the yard, asleep under a tree, dreaming of plate scraps. She tried to picture his long nose, and those gray hairs that came off in her hand when she touched it.

When a fan of moon appeared in her window, Carol felt the covers moving backwards like a slow, unstoppable tide.

He was speaking again, but too quietly for the words to rise above the creaking springs. Then she felt a hot weight on top of her, droplets of sweat that were not her own, and the whites of his eyes, slick and veined.

She pushed back on his meaty shoulders, but it was like a stone, grinding out the air from her lungs. Then a sudden tearing pain at the top of her legs, and a wetness she knew was blood. For a few moments it was like a barbed hook, ripping out her insides. She couldn't breathe. Splinters on his cheek tore at her face. It was like being murdered, she thought, except somehow part of you was still alive.

When he was done, Travis Curt got up and went out of the room, pulling the door closed behind him. Carol could hear him outside on the porch sucking down mouthfuls of night air. The unblinking moon was in its final descent over the house, like God looking down. Watching her. Watching them all.

SAMUEL

1987

FOR MANY NIGHTS leading up to the first day of high school, Samuel lay awake by the faint glow of his digital clock. A year had passed since the accident with the flung nail.

After three painful surgeries, sight had returned but the eye would always look off-center—as if forever tethered to that one moment in the past. When looking in a mirror, the discordant gaze was all Samuel saw of himself, and all he suspected anyone else would see. He secretly wished he had lost his vision, but was too ashamed to ever admit this to his parents or Uncle Rusty.

Early one Sunday morning, Samuel heard a knock on his window, and there was Eddie in a leather jacket and tee shirt. He was back in Kentucky, after a failed year down south. He had left with his mother and her new boyfriend for Florida soon after Samuel's accident.

After Eddie wiggled in, Samuel hugged him and handed him a half-empty can of soda from the bedside table. Eddie said he'd been up all night, making sure his mother stayed awake at the wheel of their blue Chevy Chevette. Eventually, after eighteen hours of driving, with everything they owned packed into the car, they had gotten to their new home, a trailer park on the county line that was known for bootlegging. Eddie told him about Florida. How everything went wrong.

His mother and her boyfriend had always been physical, he explained, mostly pushing and shoving when they came home late from bars. But one evening, after fighting in the kitchen, her boyfriend stormed into a closet, grabbed a ruby-red bowling ball and dropped it on her foot. Eddie was on the can with a hot rod magazine but rushed out when he heard the thud. His mother lay on the floor. Her makeup was smeared and clownish. Her boyfriend was now holding the bowling ball over her head—threatening to let go if she didn't admit she had accepted a drink from some guy at the bar because she secretly wanted to fuck him.

Eddie stormed into the kitchen and drew a carving knife from the wooden block by the sink. This made his mother's boyfriend stand up very straight and laugh, as though he didn't completely understand what was about to happen. When Eddie moved forward with the blade glinting in the raw kitchen light, a frying pan hit him square in the face, knocking out a front tooth and splitting his nose. He stumbled backwards, grabbing at a curtain, which came down, rod and all. Then his mother was standing over him, still holding the pan.

I'm sick and tired of you two fightin', she screamed. I don't deserve any of what you both put me through.

Eddie smiled to show Samuel the gap.

Is that why you come home? Samuel asked. 'Cause of the fight?

Most likely, Eddie said, peering around Samuel's room at the Budweiser pennants and Guns N' Roses posters.

But she must have felt bad later on, don't you think? Eddie asked. About hitting me with the skillet, 'cause she went out a week after my birthday and bought me this leather jacket from a pawnshop in Jacksonville.

It's cool, Samuel said.

Eddie unzipped it. That's pure silk. You can touch it.

Samuel brushed the lining. You always wanted a leather jacket.

But what happened to your mom's boyfriend?

He came to get his things one day when we were out. Momma was heartbroken. She took the wooden jewelry box I made her and stomped on it. Said I always found a way to ruin things for her.

She didn't mean it, buddy.

Oh, I know, 'cause if she didn't love me, she wouldn't have gotten me something like this. It wouldn't even cross her mind.

Well I love you, old buddy.

Even though I fucked up your eye?

Could have been me that done it to you. Even my mother said that. You heard her.

I wish it had been my eye.

Well now you're back, we can walk to high school together on the first morning.

Eddie sighed. Here I go lettin' you down again...I gotta go to Louisville that day and help Momma fill out some court papers. She can't do it without me, Samuel, I swear. She don't see words so well, you know that.

Samuel felt fear rising into his throat. Are you sure you have to go? Be great if we could be together, at least on the first day.

We can walk to school together ever' day once I'm back. Eddie laughed. Though I figured you'd hate me by now 'cause of your eye.

I'm used to it, Samuel said.

It was a lie, but his best friend's life was already so broken, Samuel felt it would have been like stepping on the pieces to tell him the truth. The worst disappointment was when he found out he would not be able to follow in his father's footsteps and join the army—even a slight visual impairment rendered applicants ineligible. His father had told him it was all for the best, giving Samuel the impression he was relieved and did not feel let down. Then one day he came home from the Ford plant with a stack of survival magazines. They flicked through them after eating dinner.

See that knife, Samuel. That's a good knife. I could teach you how to use that in the woods around here.

Sure, Dad.

Alfredia looked over from her television program. Just be careful is all I'm gonna say, then I'll shut up.

Samuel would tell Eddie all of this in time. They could explore the forest together.

When Uncle Rusty heard voices in Samuel's bedroom, he lingered outside the thin door, then began shouting.

Eddie's back! Eddie's back! Eddie's back!

Upstairs, over eggs and coffee, Alfredia brought a photo of Eddie and Samuel from her dresser to the kitchen counter. It had been taken on Samuel's ninth birthday, at the back of the house where Uncle Rusty liked to sit when it was sunny and he could close his eyes. In the picture, the boys were wearing blue jeans and holding the neon grips of their BMX bikes.

Those two little boys went off on their bicycles one day, Alfredia said, and came back as young men.

I had a red bicycle, Uncle Rusty told everyone. And my daddy tied my feet to the pedals because my legs were no good then. Daddy wanted 'em fixed. Remember that, Alfredia?

Alfredia glanced up from the photograph of her son and Eddie Walker. No, Rusty, I don't remember. Maybe it was before my time.

Rusty frowned. Before you was born you mean?

That's right.

You were born on a Tuesday, Alfredia. It rained, but then it got sunny. We went outside with lemonade.

Wow, Eddie said, leaning back in his seat. That's awesome you can remember stuff like that. I forgot you could do that.

Uncle Rusty looked at his breakfast plate. Eddie's back, he told everyone sitting at the breakfast counter. Then he pointed at his nephew. And Samuel's eye is all better, except that it's crooked.

Oh Rusty, Samuel's mother said quickly. He's fine. He's handsome as ever.

But—

Samuel's father lit a cigarette. June 21, 1979. What day was that, Rusty?

A Thursday. Seventy-five degrees and sunny.

Samuel's father looked at Eddie. He don't even have to think about it. Doctors told his folks he got the mind of a six-year-old... but I don't know any kid what can do that. The smoke from his cigarette was like slow, blue velvet.

Eddie's back, Uncle Rusty said again. He went to Florida, but he come back.

How long you back for? Samuel's father wanted to know.

It's for good this time, Mr. Roberts. Momma said she gonna find some work in town, hairdressin' or something...and we'll get a house in the country eventually. I got it all planned out.

What are you boys fixin' to do with the time left before high school begins?

I have to help Momma unpack our boxes of things, Eddie said. That we brought up in the Chevette.

And we're gonna play some cards, too, I expect, Samuel told his parents. Like we always do.

I got a thing of pennies under my bed if you want it.

Randy! Alfredia snapped. You don't need to encourage them.

Her husband winked at the boys. Oh, it's just poker, sweetheart.

It's gamblin' is what it is. I don't know why but I hate it.

Eddie cleared his throat. If you think it's wrong, Mrs. Roberts, we could just play Uno.

Eddie's back. Rusty announced calmly to everyone sitting at the counter. He was in Florida, but he come home for high school. They went off as boys on their bicycles and come back young men.

When breakfast was over, Alfredia went around to Eddie before he could stand up. She put her hands on the shoulders of his leather jacket and kissed the top of his head.

You're an angel, she told him. An angel sent to us from heaven.

CAROL

1934

ABOUT A YEAR after she was lost in the card game, Carol thought she was dying.

She went into the woods with the yellow tablecloth and Mary Bright, moving slowly because she felt weak and dizzy. Rain was pelting the ground, but she lay flat against the earth and called out to her mother, pleading with her to do something.

Some weeks later, after Carol understood what was happening, she kept going over in her mind what life would be like, forever shuttling between two houses in the dark. The child would be a curse to them, a creature to be hidden away from the world. It would have no schooling, and no companions but for a doll and a dog. If it was a boy, he might grow up to be like them. When she thought about how it might be a girl, she knew what she had to do.

On the day it was to happen, she lingered in her room, looking at all the things there as though seeing them for the first time. The picture of fairies she had torn from a school book. Her mother's shoe, wrapped in tissue and hidden under a loose floorboard. Carol even kissed her pillow and stroked the fraying blanket pulled flat over the bed. The next person to touch them would most likely be a stranger with no sense of the journeys she had taken in dreams.

She scrambled through deep forest toward the river, not thinking of much, just a gnawing sadness for Russ, who would wait until his own life was at an end.

After several hours Carol reached a place she felt she could do it. She let her body flop down on some loose river stones, which clucked as she stretched out her limbs after the long walk.

For a time she watched the brown water, passing quickly with a kind of laughter that was not laughter, but which hypnotized her, allowing her mind to drift. She let it. And began to see things without any feelings attached. Her life could have belonged to anybody, she thought, except that it was hers and had come to her by chance.

Still, she clung to the idea that it was no good, and she no longer wanted it. After a while she set Mary Bright on a flat rock, then hunted for stones to fill their pockets. When there was a pile, Carol picked up her doll and squeezed pebbles through a hole in her cotton dress. That way, Mary Bright would see Momma again too.

When the task was finished, she could tell that her doll was afraid. But such was Carol's determination that she held Mary Bright with one hand while chunking stones into the pockets of her own dress with the other. Then she stood, faltering at first with the shifting weight. It took time to reach the water without falling, but when Carol stepped in, the river was ice cold and the power of it—like a thrashing muscle—was ominous and frightening.

Carol laughed through her chattering teeth—more afraid of water than of the dying she hoped to do.

At some stage of it, she wondered if her mother would come and remain at her side until the end, perhaps even willing her on to where the river was deep and slow, as though thick with the sleep that would soon fill her body.

She took another step. Then another.

When the icy water swept over her knees, Carol considered releasing Mary Bright to the fast current, but that gave her the idea that the baby growing inside might also get released, then somehow splash to the riverbank, where it would sit, crying as it licked its tiny hands and feet. Then something worse: that it would find its way to the house, where her father was.

That thought made Carol give up, and she began to slowly free the stones from her pockets, one at a time, savoring the gulp as each broke the river's cold skin.

It was much longer going back. Carol conjured Russ's face. It hovered over her in the dusk. She yearned to bury her hands in his coat and say things he did not understand but which made him touch her with his eyes.

When the house finally appeared, it looked different, as if it were no longer her house, but only a place she had visited. Her legs were still numb from the water and stung where they'd been whipped by dead branches and vines.

Her daddy was chopping wood in the front yard. Where the hell you been?

Nowhere, she said, hiding her doll.

Well, get some supper on then.

Okay. I will.

He watched her go into the house. You let the fire go out too, goddamn it. You hear me?

Sitting over the warm meal she had quickly prepared, Carol pushed beans around on her greasy plate.

If you ain't gonna eat that, you sure as hell ain't gonna waste it. You bin spoiled by Travis is what's the matter.

Carol set down her fork and looked at it there on the table, a dull silver, but straight and hard with even spacing between the prongs. Most people never gave a thought to the small things, Carol said in her mind, but that eating utensil may very well have been in my mother's mouth once, long ago.

She watched her father rip the last bits of flesh from his pork rib, then suck on the bone. The sound of it made her feel sick, so she got up from the table and went upstairs to Mary Bright, who was waiting with a slightly bigger hole in her cotton dress from where Carol had picked out most of the stones on their journey back.

Over the next few months, as the bump in Carol's belly grew, there were small beatings. Her daddy even tried to push her down the stairs, but she was too quick. He was also arguing with Travis Curt, who wanted Carol to stay with him the whole time. For weeks she had not been allowed outside, except at night. And Travis had to drive her back and forth in the dark with broken headlights. Carol had been asking who would be there to help when the time came—but neither her daddy nor Travis would tell her anything.

One evening when she was in bed, she heard raised voices in the front yard. Her daddy and Travis had been out there drinking. There were shuffling footsteps on the porch, then muted thudding, as if the two men were rolling around on top of each other. Then something went smash, a paraffin lamp maybe, which was followed by a heavy thump. Then silence. Not even voices.

Carol was too afraid to go downstairs, or even close the window, so she lay there, slowly sinking to the bottom of night, where dreams would evanesce the life that she knew.

At dawn, she got up and stared from her window into the yard. Her Daddy's truck was in its usual space, but Travis's pickup was not there. She figured he'd driven home, where Russ would be out of his kennel, ready for his first meal.

After quietly peeing in the bedpan, Carol crept down the hallway to her daddy's room. The door was wide open, and she peeked in. The dirty blanket he slept under was crumpled in a ball at the end of his mattress.

She went downstairs, but he was not there either. He must have gone somewhere on foot, maybe into the woods looking for a rabbit to shoot for his breakfast.

Carol stopped in the hallway and imagined the rabbit, plunged into its small, hot heart thumping fiercely as the burning rash of metal entered its stomach and ears. She saw blood clotting on fur, and felt its eyes, wincing, trying not to close, then turning to glass for the long journey home. Soon its body would dangle from the porch, pink and glistening after being skinned by her father, separated from its life to satisfy the needs of a man for just a single day.

That was when Carol knew what to do. It was not a thought, as it came to her without words, but she had never felt more certain of anything in her life. She rushed upstairs and began pulling out drawers, grabbing what few items she would need. She slipped the fairy picture from her pillowcase, then packed Mary Bright and some possessions into a small, green suitcase. Before going downstairs, she closed the drawers and straightened up the room so everything appeared normal. On her way out, Carol touched the yellow tablecloth for good luck, then slipped out through the back door. Leaving her mother's cloth behind saddened her, but if her daddy saw it was gone, then checked her drawers upstairs, he'd know she had run away and come out to the highway, which was where she planned to go.

Soon her ankles were soaked in dew. With the instincts of an animal, Carol moved silently over cow pasture, through meadows of tall grass, between folds of plowed earth—holding, always, her swollen stomach, that world within a world.

By sunrise, Carol had reached the main highway.

There she stood, in clouds of her own breath, wondering who would pick her up and where she would land by nightfall. She wondered if she would ever see Russ again, and asked her mother to watch over him in his kennel on the nights that lay ahead.

Carol: 1934

. . .

After a couple of hours, it was clear that nobody wanted to help—especially when they saw what she was carrying. Some people slowed down as though they were stopping, but it was just to look. Others would roll down their windows and spit, or call her names.

Eventually, Carol dropped down on the gravel with her legs splayed in front of her. Her throat was cracked from thirst and her cotton underwear felt rough and crusted.

Time passed, and the noon sun was soon beating down on her head like a fist. Carol felt like rolling her body into the ditch and lying flat on her back under some dark green leaves. She was now hurting in places she had never even thought about.

But then, through wet, stinging eyes, she noticed a pickup creeping toward her. At first, she thought it was her father. But this one was black and much older.

When it was only a few yards off, the truck lurched to one side, then creaked and spluttered to a stop.

A wizened, birdlike head poked out.

Come on, what'd ya waiting for? Christmas?

Carol picked up her case and hobbled toward the decrepit vehicle, so sore were her feet with the weight of a child.

Inside the truck was the oldest, most sour looking Cherokee Indian Carol had ever seen. His clawlike hands shook on the steering wheel. I know who you are, he barked as she clambered in, and I've come out here to get you.

UNCLE RUSTY

1987

WHEN THE FIRST day of high school came, Samuel put on the clothes he had chosen a week before and went upstairs from his basement bedroom to where breakfast was being made. His father stubbed out a cigarette and looked at his boy. His mother was dressed for her job at the elementary school and stood at the stove stirring sausage gravy. The familiar aromas of the kitchen filled Samuel with a sudden remorse, as though starting in the high school meant the loss of something he hadn't realized was precious.

Oh, my goodness, Alfredia said. Don't he look like a little man, Randy? Don't he?

He ain't so little no more, said Samuel's father, reading the words on his son's tee shirt. Def Leppard, that a rock group?

You drove me to their concert in Nashville.

I thought that was Dolly Parton.

Randy, don't tease him on the first day. He's nervous enough.

Where's Uncle Rusty, Mom?

His mother plated the scrambled eggs, then lifted a platter of hash browns from the oven.

Probably still in his room.

Samuel's father unfolded the morning newspaper. Licking his wounds, I expect. I had a word with him yesterday about the whole thing. He'll get over it.

Samuel peered at the soft yellow mound on his plate but did not start to eat.

I'm sure he understands deep down, Alfredia said. In fact, I know he does. He's my older brother after all. We've been together our whole lives.

Then why is he still in his room?

Randy lit a cigarette. He's just a little disappointed, son. You know what he's like.

He's proud of you is all it is, going to the high school.

Samuel pushed the plate of food away. It's just better I go with kids I knew from middle school on the first day, Mom. I mean, if I can't go with Eddie.

The high school was a neat brick building on the other side of town. Too close to take a bus, but twenty minutes on foot. A few of Samuel's old classmates from middle school were meeting at Druthers' Pharmacy, where they would make the journey as a group on their first day. It had all been arranged at the arcade, between winning and losing on the flashing and beeping machines. Samuel had asked if he could walk with them.

A week ago, however, when Uncle Rusty heard that Eddie would not be at school on the first day, he hatched an idea. Samuel was on the back porch trying to fix the steering on a radio-controlled car.

For a few moments, Uncle Rusty just stood behind the screen, watching his nephew fiddle with a mini-screwdriver.

That you, Rusty? Samuel asked, catching a glimpse of his uncle in the doorway.

Yup, right here, Samuel. It's me.

Ain't you at work today?

Not today.

How come?

'Cause I'm here.

Even after turning fifty, Uncle Rusty still worked at the local Walmart as a greeter, giving children yellow stickers with happy faces and telling everyone to *have a nice day* or *come back and see us* when they had finished their shopping and were laden with goods.

Samuel, I want to talk to you, he said, opening the screen door just enough to slip through. Samuel turned to face him, but Uncle Rusty was looking down at his sandals. There were soft hairs on his toes. Everything about his body seemed gentle.

Samuel, I'm gonna walk you to the gates of high school on your first day.

Samuel put down the tool in his hand. He didn't want to hurt his uncle's feelings. You don't need to do that, Rusty. I'll be fine.

I'm here to serve and protect, Samuel.

Protect from what?

Rusty pointed to his face. From people looking at your eye.

Samuel blushed and let his gaze fall upon the broken toy car that he was trying to fix.

But I don't care about it anymore, Rusty. I can't change who I am.

Well they're gonna stare at it, Samuel. You betcha.

I'll be fine, buddy.

With me there, I could tell them to have a nice day like I do at Walmart. I even got stickers. As many as you want. I borrowed a whole roll.

A few weeks after the final operation, when the bandages came off, Rusty couldn't stop looking at it and kept asking how come it didn't move with the other one.

That's a kind offer, Uncle Rusty. Can you let me think about it?

Okay. I went with my sister Alfredia on the bus to school on her first day. Did you know that?

No.

Well, that happened. It was Alfredia's first day of school. I went with her on the bus and was forgotten about.

. . .

When Alfredia came home from a staff meeting at the same elementary school she had attended almost thirty-five years ago, Samuel told her everything that was going on.

He's jus' so proud you going into higher schooling is all. Rusty never had but two grades' learning.

I know, Mom, but it's the first day.

Alfredia's face softened. Is it because he's special?

No! It would be the same if you or Dad walked me! That's what I'm trying to say!

Did you tell him that?

I said I would think about it.

Maybe he'll forget the whole thing. Then she chuckled. But I doubt it...you know his mind, Samuel.

When Samuel's father took him to buy school supplies at Walmart, Uncle Rusty left his post at the entrance and followed them through the aisles in his blue vest with the roll of smiley-face stickers in his hand.

Gonna help us pick out some pens and pencils, Rusty? Randy asked him.

Yup. We'd better leave early, Samuel. Can't be late on the first day.

Samuel and his father exchanged a glance.

Say, Rusty, Randy said, I need you to help me with something on the Ford next week. Why don't you walk Samuel to school another day?

Uncle Rusty turned the roll of yellow stickers in his hand, eyelids fluttering as he searched for the words he wanted.

Well, now, I think I'd sooner not help you with the truck, Randy, 'cause Samuel, he got to get to school. He's gonna be afraid 'cause of his eye, so I got to take him. I have to. I'm his uncle.

Randy sighed. That so?

Rusty nodded. It's actually a fact.

. . .

Samuel prodded the eggs, releasing folds of steam.

His father lit another cigarette. Ain't you gonna eat your break-fast, Samuel? Gonna need your strength for the first day.

I don't have much appetite.

Alfredia took her hands from the pocket of her green apron and set them on her hips. You want a hot biscuit then? Grandma Carol's recipe?

Sorry, Mom, I'm just not hungry.

Well, grits are good when you're nervous. Maybe 'cause they're plain.

No, Mom, really, thank you. I don't want any grits.

Alfredia fiddled with her strawberry oven gloves.

You wouldn't turn down a waffle if I made one?

Alfredia, sweetheart, said her husband, folding his newspaper, the boy ain't hungry. But I'll take a waffle with me to the plant, if you have a mind to fix some.

Alfredia looked from her husband to her son.

Guess I could try and eat one, too, Mom.

Within a split second, the waffle machine was plugged into the wall, and out of the refrigerator came eggs, butter, and milk in rapid succession.

What time you meetin' your buddies? asked his father.

In about twenty minutes, outside Druthers'.

Wow, Druthers', said his father. That place still goin'?

Alfredia was mixing the batter briskly in a white bowl. That's where Rusty had his first job, she said. And you know something? They paid him in bottles of Coca-Cola.

That's illegal now, Mom.

Well it was a long time ago, but he was over the moon about it. Free Coca-Cola, can you believe that?

Randy pulled a fresh pack of cigarettes from a green carton in the refrigerator.

He must have been in heaven, Alfredia.

He was. Anyone we met in the street that would talk to him, he promised to share it with 'em if they would only come by and sit at the counter. Eventually word got around, and the place was full of people drinking Rusty's wages.

Samuel was watching the whisk go around. Next to the bowl on the counter, sitting empty, was his uncle's Winnie the Pooh donkey mug.

He must be waitin' until you leave to come out of his room and have some breakfast, said Randy.

Alfredia glanced at the door that led down to Rusty's small apartment. Her brother had moved in fifteen years ago when she was pregnant with Samuel and Randy was away for weeks at a time on a military base. Rusty learned to take walks by himself in town and got a part-time job setting spokes onto bicycle rims.

After Samuel was born, Randy converted the garage into a one-room apartment to give his brother-in-law a sense of independence. Outside there was a Coca-Cola welcome mat and a Coca-Cola OPEN sign that Rusty would flip around to CLOSED when he was going to bed.

When it was finally time to go, Alfredia put Samuel's waffle in plastic wrap and tried not to comment as he stuffed it into his bag with the new pencils and pens from Walmart.

There were many cars going by on the street now, and when the diesel engines of school buses rattled the hall mirror, Samuel turned toward it instinctively.

You'd better go, said his father. Your friends might leave without you.

But it was too late.

He'd caught a glimpse of himself in the glass—a distant reflection, but enough to feel foolish and vain, a coward who, above all, feared the judgment of others. He stood there in his rock tee shirt and new Converse, on the first morning of high school, burning with the shame he had hoped to elude.

He rolled the backpack off his shoulders and moved quickly.

His uncle must have heard feet on the stairs because Samuel didn't even get halfway down before a door opened and a head appeared.

Did you come to say goodbye, Samuel?

No, I came to ask if my uncle would walk me to high school.

Rusty pointed. Because of your eye?

Just c'mon Rusty. Hurry up.

But I haven't had breakfast.

There's no time for eating, we've got to go.

Okay then, Rusty said, flipping the Coca-Cola sign to OPEN, then stepping out onto the staircase.

Samuel grimaced at the sight of his uncle's Coca-Cola pants, Coca-Cola sweatshirt, and Coca-Cola Velcro sneakers. Is that what you're wearing, Rusty? All red?

Rusty looked down at himself as though confused. Yes, he answered. It's what I'm wearing.

In town, disorderly clusters of children drifted toward the squat brick building surrounded by sports fields and parking lots. Many people passed them in station wagons and trucks. The road winding up to the entrance was a yellow chain of buses.

Uncle Rusty walked quickly without speaking. It was a warm, cloudless day. They could hear their rubber-soled shoes on the sidewalk and the rhythmic sigh of breathing. Samuel tried to keep his eyes fixed on the path ahead and not look to see who might be watching.

When they got close to the gates, vehicles were lined up waiting to release the children inside.

Samuel stopped walking at the end of the line.

Okay, this is good enough, Rusty.

His uncle pulled a roll of yellow stickers from his pocket.

Do you want these to give out?

Jesus, no, put those away, Rusty. Then he pulled the waffle from his bag. Eat this on the way home and don't tell Mom I gave it to you.

Uncle Rusty looked at the brown square in his hand, still warm from the machine. What if I drop it?

You won't drop it.

It could slip from my hand.

Well, keep it in the plastic wrap.

That's what I mean. Rusty turned the waffle over. Where did my sister put the syrup?

I'm going now, bye.

Okay, Rusty called after him, still transfixed by the waffle, come back and see us.

OLD MAN WALKER

1934

THERE WERE SO many holes in the floor of the truck, Carol had to be careful where she put her feet. The seat fabric had ripped away down to sponge and a few of the springs had uncoiled and stood erect between her and the old man.

Don't you wanna know where I'm takin' you, Carol? Old Man Walker said without turning to look. They'd been trundling along for hours with hardly a word.

How you know my name?

I was at the card table the night your daddy bet you and lost.

You know Travis Curt too? Carol said, feeling her voice falter.

Well I knew him, if that's what you mean.

Don't y'all talk anymore?

The old man stared at Carol for a long moment, then turned back to the road without saying anything else. He had long gray hair and squinted to see anything close enough to touch.

It don't matter to me where we going, said Carol finally. So long as it's far'way. She imagined Russ then. He was next to her mother and they were both looking at her.

Old Man Walker coughed. It's far'nough that the truck might'n make it all the way.

Carol looked down through a hole at the road passing under them. It's an old one, ain't it?

Old? asked the old man. I only had it sixteen years.

I mean it's well-used.

Most of the time it goes anywhere I want it to, if you feed it just like a horse. But I don't care for it the way I care for an animal.

I know what you mean, Carol said. Animals are jus' like children.

You ever leave the county before, child?

I've been to Lexington. When my momma was alive. But I don't remember it.

Well, we're going the opposite way, to a place you surely ain't never bin, and would never find by accident.

He turned to glance out the rear window, which was yellowed and webbed with cracks.

And if any folk got a mind to follow us—then I gots somethin' for 'em.

He reached down and pulled out a bone-handled knife from a wooden box on the floor.

You gonna scalp 'em, mister?

Old Man Walker laughed. You read too many books, child.

I only ever had one book, but I loved it.

Tell me the story.

There weren't no story, it were pictures.

Pictures of what then?

Fairies.

What?

Little folks, tiny creatures with wings that are always near us.

You mean flies?

No, I mean fairies.

Hmm. So no schoolin'?

Not much.

Old Man Walker went quiet then, as though talking had tired

him out. For a time Carol looked down again, at the road passing beneath them. But then she thought of something that made her feel afraid. She turned quickly to the old man, determined to ask, even if it meant finding out he was in the service of her father.

How did you know where I was, mister?

Heh, heh, I was wonderin' if you'd ask that. Luck or fate is what it was. I heard some folks outside the feed store, jabberin' about a young gal wi' child out there on the highway who looked to be runnin' away. I knew it had to be you and I was right. He laughed as if pleased with himself.

Does my daddy know? Is he gun' give chase?

The old man cackled wildly, then pointed at the box with the bone knife. I'd hate for it to happen that way, Carol, but so be it.

For what to happen?

For your daddy to meet me at them crossroads.

What crossroads? Is that where we're goin'?

No, no, child. Ever'body gits crossroads in their lives. It's where a person has the chance to choose another way.

Will I have to go back if he meets us there? I don't want to go back.

The man spat on the floor. It ain't no real place is what I'm tryin' to tell ya—but you ain't never goin' back. Not for any reason. Better to throw yourself on a fire and burn alive than go back to your daddy.

Carol felt for Mary Bright, who she'd hidden under her leg. But I ain't got no money and don't know a soul but you.

How old are you? Twelve? Fifteen?

I guess around fifteen. I ain't never had a birthday, except when Momma was alive, and I was too young to know my numbers.

The old man took one hand off the steering wheel, reached into his coat pocket, and pulled out a stack of money tied with string. He threw it into Carol's lap with a laugh.

That's ever'thing I ever won from your daddy at cards.

Carol had never seen so many bills in one place.

The old man stuck his hand out, and Carol returned the wad of money.

Just so it don't fall through one of them holes in the floor. I'm gonna hold it until we get where we're going. But it's yours, I promise.

You're jus' givin' it to me?

Old Man Walker turned to look at her then. What you give in this world will be given back to you. And what you take will be taken from you. Them's the oldest words I know. I was just a lil'un when that got told to me, but I always remember to pass it on.

When it got dark the headlamps of the truck flickered ahead on the road like two candles. Carol dozed for a time, then woke and noticed the old man's face was all puckered in, not moving. His mouth hung open, too, and his breathing was loud and forced. Carol grabbed his arm.

Wake up! Wake up!

The old man's body flinched, and they veered violently to the side of the road, spraying rocks into a ditch.

What the hell you tryin' to do? Make me wreck, woman?

Your eyes were closed! You were sleepin'!

Tsk! I wasn't sleepin', this is just how I look, if you hadn't noticed.

Well you were breathin' funny, like you was snorin'.

We ain't bin together but half a day, and you're tellin' me how to breathe. Typical woman.

I didn't know...

Well, said the old man, squinting at the road ahead. I guess it is kinda funny. You're not the first person to think I was dead.

I didn't think you was dead mister, I thought you was sleepin'.

The truck, still rolling through the darkness, filled with the sound of their laughter.

I had me a daughter once, Carol.

When, mister?

Long ago. Before.

Before what?

Before I changed. I was once like your daddy. Especially after the things I seen in the war.

What war?

Old Man Walker flinched angrily. What war! Christ, child, the American Civil War.

Oh, yeah, I heard of that.

I should think so. How about Nunna daul Tsuny? The trail where they cried?

Carol had only heard Cherokee a couple of times in her life, but tried to imagine what it could be. She pictured Hansel and Gretel lost in dense woodland with only the fairies to help.

Outside it was very dark. Night was just beginning.

Then Old Man Walker noticed something moving in Carol's hand. He turned sharply then jumped back in his seat.

What the hell's that! What you holdin' there!

It's jus' Mary Bright, my doll.

The old man squinted as he leaned down toward the small figure in Carol's hands.

It's a doll you say?

Yes sir, Mary Bright.

Jesus Christ in heaven, I thought you'd had the baby while I was talkin' to you.

Carol stroked the top of Mary Bright's head. I hope it's gonna be that easy, she said. I got her name from Momma. She said that since I bin' born, ever' day would be merry and bright.

Sometime in the middle of the night, they turned down a dirt road and bounced along for almost an hour. When they finally stopped, it was before a large house that had once been something grand but was now crumbling like an old wedding cake.

Carol woke when the engine ceased turning over. She looked out and saw a Black woman smoking a cigar on the porch. The woman raised her hand in the weak glow of the truck's lamps. Then another woman, tall and white, stepped forward from the shadows. She had a shotgun in the crook of her arm and a sharp, mean face.

Who are they? Carol asked.

Bessie and Martha.

Am I gonna stay with them?

That's right.

Carol sat in the truck, not knowing what to do. Her throat felt rough from the engine's fumes, and her swollen legs ached without mercy. The sight of the women filled her with dread. She wondered if they were going to kill her, and if this had been her daddy's plan all along.

Old Man Walker climbed down from the truck and came around to her door.

When he helped her out, Carol was surprised at the strength in his sinewy hand. If he *was* on her side, she felt instinctively that her father could never win against a person like this.

When he led her toward the house, she felt like a small child. He held onto her with one hand, while in his other dangled Carol's small case, containing a doll, a few clothes, a page torn from a book, and a single shoe.

EDDIE

1989

THE GIRL IN Samuel's sophomore history class had chestnut hair and a long, dark face with deep pools for eyes. Jennifer Hutchins was taller than most boys in the grade, and wore a silver retainer that imprisoned her teeth and her gums. For the last three months, Samuel kept a high school yearbook open to Jennifer's class photo under his pillow. A late night TV ad for the psychic hotline had guaranteed this as a way to awaken love in another person.

At the beginning of each history lesson, Samuel waited until she found a seat, then rushed to the nearest empty desk. Once settled, he'd watch her wrap hair around a finger or pull at the gum in her mouth, wishing he were close enough to feel her breath or inhale the flowers of her shampoo.

He spotted her from time to time at the arcade. Once, she was outside wearing stonewashed jeans that were rolled at the bottom. She was holding a large flat box with leftover pizza and waiting at the curb for someone to pull up. Samuel imagined her in the summer without shoes and socks, riding in her parents' minivan with her feet on the dash, wearing turned-up shorts and a thin, delicate blouse through which he could discern softness.

We don't know exactly how many died, the teacher told the class, looking at some dates he'd written on the chalkboard, but it was a lot, a whole lot of people. Try and imagine it by picturing stadiums full of men, women, and children. All dead in their seats.

That's gross, said a girl in the front row.

A boy at the back raised his hand. The students followed their teacher's gaze and turned to look.

Yes, Raymond? You have a question?

Er, did they have stadiums back then, sir? In the olden days?

A few people chuckled, then waited to hear what the teacher would say.

Well, yes, actually. But not like the ones you see on TV. The idea of an arena or stadium is actually very old. Does anybody know how old?

A thousand years? suggested a girl beside the window.

Everyone laughed at that.

King Arthur! said someone in a fake British accent.

The teacher smiled. Older. Much, much, *much* older, folks.

Most of the class was now paying close attention.

The teacher leaned toward them. Who has heard of ancient Rome?

The students looked around to see if anyone was nodding or had their hand up.

The Romans didn't play football or baseball...but they did have gladiatorial combat.

There was a shuffling of approval among the boys.

The teacher nodded. You've all seen movies about that, I guess.

Jennifer Hutchins was just two seats ahead. Samuel raised his hand in the hope she might turn around.

Yes, Samuel?

It was a fight to the death, wasn't it? In the Roman stadiums?

In most cases that's an accurate statement. Then the teacher looked around the room. People were starting to lose interest and talk amongst themselves.

Now listen up, everyone, listen to this, please, because this is a hard question but will get us back on topic: How do the Romans

have anything to do with smallpox and how it decimated the indig-
enous population of Native Americans?

The teacher meant it for everybody, but his eyes had come back to
Samuel. The class waited for him to say something they could mock.

Suffering and pain, Samuel said with a confidence that took the
teacher by surprise. Jennifer Hutchins was still looking, her dark
eyes just pouring into him.

Now that's interesting, the teacher said. Care to take it further, Samuel?

Well, I guess both the Romans and the European settlers
were invaders, right? They both brought suffering and pain...the
Romans through war and the Europeans through disease.

That is a thoroughly accurate statement, everyone. And in
most periods of history it's safe to say that ordinary folks like you
and me suffered the most, not the leaders who gave the orders, or
the rich, the powerful, and the famous.

Like Michael Jackson, sir?

How about Madonna? Like a virgin!

The teacher was holding chalk up to the board, about to write
something. He waited for the waves of laughter to pass.

Settle down, everyone. What I meant to say is that history has been recorded by the victors, not the defeated or
disenfranchised.

Then Samuel felt his mouth moving impulsively. I think that's
wrong, sir.

The class fell silent. Jennifer Hutchins twisted around again.
She was biting her finger this time. After meeting her eyes, Samuel dropped his gaze to the almost imperceptible lines on her lips.
Her body was fully turned in its chair and light from the window was breaking on her shoulder in tiny, dazzling pools. Samuel
rubbed his forehead to cover one side of his face.

The teacher was looking at him and everyone in the classroom
was quiet.

What I mean... Samuel said, his voice hesitant now, is that if the
victors write history, how can we trust anything we read?

56

The teacher put down his chalk and sat on the corner of his desk. He closed his eyes, and the children thought he was angry, but when he spoke, it was in a tone that surprised them.

To be honest with you all, what Samuel's saying is really the most important question any historian can ask. If you leave school with one thing from my class it should be this. If you open that book on your desks, it'll still tell you that Christopher Columbus discovered America.

Why is that wrong, sir? a boy at the back wanted to know.

It's not wrong, but it tells us that the history we read today is from the perspective of Europeans. Otherwise, it would say that America was discovered by people during the last Ice Age, walking across what was then a frozen sea. The European settlers would not be at the beginning of the book, but somewhere near the end.

Most of the students went quiet, but others were starting to quietly pack away their things. The teacher looked at the clock, then jumped up from the desk.

Homework tonight is to finish chapter fourteen and *please* pick the Native tribe you want to study. I'd recommend Cherokee, as this is Kentucky.

He looked to the back of the room, to a student who seldom raised his hand or spoke to others. We've got at least one student here descended from the Cherokee Nation, isn't that right, Eddie Walker?

Everyone stopped what they were doing and looked at the boy in the black leather jacket, who was staring at his desk, not moving. There were names and curses etched into the wood, and Eddie read them, said their names in his head.

The room filled with excited chatter and the sound of schoolbags being zipped.

Listen up! said the teacher, trying to speak over the din. If you do choose the Cherokee, start with the Trail of Tears section in the book and work backwards.

When the bell finally rang, there was a mad scramble. But Samuel hung back, waiting for Jennifer to put away her things. He wanted to stand behind her in the lunch line.

At the back of the classroom Eddie rose from his seat with a yawn. He seldom brought any supplies to school, except for a crumpled piece of paper that remained blank. He stuffed it back into his pocket. Since his arrest in the middle of freshman year for possession of drugs, most students avoided him. At recess he went outside and hung around the gym, smoking cigarettes. None of the teachers seemed to care, so long as he kept out of their way.

When Samuel's parents found out Eddie was on drugs, they warned their son to be kind but keep his distance. Almost every night, there was something on the television news about young people, addicted and dying.

It's his choice if he wants to fill himself with that junk, Samuel's father had said. But I don't want you involved, do you hear, son?

But Dad, Samuel protested, he's my best friend.

Well, then, give him the space to figure this out.

A mass of students moved slowly through the bright halls, past rows of gray, dimpled lockers. The aroma of food filled the air, and two lines began to form in readiness for a hot meal and a plastic cup of soda.

Samuel had timed it perfectly and was one person away from Jennifer Hutchins, who stood beside her best friend Megan. He wondered if she would say anything about his comment in class, or about their teacher sitting on the desk and closing his eyes. But the girls seemed preoccupied, giggling and covering their mouths. Samuel repeated to himself over and over that it wasn't his eye they were talking about, but something he could not imagine that was amusing only to girls when they were together.

The two lunch lines were made up of students who paid for food and students who received free meals. Although Samuel and Eddie didn't spend much time together anymore, they sometimes met up when both lines converged at the trays. Then they would talk for as long as they could. Eddie had gotten thinner in the last year. There were shadows under his eyes and a hot rash of acne that circled his mouth. He was in Louisville a lot with his mother and sometimes missed weeks of school. Nobody knew why. But

when Samuel saw him smoking behind the gym, he would sometimes go over to talk—tell his friend he loved him and that they
would always be brothers. Eddie would nod and touch his gelled
hair. There was nothing to say because everything that had once
mattered to him and that he found beautiful had long been hidden
away from the surface of his life.

Since his drug arrest, Eddie had not been allowed over to Samuel's house. Alfredia had treated the boys to a Mexican dinner three
months before for Samuel's fifteenth birthday. When they got to
the restaurant Eddie was already there, and had been in the booth
long enough to drink a pitcher of water. Country music played in
the dining room and Eddie said they should go to McDonalds and
play Mexican music. When everyone laughed, his face lit up.

Samuel and the other students inched toward the hot, wet trays
being stacked by the cafeteria crew in coveralls and hairnets. Then
Samuel heard laughing and saw students being pushed aside, as
though a small tornado was winding its way between the lines.
A backpack was suddenly flung through the air, and somebody
darted from the line after it. A moment later, Taylor Radley, a
senior wrestling champion, pushed in behind Samuel with two of
his friends. The lunch monitor had left to put a fresh box of milk
in the machine, so there was no one to say anything.

Taylor's hair was curly blond and long at the back. There were
tiny moles on his face and arms. He had once pinned a boy's head
against a window of the school bus just to make everyone inside
the bus laugh. Samuel could feel Taylor's eyes boring into the back
of his head. He continued to look straight ahead, at Jennifer and
Megan, toward where hot food was being served and plastic cups
were being placed upside down on trays.

Hey, Samuel!

Samuel feigned distraction by looking at his Casio survival watch, a recent birthday present from Grandma Carol and
Grandpa Joe.

Samuel! Roberts! Hey!

Having no choice, he turned.

Do something for me Samuel, huh?

What's that, buddy?

Ask Jennifer Bitchins something for me.

The two friends bobbed their heads with excitement.

Oh Jennifer? I don't know her that well guys.

Taylor laughed. I bet you'd like to though, right?

Samuel laughed weakly.

Ask if her cherry's been popped.

People in the lunch line stopped talking and turned to listen.

C'mon, Samuel, ask her that. You know what a cherry is, right?

Samuel felt his heart fluttering as though a small bird was trapped inside of it. The meal he had been looking forward to now made him feel sick.

You can see me, can't ya, Samuel? Taylor said, moving his head from side to side. With that funny little eye of yours swirling around in there.

He looks like a clown!

Shut up, Jesse, Taylor said. That ain't right. Don't say that about Samuel. C'mon, what's wrong with you?

Samuel rubbed his forehead and looked down at the new sneakers his mother had bought for him at the mall last weekend.

He don't look nothing like a clown, Taylor continued. To be honest, he looks more like a retard.

People in the lunch line gasped with horror and excitement. In Samuel's mind flashed an image of the Native Americans from class, their bodies rotten with smallpox, a disease wished upon them by men and women, who the teacher had said, felt little to no remorse.

Well, you gonna do it, chicken shit?

Samuel looked and could see that Jennifer Hutchins was embarrassed and afraid. Her long arms were folded across her body. She was no longer laughing or covering her mouth, but closing like a flower at dusk.

C'mon, fuckhead! Ask Bitchins if her cherry's bin popped!

Taylor and his friends jeered. Whatcha waitin' for?

Samuel tried to think of something to say that would make everything go back to the way it had been. But his voice felt small, and his limbs weak and empty—as though in a dream and bound by ropes of sleep.

He's just another retard like his Uncle Rusty, Taylor said, turning to his friends. I've seen him at Walmart greeting people like a big, dumb piece of shit.

Samuel felt anger rise up like a fiery head, consuming all the fear in its path. He surged forward and shoved Taylor hard in the chest. The boy was stunned for a moment, then reached an arm around Samuel's neck and pulled him down into a headlock.

Think you can fuckin' push me, Roberts? You retard!

Samuel's head filled with blood. He was looking at the tiles of the cafeteria. Each one was slightly different. Suddenly it was hard to breathe.

Tell everyone what a retard you are, Roberts. Go on, say it.

But Samuel couldn't speak or open his mouth.

There was a loud bang and Taylor's arm released. Samuel straightened up, gasping for air, as a lunch tray was smashed again into the boy's face. With the third blow he fell down, blinking madly and trying to shield himself from the onslaught. One of Taylor's friends tried to grab the tray, but Eddie shoved the edge of it into the boy's throat and he went down too, with a spluttering sound that made people scream. There was blood on the tiles of the cafeteria and on the back of the tray. Taylor's face was soon a red mask. Eddie dropped the tray then and took off.

Everyone was trying to make sense of what they had seen. Two of the cooks burst from the kitchen and shoved everyone aside. A moment later they heard shouting, and the school nurse appeared with her bag at the end of the corridor. No one had ever seen her run before. She got down on her knees and began fumbling with rolls of gauze. The cafeteria workers were trying to get everyone to move back.

Taylor was crying and trying to speak. He had lost a tooth and there was blood in his eyes.

When the ambulance pulled up outside with lights blazing, paramedics wheeled a stretcher through the cafeteria's emergency exit doors. Food service had stopped, and students were being told to leave the area and go back to their homerooms.

A girl standing near Samuel turned to her friend. Oh my God, he's psycho! she said. I hope they lock him up. It didn't occur to Samuel they weren't talking about Taylor Radley.

At the beginning of next period, the teacher came in and told everyone in a monotone voice to take out their books and start reading from page fifty-nine. Samuel had looked everywhere for Eddie but figured he was halfway back to the trailer park by now.

Then a few minutes into the lesson, the door opened very slowly. Eddie slinked in and went quickly to his seat without looking at the teacher or any of the students. No one said anything as he took the crumped piece of white paper from his jacket and set it on the desk. The teacher watched Eddie settle in and then went out. A moment later there were rapid footsteps in the corridor. The door opened quickly. It was the principal with two police officers. Eddie stood at the sight of them. The two cops unclicked the straps on their gun holsters. Two students near Eddie slid down under their desks.

Easy now, one of the cops said. We just want to go outside and hear your side of the story, that's all.

Eddie spun around and put his hands on his head with a casualness that made him seem too old for high school.

The cops rushed forward and handcuffed him. Eddie's black Levi jeans and leather jacket were dusty from where he had been hiding in a storage closet. He looked tired and hardly able to walk. It all seemed unfair somehow to Samuel, that some people were allowed to be violent and others were not. He would have told his history teacher it was injustice in their own time. But knowledge felt useless to him in that moment, like a key without anything to open.

Then as Eddie approached the classroom door he jerked out of the officers' grip. There was a scuffle and he was pushed to the ground as the police fought to regain control. Samuel could hear the leather jacket creaking as his best friend struggled in vain to be free.

BESSIE

1939

A LARGE MEAL of hush puppies, collard greens, cornbread, and chicken was spread across the table in mismatched dishes and cloths. When Bessie asked for the salt, Carol secured her son with one arm and reached for a tarnished shaker with the other. Then she watched as Bessie tapped white flecks onto her food.

You know we got a girl comin', Bessie said.

I already aired out the room.

D'you make up the bed?

I was fixin' to.

Maybe put some flowers in a jar.

I know, Bessie. I'll make it real nice I promise.

'Cuz this gal, she way past quick'ning, so I can't do nothing except explain to her why I can't do nothing. Now, if she ain't goin' home, she gonna stay with us until her baby's in the world, which could be a while.

Carol was trying to restrain the boy in her lap. His wish, as always, was to slide under the table where he would find things on the floor to amuse himself or to put in his mouth.

Carol scowled. Quit it, Rusty!

Bessie dropped a chicken wing onto her plate with a hollow clunk. Lord Jesus in heaven, Carol, jus' let him go. If that's what he wants, where's the harm in it? Lord knows I wish I could hide under the table, some of the folks we get comin' round here.

Rusty slithered through his mother's arms and disappeared.

He jus' gets so grubby. And it ain't normal that he can't walk yet.

Bessie motioned to the window with a piece of corn. Have you seen the world, child? There ain't nothing normal. In fact, if you were sane people would think you was crazy.

But he don't talk so good neither. Have you noticed that?

Bessie wiped her mouth with a clean cotton square. There's a chance that boy is special, Carol, like I told you last year.

Slow you mean?

Slow, fast, makes no difference. God turns the world at one speed.

Carol was many months past quickening when she arrived in the truck with Old Man Walker. Bessie had seen it right away and told the Cherokee that she hardly ever got any so young in such a condition. It must have been a nasty and dangerous situation he'd plucked her from. He stayed that night in one of the empty rooms, then got back in his truck at first light after Martha fed him sausage and biscuits, with a tin cup of black coffee to wash it down.

Carol's delivery took place a short time later on the first hot day of summer. There were towels everywhere, with Martha hovering by the door, as she always did. In the end, Bessie didn't need any help. Martha said it was like watching someone pull a catfish from a mud puddle. Carol felt the baby leaving her body. He was a big boy and she ripped during delivery. Despite the sweat-soaked sheets and blood from the tear, Carol thought Rusty was the most precious thing she had ever seen. Bessie made her stay in bed a whole two weeks after, drinking special tea, and making sure every day that everything down there was clean and dry.

. . .

Bessie picked up the salt again and shook it in her hand. A few dry pieces tumbled onto her palm.

Is there anything even in this? I need my glasses. And where's Martha at. Martha!

Pans clattered from the kitchen. Then the woman who did most of the cooking appeared in the doorway, wiping her hands on a rag. She was tall and bent slightly at the very top of her body as if from always having to look down. Martha was Polish, but had learned to make the food Bessie liked, and even enjoy it herself.

What you want Bessie? I'm busy.

I'm going to get fatter than I am now if you don't eat some of this.

That's what you call me in for?

No, but leave the kitchen and come sit with us.

But when is girl coming?

On the evenin' tide, Bessie said. Like I told you. That's why we're eatin' our main meal now instead of at supper. Carol gonna make up the back room.

But that room needs airing out.

Carol's doin' it. Now *please* stop fussin' and sit.

Martha tucked the cloth into her apron and joined them at the table.

I can help in the kitchen when I'm done with the room, Carol said.

After most of the procedures, Martha would spend hours scrubbing blood out of the linens. Her hands were like gray rags. She had taught Carol a good many things about cleaning and cooking. But when it came to baking, no one could compete with Carol's biscuits.

Thank you, Martha said, spooning small mountains of things onto her plate. I could use help with all towels we have this week.

You're gonna work that girl to death, Bessie said. Soak longer and scrub less would be my motto.

Martha huffed. Some of those towels want putting in trash.

With Rusty occupied under the dining table, Carol began to eat something too. I'll take all the work you can give me, she told the two older women, seein' as I don't pay a cent for food'n lodgin'.

Bessie sighed as if she were annoyed. There you go again, Carol, worryin' about nothin'. In case you ain't noticed, this is not a hotel. It's a home. I ain't much travelled 'cept to Tennessee for trainin' purposes—but the difference is you don't need money to stay in a home.

But—

But, but, but, Bessie said. *But* ain't gonna find my glasses, Carol, 'cause *but* never did nothin'.

After almost four years with Bessie and Martha, Carol had learned to milk a cow, milk a goat, catch an escaped goat, plant beans, dig potatoes, plant squash, harvest squash, and get blood out of almost anything.

Poultry or hogs usually came to them as gifts from the calloused hands of working men or grateful wives already struggling to look after the children they had and not wanting more. At first Carol thought that Bessie and Martha lived secret lives in the community, but Bessie's old plantation house was well known, and people usually waved when they saw her out walking the fields with a heavy stick or grumbling past in the old truck.

Once, when they were chopping wood, Carol had asked Bessie if she was worried about the Ku Klux Klan burning something in her yard, or coming at night in their hoods to preach and holler. Near where she grew up, whole families—with babes in arms—had been dragged into their dooryards and beaten by gangs of men at night.

Well wouldn't you know, Bessie said, one of those nasty ol' Klansmen brung his daughter to see me couple of years back. She swung the axe and split a log with a single blow.

Carol's eyes widened. He came here?

Yuh. From the next county. And I'm sure you can figure out why. Bessie put down her axe. Her forehead and cheeks were glistening with sweat. It's what I hate the most. I'd chop their filthy bidness clean off if it were up to me.

Was she past quick'ning?

No, she weren't, and I told him I would do it only, *only* if he keeps his dried up posse o' white fools off my doorstep. I told him if I see just one flash of pillowcase, well, then ever'one is gonna know what he done to his poor child. And I mean ever'one, preacher, farmers, wagon drivers, bootleggers, the Civil War general who lives alone on Victory Hill talkin' to hisself all day...even president of the United States if I have to.

Well if he'd bin like my daddy, Carol explained, then he'd probably be fixin' to trick you in some way.

The big woman smiled. I ain't nobody's fool 'cept my own. I gave him a pen and a piece of paper to sign that said he got the pro-cedure in return for my protection from the Klan.

Carol laughed. I'll bet he was mad about that.

He didn't say a damn thing—just scratched out his ugly ol' name right there on the paper that Martha wrote for me. It looked like a snake too, like the devil's serpent when he told Eve to try that juicy ol' apple. He knew his sin was about the worst kind. The Bible got whole chapters on it somewhere I'm sure.

Bessie sat on the thick stump she'd been using to split the wood. She lay her axe on the ground with the edge pointing away. Then she pulled a cigar stub from her pocket and lit the end.

That lil' girl was here about a week. When her father came back, he was real bossy and short. I knew he would be and I was ready for it. It's what men do to hide their shame and stupidity. I told him, there and then, that I sent that paper wi'his name on it, explaining everything what gone on, names and dates, what have you, to my sister in Illinoise with instructions to be opened in the event of my untimely demise by lynching or some such other nonsense. Well, Carol. You. Should. Have. Seen. His. Ugly. Ol'. Face.

You got family in Illinois?

Bessie chuckled. I'm an only child so far as I know, may the Lord bless my momma, born into shackles as she was. Anyway, his daughter, she run off six months later. May the Lord Jesus hisself help and guide that lost soul. Robbery, Carol, even killin' I can forgive if there's Christian cause…But not that…never, *ever* that.

Maybe you should've told the sheriff? About what he done?

That's a good idea, Carol, except that he was the sheriff.

Once Carol had made up the new girl's room and put some wild-flowers in a glass vase, she helped Martha as promised with a mound of bloodstained towels that had been soaking in vinegar and cold water. Rusty was outside crawling around with the chickens. Carol could see him through an open window. How she wished he would stand up and walk like other little boys.

He's turning four soon, Martha said, her hands deep in the basin of water. I'm trying to decide what cake is Rusty's favorite.

It's anybody's guess, 'cause he don't talk and he don't walk.

When is your birthday, Carol?

I have no idea.

So how old you are?

Carol shrugged. Maybe eighteen? Maybe twenty?

Oh my God, so young!

Well, I don't feel young, seeing ever'thing that goes on with people. I never imagined even a half of it. I was still playing with dolls when I first come.

Carol thought then of Mary Bright upstairs on her bed, and her mother's shoe that lived now in the closet, in a box with some dried summer flowers. Carol hadn't taken it out for a long time. The memory of her mother had become like a distant music that she strained to hear.

You don't feel young, Martha went on, but you are still in begin-ning. Trust me, I know. You will have good life, maybe more children.

Carol blushed but went on scrubbing. I actually think about that. What it would be like to live in a town, come and go as I please.

What's first thing you want to do in town?

That's easy. See a movie.

Martha nodded approvingly. Ok me too. Maybe we all go.

I want to live in a town so bad, Martha.

And get married?

To a man? I doubt it. It's jus' so hard to trust anybody. Maybe a movie star from a magazine is what I need, someone gentle, but strong when he has to be.

Sounds like my brother in Poland.

What's his name?

Jakob.

Well I wish he were here so I could marry him.

I was married once, did you know that?

Carol looked up from her work. No I didn't.

Martha stopped scrubbing and picked something from the bristles of her brush.

I'm surprised Bessie not tell you. There's not much to say. He wasn't nice man. I came here because I get pregnant but knew I couldn't bring child into same world as him to get same treatment.

You came to Bessie for a procedure?

Yes, but Bessie wouldn't do it.

Why? Was you too far along?

No, but Bessie said not wanting husband was different from not wanting baby. So, if I want, I can have baby and then live in house until I find good situation.

What happened to your husband?

Martha folded a wet towel over itself. After one week he found me. I was so afraid.

What did he want?

To take me back, like I am dog. But Bessie wouldn't let him come in house. He called her names, dirty *this*, dirty *that*, and told her he had gun in glovebox of car. Bessie said that no matter how big his gun, hers was bigger. He went away but came back next day and said he was going to call police. Bessie walk right up to him with piece of paper in hand which she let him look at for few moments. She told him it was signed document from state judge saying that as favor for helping his sister, the judge was willing to put one man of her choosing in jail for rest of life.

For real?

Martha's face softened into a laugh. It was certificate of guarantee for new Maytag refrigerator—but my husband couldn't read.

What happened to him then?

Well, it was hard time, so he went in California to pick fruits. Many men went. Then almost one year after Bessie chased him off, he was killed by policemen in workers' camp.

But what happened to your baby?

Martha let the towel she was holding slip silently back into the gray water. She left the sink and sat down at the kitchen table.

Carol followed, pulling out a chair as quietly as possible.

He was born in morning, and we buried him in afternoon at the edge of meadow.

Martha stopped talking and held her breath until the impulse to cry had passed.

Bessie read from Holy Bible, I will never forget, *Let the little children come to me, and do not hinder them, for the kingdom of heaven belongs to such as these.* That means he didn't suffer, don't you think?

Carol reached over and touched her hand. That's *exactly* what it means.

Eventually Martha got up from the table and went back to the sink.

You don't have to feel sorry for me, Carol. I like it here. Especially now with Rusty taking our shoes off under table, oh, how he makes me laugh.

Before the last rays of sunlight could dim and be forgotten, Carol took Rusty in his wagon to the woods so they could pick more wildflowers—the colorful ones that grew only in places where light could finger the ground in a dazzling spray.

Once back home, Carol found a clean Mason jar in the pantry and filled it with cold water from the pump outside. Then she gently shook out the flowers before dropping them into the jar and arranging each little head so that none were hidden or crushed. When that was done, she carried the vase up to Martha's room. Bessie saw her on the landing and said that flowers were proof God made the world to be enjoyed.

At dusk, the three women sat on the front porch with a platter of cut peaches, waiting for the lights of a car. Rusty was on the steps playing with his rubber ball. Deep in the woods, a lone whippoor-will sang at the edge of night's curtain.

When the fruit was eaten, Bessie lit her evening cigar and Martha went inside for the shotgun. Once or twice, there had been no girl at all, just a man full of rage and bitterness for what he himself had done.

As they waited, calmed by the sizzle of Bessie's cigar, all around them in the trees, insects chirped and rattled in an overlapping rhythm, and Carol wondered if everything in this world wasn't just a rehearsal for some other more perfect place, where there was no cruelty or suffering, but no kindness or salvation neither.

SAMUEL

1991

FOR GRADUATION WEEKEND, Samuel's parents decorated the yard with banners and laid out a Mexican taco buffet on the back porch. Uncle Rusty's job was to set utensils beside the steel pans and arrange the soda so there were always cold cans available to Samuel's friends.

Grandma Carol and Grandpa Joe had come early to spend time with their grandson. When their car pulled up, Samuel went over and walked them through the yard to where lawn chairs were unfolded.

When he was in elementary school, Samuel had loved seeing his Grandma Carol, but since he'd become a teenager, they had grown apart. She had been tyrannical with her daughter about Samuel playing cards. And he was never, ever to take a drink of liquor while she lived. The family was cursed in that way, she believed, with the sins of past generations just waiting for a door to reenter their lives and take over the present. And she'd hated it when he grew out his hair. A year ago Samuel had gone to her house for supper in ripped jeans. Grandma Carol left him standing at the door to call her daughter and say a vagrant had shown up on her property.

When his grandparents were seated comfortably, Samuel fixed two plates of food from the buffet and carried them over.

But this is your special day, said Grandpa Joe. We should be serving you, graduate.

Grandma Carol poked the refried beans on her plate with a plastic fork. What is this?

Mexican, Grandma.

She handed the plate back to Samuel. I never much liked beans. Ask Alfredia to make me a sandwich when you go in the house.

Excited to start college in the fall, big fella? asked Grandpa. What do you want to study?

Samuel set the uneaten plate of food down on the grass. Engineering maybe. Something where I can use my hands.

Grandpa Joe nudged his wife. She was holding a can of soda and some of it spilled out.

Ain't I the same way, Carol?

Yes, you are, she said, pressing a napkin into her dress. First the paint factory, then the farm. You always used your hands for ever'thing.

I sure worked hard my whole life, said Grandpa Joe. But there wasn't a day I didn't get some joy from it.

Not too many machines back then for farming like there is now, right Grandpa?

Oh, it's a different world now. A whole different ball game.

Then Grandma Carol reached out her hand. I'm proud of you, Samuel. I might not seem like I am. But that's just my way. Now tell me, you gonna cut your hair for college?

At dusk, Alfredia made Samuel's friends line up so she could take pictures. Then everyone drove away in small cars or borrowed trucks with graduation flags and banners flapping from their vehicles. Some of Samuel's friends had scribbled SENIORS on the back windows in spray-snow. Others had written MISTY, the name of a student killed junior year by a drunk driver.

Samuel asked Uncle Rusty to be his passenger for the cruise up and down Main Street, that way he could see and feel the excitement of a graduation for himself. When they were belted into Samuel's red Ford Mustang waiting to pull out of the driveway, Rusty began to rock back and forth in his seat.

I'm nervous about the cruise, Samuel.

How come?

I never bin in one.

It's easy, Rusty, you just sit there, and from time to time scream something out the window.

Scream out the window? When?

Just whenever you feel like it.

What though? A word?

Anything you want, Rusty.

Can I curse?

How's about Coca-Cola?

Ok. Just tell me when.

All over town there were signs and billboards congratulating the senior class. Every business had something colorful hung up in the window. For the dance, the high school teachers had turned the gym into an enchanted underwater kingdom. The students believed the hardest time of their lives had come to an end.

When the cruise was over, Samuel dropped Uncle Rusty back at home. After eating his supper, Salisbury steak, Cajun rice, and creamed corn, he went downstairs and stayed up late arranging his model cars on the floor of his little apartment. When people in the street revved their engines or screamed through the open windows of their vehicles, Rusty would look down and touch one of his cars. Then he would move them all forward an inch or two. It was a cruise for graduates, just like the one he had been in with Samuel, but with free Coca-Cola at the end for all the tiny, invisible people.

. . .

By the early hours of the morning it was all over.

Vehicles were back in their driveways. Houses muted by sleepers held steady against the passing night. At school all the lights had been switched off. The classrooms dark and empty but for neat rows of desks and the aroma of polish which hung in the air like childhood suspended. The sparkling underwater kingdom that had made everyone nervous and then confident was now just a place of trampled cups—a school gym hung with old bedsheets that someone had painted and then sprinkled with glitter.

Around three o'clock in the morning, Samuel stumbled in through the basement door and tripped over something in the darkness. There was vomit on his clothes and on his shoes. When the basement light flicked on, Samuel saw Uncle Rusty sitting upright in a wicker chair.

Congratulations graduate!

Jesus, Rusty, you scared the piss out of me. I'm drunk as hell.

You want a Coca-Cola, Samuel?

No I'm going to bed. Don't tell Mom and Dad you seen me like this.

Okay, Rusty said, getting up and turning his sign over to CLOSED.

A week after graduation, Samuel started work at an auto-parts store. His job was to look things up on an oil and coffee stained keyboard, then give estimates for parts. When there was no one in the shop, he would count the tires and batteries, then place orders from suppliers on the phone.

After a month, he got into the habit of an afternoon smoke break out back near the dumpster. On hot days he would chug down a beer if no one was watching. He kept some cans in his locker and they managed to stay cool from the air conditioning.

One afternoon, just as he was finishing a smoke, Samuel saw something move in the trees. He stubbed out his cigarette and crossed the parking lot quickly.

That you? he said, leaning into the tree line.

Yuh, Sam, it's me.

But Eddie, you ain't supposed to leave the shack.

I know it, but I've been dreamin' of somethin'.

What?

Pizza.

You'd risk getting caught for a slice of pizza? I love you man.

I'm lonely out there in the shack, Samuel.

Well you ain't supposed to come to town. The cops will find you. Just wait a couple more hours until five when I get off.

You want me to go back?

Samuel thought for a moment. My car is open, go lay down in the back seat. Crack the window so you don't burn up.

But it's electric.

Jesus, Samuel said, digging for the key in his pocket.

He had not seen Eddie for most of high school. After the assault charge sophomore year, he'd been transferred to a juvenile home in Bardstown, fifty miles away. After that he went to live with his mother in Frenchburg. When she left for California to meet a man she'd known in high school, Eddie stayed there alone, watching television and rehydrating packets of noodles he bought at different gas stations with forged checks.

One afternoon he came home and there was an eviction notice on the door. Eddie ripped it down quickly and tried to get inside, but the locks had been changed. All his stuff was in the house, so he went around the back and bust open his bedroom window.

A neighbor must have been watching, because soon the police came and Eddie had to jump the back fence to get away. A cop shouted at him to stop. But Eddie didn't even turn around. He crossed the freeway and kept going until he was deep in swampy woodland. There he unzipped his leather jacket and collapsed on a fallen tree, panting and clammy with sweat.

After sleeping in a tractor shed for two nights and filling his pockets from the trash of a sandwich shop, Eddie hitchhiked west to where his best friend lived. His idea was to live in the woods until cold weather came. There was a shack he remembered past the old BMX track, near a river. He figured Samuel could teach him how to survive like his Cherokee ancestors. Then he would go up to Cincinnati where he had a friend from the youth home—or maybe down through Alabama and Florida like his father, on the run from the law.

When Samuel's shift at the auto-parts store ended he walked to his car. Looked around for a moment, then got in.

I'm takin' you back to the shack.

What about the pizza? Eddie said. He was stretched flat on the back seat. That's why I come to town.

I thought you were lonely.

Yeah, that too, Eddie said, sitting up.

Stay down goddamnit. You're a fugitive.

I am?

Samuel lit a cigarette and passed it back. That's what you told me.

'Cause I was chased by the police, which means they found out about the checks.

But did they recognize you?

All my stuff was in the house. The landlord prob'ly give'um my name.

Well then, don't leave the shack. Quit jerkin' off and set the traps like I showed you.

Eddie shrugged. But rabbits are kinda sweet, Samuel. I feel bad for 'em. I'd rather eat coyote. Can you teach me how to catch a coyote?

You're the coyote, Eddie, coming here tryin' to sniff out pizza. You're supposed to catch your food. What about the fishin'?

I went to the bend where you told me.

Catch anything?

Snappin' turtle.

Seriously? No catfish?

I reckon I might need some bait for that.

Dumbass, you're kiddin' right?

Eddie laughed. I don't wanna tear open some poor creature's mouth when I can have pizza. How many cigarettes you got?

Samuel reached into his pocket and gave Eddie his box of Marlboro Reds.

You're a lost cause, Eddie, at least when it comes to huntin'.

Although Alfredia didn't know what was going on, Samuel had told his father about Eddie living wild in the shack beyond the old BMX track.

Does he have a gun, Samuel?

No.

Good, don't give him one. He'll be alright so long as he don't have a gun. There's nothing out there but skeeters and ticks.

Several nights a week, Samuel would park his car at the convenience store on the edge of town, then disappear into the woods. It was a half-hour walk to the shack. He had taught Eddie many things, including how to purify water and which plants he could pick and eat.

Some nights they'd just sit in the dirt and dead leaves, getting drunk on moonshine or whiskey. Beer was no good to them. It was too heavy to haul and they couldn't drink it fast enough to get a decent buzz.

On a battery-powered stereo, they played Black Sabbath or Skid Row. When they got high, Santana or the Grateful Dead. Poker by firelight with small rocks or bird arrowheads Eddie found on the riverbank while not fishing.

Sometimes Eddie got up and danced in the flickering light of their fire. When Samuel was drunk enough he danced too. There was no one else for miles. Just muttering trees, water silvered by moonlight, animals tucked into envelopes of night.

On one of the last evenings in August, it was so hot their clothes stuck to their bodies. They had been drinking for several hours when Samuel got up and walked through some bushes in the direction of the river. Eddie followed.

The water was low because of the heat. They stripped down to their underwear and stepped over smooth rocks toward the knee-high water. Samuel knew a deep pool where they could lay down so that only their shoulders and faces would show.

Damn that feels good, don't it? Samuel said as his body sank.

What about snappin' turtles?

Samuel laughed. You worried about your pecker? I reckon I'm too drunk to give a shit.

Eddie looked back at the riverbank.

What you worried about now?

Just wish I'd brought the bottle.

Oh, hell yeah, Samuel said. A few gulps of bourbon and we'd be all set.

Want me to run back?

Skeeters would eat y'alive, Eddie. Let's just cool off awhile.

Sure is hot ain't it?

Samuel closed his eyes. Won't be too many more days like this.

This time next week you'll be in college, Samuel.

And you'll be with your girl in Ohio.

Yeah. Jean.

Wish I could come with you, Eddie.

You can if you want.

Mom and Dad would kill me. They already paid for a semester of tuition and a room in the dorms.

You don't want to go to Western?

Not really.

Serious?

Four more years of fuckin' school? No way…

Eddie chuckled. You'll get used to it.

I thought we'd be famous by now, goddamnit, playing poker, or rock and roll. Somethin' cool, y'know?

But college will be fun. I heard the girls at Western are smokin' hot.

Smokin' crack more like.

Well, you're welcome in Ohio with me and Jean anytime you want.

That's the problem, Samuel said, moving his body in the water. There's nothing I want. I hate school, I hate working in town, and I can't join the service 'cause my eye.

Eddie stirred in the water. Goddamnit, I told you I was sorry.

Samuel laughed and rubbed a wet hand in his friend's face. I'm just fuckin' with ya dude.

From where I'm sitting you've got it made.

What the hell you talking about?

You can do anything you want. You've even got a car, man. You could drive to Mexico if you felt like it, suck down a tequila worm and keep on truckin'.

Maybe I will, said Samuel. Because there's nothing here I want. Factories are shit. Jobs are shit. People suck. School is boring.

There's nothin' you want to do?

Get high and jerk off.

C'mon, I'm trying to help you, Eddie said, almost pleading with his friend. Samuel's despair seemed to pull on him as though everything between them was shared.

I'm serious. All I wanna do is drink. I live for it.

What about survival shit?

What about it?

You could teach that to people.

Like who?

I don't know, anybody. Me and Jean for one.

Samuel's face did not move or show any expression.

See? Eddie said. It's a good idea. We'll be your first customers if you don't mind an IOU.

Thanks buddy.

They sat without moving in the cool water. Night was settling around them.

So what do *you* want? Samuel asked his friend.

I can't say.

You don't know?

I know, but I'm shy about it.

Don't be an asshole.

Eddie spoke hurriedly, as though there was danger in admitting the things he wanted. First off, I want a job that pays enough for me to get married, have a kid, and then take it to Disney World in Florida. After that I don't care what happens.

You're shittin' me. Disney World?

And I wanna buy a real house, watch TV at night, fuckin' fix shit, mow the yard, play with my kid, grill, watch sports, go to NASCAR, fuck my wife, get drunk, try and get in touch with my mother, tell her I'm sorry, and play poker with you once a week.

Then, out of nowhere, Eddie started to cry.

I ain't never had a real home, Samuel.

C'mon Eddie, that's bullshit. What about the shack?

Eddie jumped up and splashed water in his face. You're a fuckin' asshole, you know that?

They darted back to the camp over dry rocks, laughing, then pulled on their clothes. For the next few hours, they guzzled the rest of the liquor and by midnight were passed out as two heaps on the ground.

After one semester at Western, Samuel found he couldn't go on and officially withdrew from the school. He moved back in with his mother and father, telling them he'd get his old job back at the auto-parts store. But after he'd left for college, someone had found the beer cans piled up in his locker.

Despite having dropped out of school, every Thursday night, Samuel returned to Bowling Green to drink and play cards at

Chance's house in the student village. He kept some overdue library books in the back seat of his red Mustang in case Public Safety stopped to ask why he was on the campus without a valid ID.

His mother thought these weekly trips were a sign he might return, and promised Samuel she'd call his professors and plead with them to give him another chance. He only had to say the word. But the idea of four more years of papers and homework was more than Samuel could bear. Instead he bought an acoustic guitar and a book that taught you how to play using numbers instead of notes. After learning some chords in his room, Samuel would sit out on the back porch with his uncle, brushing at the strings.

Once I get the hang of this, Rusty, I'm gonna write some ballads, then hitch out to Los Angeles and get a band together.

When's that?

Before I turn twenty. That's my goal.

But most nights, he just stayed up in his bedroom gulping shots of Jäger and smoking cigarettes with the stereo on. With liquor screaming through his veins, Samuel would stare at himself for hours in the mirror, marveling at how the drunker he got, the straighter his eye seemed to be. He read on an album sleeve that Jimi Hendrix slept in bed with his guitar, so Samuel did the same, but then one night turned over and put his elbow through the back of it.

Without anyone knowing, Samuel's father put in an application for his son at Ford, filling out the paperwork on his breaks. Alfredia cried when her husband told her and Samuel about what he had done. She had always dreamed her son would work in an office, wear a necktie, and drink coffee out of a machine.

Waiting to be called for an interview at the auto plant in Louisville, Samuel was drinking more than ever in his parents' basement. In the afternoons, when Uncle Rusty got home from Walmart, they would sit together on the back porch with the sense that life would always go on in the same way.

Samuel rarely left the house but for his Thursday night card game at Western.

Chance was captain of the softball team, so there were always girls at her parties. Everyone drank from plastic cups, listened to Alice in Chains, Nirvana, and Nine Inch Nails, and talked about life in another state, where it was always warm and people were open-minded. Most of Chance's guests used the playing cards for drinking games, but Samuel was there to gamble.

At first it was just coins, but after months of regular play, people began showing up with small rolls of bills. Samuel liked how drinkers would stand over the table and watch. Lifting bottles of beer to their mouths. Not speaking. It made him feel important to be looked at, long hair falling over his right eye so it was hard to tell straight away there was anything different.

But one night he got too drunk to play and hit a streak of bad luck.

Give it up, Chance said when his money ran out. Go smoke it off on the patio.

The other players waited for Samuel to leave the table, but he didn't budge. There was a girl at the party he recognized from freshman biology. She had very straight hair, freckles, and a nose that turned up at the end. Samuel had seen her earlier in the hall, laughing into her Dixie cup. Chance said her name was Dorothy Sales. Earlier that night, before sitting down to play cards, Samuel had talked with her for an hour about everything from teachers to their favorite things in the cafeteria. He could speak freely in the dark hall with his face veiled by shadow.

Dorothy was from Lexington, where her mother lived in a big colonial house with a paddock to train horses. She told him about her parents' vicious divorce and why she was changing her major from accounting to anthropology. She told Samuel to come back to Western, give college another go. Her soft, light voice made anything at all seem possible.

He was drinking Jäger from a bottle but put it down on a counter beside some empty cups when their conversation turned serious. He told her about his best friend. Their summer after high school. She listened and laughed at how Eddie had risked jail for pizza. But in the end, there was never even a warrant out for his arrest. It had all been for nothing. He told Dorothy about how Eddie and Jean were living together now that she was pregnant with his baby.

When Dorothy's boyfriend arrived with a tray of vodka Jell-O shots in clear plastic cups, Samuel excused himself to play cards. He had known there was someone but hoped he would not come. Dorothy's boyfriend was on the soccer team and from England. He was skinny but had a muscular body and hair just a bit longer than Samuel's. He looked like someone Samuel could be friends with, but in his voice was a mocking tone, as though beneath the long hair and cool clothes, he loved only the things he could dominate.

Samuel watched him touch Dorothy as he played poker at the table in Chance's kitchen. But then the liquor got to his eyes, and even the cards were hard to look at. One suit was the same as another.

When he'd run completely out of money, Samuel pulled out the key to his red Mustang and threw it on the table. Chance grabbed it. Samuel jumped up from his seat with a sudden, uncontrollable rage, and Chance slapped him hard, then immediately laughed. Samuel stood there touching his cheek. People were staring, excited by what had happened.

C'mon asshole, Chance said, being hit by a girl is still better than losing your car.

Samuel could hear people laughing, but their bodies were just a blur of colors. When he tried to speak, the words came out of his mouth in slow motion. Chance took his arm and helped him across the kitchen and into the hall.

Dor'thy, he said. Shewashere. I needtotellhersomething.

Dorothy is with her boyfriend, Samuel, so forget about that. You're too cool for her anyway.

Whataboutyou?

Chance laughed, and put the car keys back in his pocket. Sleep it off in my room. And don't do anything stupid like that again...please.

Samuel thought he could hear people talking then, behind Chance, saying things about his game, that he had lost everything and couldn't play cards, and that he shouldn't be on school grounds because he was a dropout.

Then Dorothy passed them in the hall. Samuel knew because of her perfume. He opened his eyes wide, forcing the muscles to focus. Her boyfriend was behind her. Drunk, his hands traveling greedily over her body like small, hungry animals.

C'mon Samuel, Chance said, opening her bedroom door and bundling him in. Stay here and sober up. And don't pee on the comforter, use a cup if you have to.

Samuel flopped his head up and down like a cloth doll, but after she'd gone, found that he couldn't lie down at all. His head was spinning and it took every ounce of his will to keep from throwing up. He held the image of Dorothy in his mind and imagined pulling her boyfriend away by force. He could drive them somewhere far away, like Daytona Beach, or Austin, Texas. He remembered Taylor Radley then, that day in the cafeteria at high school. The things he'd said about his eye and the names he'd called Uncle Rusty.

When he opened his eyes it was night. The music from the party was louder but the room very dark, as though everything around him had been sketched. He wondered how long he had been asleep, and if Dorothy was in the next room and if she needed him. His head hurt and he was dizzy, unable even to sit up. He rolled over and reached for a half-finished bottle of beer. It broke the dryness on his lips, but the sweet, warm bubbles brought the contents of his stomach surging into his mouth.

He sat there over the orange pool, his nose and throat still burning. Then he vomited again, this time with a growl. The door flung open and there was suddenly a crowd. Vomit had pooled on the carpet and dripped off the bed, some had even reached the shelf with Chance's softball trophies and spiral bound notebooks.

Samuel stood shakily and stumbled toward the door. People parted without speaking. He had to get out and into the cool evening air where he could breathe again. By the time he reached his

red Mustang, people were calling him back. He unlocked the door
and got in. Then he heard clapping and in the mirror saw Chance
running toward him in her striped athletic flip-flops. He slotted
the key, turned hard, and rammed the shifter into drive, peeling
out of the parking lot full of liquor and rage, determined to exit a
world governed by shame and disappointment.

Once out of the city, he lowered the sun visor and took out a ceramic
pipe. It was white and orange to resemble a cigarette. Packed inside
was a pinch of marijuana. Fumbling with his lighter, he lit the pipe
and held the smoke in his lungs for longer than usual.

Through habit he was able to go on for many miles toward the
county where he had once been a child. A ghostly moon hung over
the car in a sky too bright for stars.

He could barely see the road but followed as best he could a
white strip, that from time to time would disappear. He did not
know how fast he was going, or if he was even driving in the right
direction. His thoughts bobbed, just out of reach. Only the present mattered, the shallow moment where memory had no place
or power.

Soon his will to grasp thoughts began draining away. It was
just a few lapses at first, then the world he knew—the sound of the
engine, Dorothy holding her red cup, the cards he had been dealt,
Chance's hand on his face, the warm beer, the dark road under
headlights—all plunged soundlessly into a deep tunnel of sleep.

The Mustang continued for a mile or so, seeming to steer itself,
until his hands dropped slowly from the wheel the angle shifted,
and the car drove another mile on the wrong side of the highway.
When the road bent right, the red car continued straight. Then
both tires hit dirt. Then rough grass. Then a sudden drop down
an embankment toward a dense patch of trees.

For about forty or fifty yards, with Samuel's Converse shoe
still on the gas pedal, the Mustang rattled violently as tree limbs
slashed and tore at the body.

If he had been awake Samuel would have remembered the sound of whipping, then a moment of weightlessness as he slipped down the soft mud of a riverbank and flipped over with a splash, the trunk disappearing into a deep pocket of water.

It was almost dawn when the river caused the car to shift.

The submerged back end, heavy now, was being dragged away from the bank. The creaking of metal and glug of empty spaces filling caused Samuel to open his eyes.

Although he'd hung in his seat belt for hours, swimming in and out of dreams, the terror that seized him upon waking made him shriek and flap his arms. Then he remembered and forced open his door, splashing into the cold river that was now filling the shell of his car. Like an animal awake only to fear, he waded through the cold liquid, then pulled himself onto the bank by grabbing handfuls of reeds. A moment later, the water boiled and the car disappeared into a deep channel.

Samuel gasped for air, still too cold and panicked to feel the cuts on his hands and face.

Around him the world was a deep, dense violet.

Then a terrible thought took hold.

He pulled himself up and squelched through the trees, tearing through bushes and low branches in the direction of the road. With his mind squeezed by fear, Samuel pushed his weak, freezing body up the steep grass slope to the road. Then he stood and let his gaze spill onto the tarmac at the other vehicle he feared was there, jagged and crushed, its occupants all around, torn open in pools of glass and blood.

But all Samuel could see was empty road, trees, and a sky dotted with distant birds.

He went a little ways down the road and was surprised to discover he was wearing only one shoe. A pink, wet sock made him stop and stare until he realized there was blood running down his leg from a deep gash. He was still too cold to feel any pain, and so stumbled back down the slope, following his tire tracks through the shallow woodland. When he got to the river, Samuel lay on his back in the wet mud, breathing hard, his entire body shaking with cold but brimming with a kind of mad joy at what he had *not* seen on the road, at what he had *not* done.

He thought of his mother then, imagined her face the moment she realized her son was dead.

He saw his father at the kitchen counter smoking cigarettes, feeling packed down into some chamber of grief, where lived the faces of those he had killed in war.

And Uncle Rusty in his little room, brushing the strings on Samuel's broken guitar, listening for a music that seemed just one breath away.

When it was time to start walking, Samuel got up and stood at the water's edge, gazing hard at the black smudge of his tires a few inches below the surface of the river. Samuel had not believed in God since he was little, but at that moment he felt in his body the presence of something, like a thick, unflexed muscle.

Then he looked all around because the trees were moving.

Not a single trunk was still. Everything was moving.

An invisible force was everywhere and made everything touch.

BESSIE

1942

So MANY NIGHTS they sat out on the porch, listening to news of the war on the wireless, as Bessie puffed on a cigar and Rusty fiddled with the wooden blocks Bessie had cut for him in the shed and Martha had stained in the kitchen one snowy afternoon. They had been wrapped and placed in his stocking last Christmas, along with some chocolate, an orange, and a wooden airplane that could fly with a rubber band.

As usual, after the president made his speech, Bessie turned the knob of the wireless and they all went to bed. For the first time in a week it was just the four of them in the house.

In her bed Carol lay awake, wondering how far she would have to travel from Kentucky to hear the guns and the bombs. If Martha's brother had been killed, there must have been children caught up in it too, little boys not much different from her own son. Then she thought of the girl who had come to this house almost seven years ago. The life she had run from. That had been like a war.

Carol used to dream her father was out there, in the woods beyond the house, crouched down, waiting to be seen from a window. Laughing at her. Laughing at them all. There were other feelings too, smaller than fears, but bleak and persistent, that followed wherever she went, just waiting for a break in her thoughts to land.

In the morning, with Rusty still sleeping, Carol crept down to the kitchen and made a batch of fresh biscuits while the house was quiet. Their home had been unusually busy—even with so many sweethearts and husbands fighting overseas. The atmosphere of threat, Bessie said, was pushing people into each other's arms.

Martha was late coming down to eat.

We're all she's got now, Bessie said, pouring herself more coffee.

When Martha finally appeared in the doorway still wearing her nightgown and slippers, Bessie told her to sit and get served for a change.

But once seated she could only stare at the food on her plate.

Please eat the biscuit, Carol said earnestly.

Martha sank forward until her forehead rested on the tablecloth.

I think we'll go for a drive today in the truck, said Bessie. Burn up some of that gas before it goes stale.

Martha lifted her head and broke into a tearful smile.

Guess you think that's funny, Bessie said.

No, Martha replied. It's Rusty. He's tickling my feet.

Carol went red with anger. Rusty! she hollered, bending down. He even had one of Martha's slippers in his mouth.

I ought to spank you!

Please, Martha said. Let him. Just for today.

He's like a little mutt, said Carol, chewing on people's shoes.

Rusty had grown but his legs were deformed, and it took great effort to slide up and down the stairs on his belly. He was almost seven but still barely spoke. Bessie said they wouldn't know too much about his condition until he got bigger.

Carol cried about it sometimes, wondering what she had done wrong. Or if it was some curse for how he'd come to be.

Carol would tell Rusty that if he didn't try and walk soon, he'd stay a baby forever. But he'd just pull down her hand to his cheek. Or bite her fingers so that Carol would have to yell, which only encouraged him. Sometimes when she tried to teach him something, he'd listen for a moment then look away as though the room were full of people that no one else could see. Most of the time he was under the table. It made Carol think of the yellow tablecloth her mother had made. It was one of two things she yearned to have back in her possession. The other mightn't even be alive anymore. But if he was, he'd be old, with mist in his eyes and an uncertain way of moving about.

Before they went out in the car, Bessie wanted the sinks filled so things could soak awhile. She asked Carol to help her with the buckets.

The kitchen smelled of vinegar and faintly of tobacco from Bessie's evening cigar—now savored indoors, as it was too cold to sit out on the porch. Fall had begun early, startling them with a quick, heavy frost.

So, do you think the Japanese or Germans gonna invade Kentucky? Carol asked Bessie, as they heaved full buckets from the pump. Rusty was at the edge of the woods picking up handfuls of dirt and squeezing them.

We're too far, child. Now...America's gonna win this one, but after the victory come, prepare yourself, because there's gonna be big changes 'round here.

Inside, they poured the cold, clear liquid into deep enamel sinks. Water was heating on the stove so Martha could have a hot bath when they returned from their outing.

Like what kind of changes, Bessie, food rationing?

You hear about all those women in their boiler suits building airplanes, using men's tools, earning men's money? You think they're gonna go back to house-wifing? I don't think so. Not me. You can't give someone freedom then take it back. The feeling of bein' free—havin' your own money. That's goin'stick.

They each scooped a mound of sheets and let them sink like soft islands into the gray water.

Martha was in the corner listening to their conversation and holding a cigarette, which was unusual for her. She breathed out a thin line of blue smoke. Maybe we have female president too, eh?

You think I'm jokin', Bessie said, but what I can also tell you for nothin' is that Black folks is dyin' right now in oceans and jungles, even in the sky, fightin' for a freedom they don't even get at home. Somethin's gonna give. Believe you me, there's a reck'ning comin'.

After packing a lunch of pork cutlet sandwiches and potato salad, the three women drove to the river.

Rusty wanted to go outside but Carol was worried about him falling in the water. Bessie said the river was too far for him to crawl so they swung a door open and put him on a patch of dirt, where he could pick things up and pat the ground in his search for tiny creatures to play with.

That boy don't feel no cold never, Bessie said. His daddy must've been'uh Eskimo.

Carol looked at the sticky mound of potato salad on her plate. Then she felt Bessie's meaty hand on hers.

I'm sorry, child. I didn't mean to bring up the past in so cavalier a fashion.

When do you think he's gonna talk? Carol asked with more exasperation than hope. Maybe we should take him to a special doctor?

I was thinking that, said Bessie. It's a long drive to the city but we could do it. I wouldn't be able to come in with y'all. You know that right? It'll have to be you and Martha.

He does speak a little, said Martha. I heard him chatting to your doll, Mary Beth.

But he don't talk like he should, Carol said without correcting her. The strain in her voice was clear now to the other women.

Let's wait until the war's over, said Bessie.

Carol sighed loudly. That's your answer to everything. That and fooling people with bits o'paper they can't hardly read.

Bessie's eyes narrowed. That's right, she said. I'm the most dishonest-honest person you'll ever meet.

Martha put her sandwich down and they all laughed for the first time in many weeks.

After her bath, Martha said she felt much better, and over supper they put the radio on. But when the newscaster said the fighting overseas had never been so bad, Bessie got up and switched it off. Rusty crawled out from under the table to see what had happened.

Look at that! said Bessie. He understands things just fine.

Before Carol could respond, the sound of a man's screaming filled the room. They all looked at the radio, but it was coming from outside.

Bessie wiped her mouth on a checkered cloth napkin.

Carol, you carry Rusty upstairs, then get my tools ready.

On the hall landing, Carol looked out to the front yard. A woman had fallen while trying to get out of a car. The bottom of her dress was hiked over her knees, and a wire clothes hanger was sticking out from between her legs. Her boyfriend was crying for help and attempting to lift her. Within moments, Bessie and Martha were out there with the World War I canvas stretcher they'd gotten cheap from a traveling salesman.

With the sheer amount of blood on her dress, Carol felt certain the girl was coming in to die.

It wasn't the first time women had shown up this way. In the old days, Bessie said they used slippery elm drunk in tea, or gunpowder and whiskey, or tried lifting something heavy. If these methods didn't work, they took drastic steps, such as knitting needles, bicycle spokes, or bones from an old corset.

Once they had brought the girl in, Martha cut off her clothes and lay her down in a bed. As usual, Bessie was completely calm as she began the examination.

The woman's name was Marjorie.

Listen to me, child, Bessie told her coolly. This may pinch a little, but I want you to jus' breathe and relax, breathe and relax, that's all you got to do from here on out, don't think, honey... just breathe and relax, with the help of Jesus, Bessie gonna make it all better.

Martha held the girl's blood-covered hand and stroked her forehead.

Harold! the girl cried out. Harold! I'm gonna die! Harold!

Bessie looked up into the girl's eyes. Oh my sweet baby, there ain't no way you goin' die. Now Harold jus' outside on the porch. Be brave for him now. You can always be more relaxed than you are...breathe and relax.

On a small table beside the bed, Bessie's implements were laid out: a speculum, uterine sounds, dilators, curettes, wired gum catheters, and a suture kit. Carol had been taught to set them out in a special way so Bessie knew where each one was without having to look.

Carol watched from the doorway. When it was almost over, and the girl's eyes closed, Martha stepped away from the bed and washed up, then stood with Carol.

Do you think she was in a lot of pain?

Martha thought about it before answering. Probably worst pain of her life.

But Bessie said she's not goin' die, right?

Martha shrugged. She says that to everyone, typical doctor.

Ain't it strange how love can lead so quickly to pain?

Martha turned to Carol with a wry smile. It's not love that does this. But you're right: all love leads to pain of one kind or another. It's something I can't understand.

By dusk, the young woman was in a deep sleep. As they didn't know if Marjorie would survive the night, Bessie made an exception and let Harold sit in the room at her bedside. He was a tall, nervous man in thick glasses who had failed to make the war draft on account of flat feet.

When Rusty was finally down for the night, Carol took the man some black coffee and an unbuttered biscuit. As she gave him the plate, he tried to speak, but choked on the words. Then he took off his glasses and sobbed bitterly into his hands.

Carol went away.

When she returned some time later, the man was leaning forward in his seat, staring at the sleeping girl.

Carol took a chair from the corner and put it next to his.

We should've just got married when she realized, he said without looking at Carol.

Why didn't you?

Marjorie didn't want to wed in shame. My parents are quite religious and she didn't want to disappoint them.

They stared at the thin, brown-haired girl under cool white sheets that had been scrubbed many times over.

How pale she was and how very still, Carol thought, neither dead nor alive, but somewhere in between, in some crack.

I always wonder what's going on in people's heads, Carol said. I mean, sleeping people that is. We have no idea what sleeping people feel.

I've been praying all night, Harold confessed. I don't know what else I can do.

Bessie says praying is always good, day or night, don't matter. He's always listenin'.

Oh, sweet Jesus, Harold said. Please don't take my Marjorie, my sweet girl.

Carol kept the man company all night, leaving him only now and then to check on Rusty.

By morning Harold was holding one of Marjorie's hands while Carol held the other.

By noon she still hadn't woken up. Her chest was moving, they could see that. But her eyes were closed. She was still so far away.

SAMUEL

1991

THE RIVER WAS still high when it came time to retrieve the car. The first thing they saw were faint smudges of black that Samuel said were rear tires. The farmer bent down to study the current.

It's too quick for your boy to go in, Randy. Too risky. Better call my brother, Ken. He lives in the next town and could use the work if you don't mind.

The farmer was from Pennsylvania and had a direct way of talking.

Samuel's father nodded. I'm happy to pay something for his trouble...you too.

The farmer swatted at the offer. Don't worry about me. Just take care of him and we'll be straight.

They went back to the farmer's house and drank black coffee. Their shoes were wet from the tall grass and left prints on the clean tile floor.

When the farmer's brother appeared at the back door, he was skinny with long hair and army tattoos on both arms. The farmer handed him a mug of black coffee with three packets of sugar. Then Samuel's father explained what had happened. The brother seemed excited by the whole thing and kept looking at Samuel, grinning, as though the incident were part of some adventure. Randy took a hundred-dollar bill from his wallet and asked if it was enough.

See, what I tell you? the farmer said to his brother. There's paid work around here if you know where to find it.

Walking over the fields, Ken slipped off his boots and went barefoot. Everyone pretended not to notice.

Not many boys get to have a Mustang for their first car, Ken told him.

It was red too. I'm thinking it won't run again.

No it won't. But at least you went out in a blaze of glory.

He was carrying chains on his shoulder and a garden rake in his hands. Samuel asked what the rake was for.

I'm gonna thread the chain in this here rake, then go around the other side and just reach in and grab the handle. That way I don't have to swim through the cabin, where I might get snagged.

When they got to the river, Ken tied one end of the chain to a tree and the other to the rake like he said. Then he stripped down to his underpants and stepped through the slick weeds. With a look of glee he entered the muddy water, carrying the rake over his head like a rifle.

That current is stronger than it looks, the farmer shouted. I've seen animals with more meat than you dragged off...so don't be a hero, Kenny.

Where the water deepened it slowed to a sheet of brown glass. When Ken made it to the place of the overturned vehicle, they could see only his head and long hair floating behind him. Then he bobbed and disappeared under the river.

Don't let the hippy stuff fool you, said the farmer. My brother knows what he's doing.

Almost a minute later, Ken resurfaced on the other side of the car. The three men on the bank exhaled.

The radio's still playing! he hollered.

What? shouted the farmer. Can't be.

The brother was now on his way back toward them, holding the other end of the chain but not the rake.

I'm serious, he said. I heard music down there. Samuel must've had the radio on, 'cause it's still goin'.

He clambered onto the bank and dropped the chain, breathing hard. Then he lay down on his back.

The farmer stood over him. That car has been in there three days. Ain't no way in hell that radio is on.

Ken sat up. Shielded his eyes from the sun. I tell you, it was Green River by Creedence.

The farmer spat tobacco juice next to his brother's bare leg. I knew you was lying! Where's the rake?

It's in the vehicle, he said. But the end of the chain was beside him on the ground like the limp neck of a beast he had slain.

The farmer went back to the house alone while the rest of them waited by the river.

Soon they heard a tractor coming toward them across the field.

The farmer stopped at the bank, climbed down, and attached both ends of the chain to a hitch on the tractor's bucket. You might want to stand away, he advised. If it snaps, it'll give you a pretty good lick.

The farmer backed the tractor up slow to be sure the chains were locked.

Samuel could hear the low gears of the engine gritting like metal teeth as his red Mustang rose slowly from the river. He stared as it inched through the water like some docile creature. But when the car hit the bank, the chains were really grinding against the frame and it heaved a path of ripped grass and torn riverweeds. When the vehicle was fifteen yards clear of the water, the farmer turned the tractor off, then got out and stood with the other men, watching water drip from the glistening metal. A scrap dealer had promised Samuel a hundred dollars.

When the car had been dragged across the field to the machine shed, the scrap dealer had still not shown up, so the farmer grilled some chicken and they put the meat in potato buns with a spoonful of barbecue sauce and dill pickles from a jar.

Soon they heard a big diesel slowing down on the main road. Ken thanked Samuel and his father for the hundred dollars and wrote down his phone number in case there were other jobs that came up.

When Samuel's car was loaded onto the flatbed truck, his father followed the scrap dealer toward town for about six miles, but instead of turning off for home, Randy steered onto the Blue Grass Parkway past a peeling billboard that read, HELL IS REAL.

Where we goin', pop? Samuel asked.

Louisville.

Why?

You'll see.

On the highway, Samuel tried to talk to his father but the old man was quiet. When Samuel put on the radio his father snapped it off.

You mad at me, Pop?

Close to it.

It didn't seem like you was back at the farmer's house.

Well, I couldn't show it then.

I'll pay you back the hundred dollars when I get the check from the scrap dealer, I promise. I'm gonna get a job, too, so I can buy another Mustang.

Well, Auto Parts won't have you back 'cause of your drinkin' at work. And I don't want you up at Walmart, in case you ruin it for your Uncle Rusty.

Samuel hung his head and looked at his feet on the mat. I thought we went through this already, Dad. I'm trying to change.

His father stared at the road ahead. I ain't never seen anybody walk away from flipping their car like that, least of all in a goddamned river.

It was more on the bank when I…

I don't mean the angle of the car, Sam! I mean driving drunk. Samuel could see his eyes were burning now. And most likely you were goddamn, mother-stinking high too. Am I right?

Dad…

And don't you ever fuckin' lie to me, son. I'm your father. Don't you ever forget that.

Tears filled Samuel's eyes and he turned his body to the window where they would not be seen.

I thought I'd slept it off at Chance's house...I was sleeping a good while. I should have drunk coffee, I know, but—

Coffee makes you alert, son. It don't make you sober.

But Dad, you drank when you were young, right?

It was Vietnam, and we got the booze for nothing. But I never did anything as stupid as what you're doing. When I was twenty years old, I was already back from the war and working a steady job.

Samuel wiped his eyes and blew his nose with a napkin from the glove box.

Sorry I'm such a fuckup.

Samuel thought his father might yell then, but he just looked ahead at the road with no expression.

Quit feeling sorry for yourself, Samuel. That might work with your mother, but not with me. Jesus in hell, I don't know what she would have done if we lost you. It would kill her. You know that? Put her in an early grave.

Samuel imagined his mother standing over his pale, made-up body in the plush casket with organ music playing. Uncle Rusty there too, fiddling with a Coca-Cola toy, pushed to the very limits of what he could understand.

I really have been trying to change, Dad.

Yeah, I know. But it ain't soon enough for me, son.

He wanted to tell his father that he just couldn't imagine his life without alcohol. The feeling it gave him was the only thing he looked forward to. And anything, absolutely anything, felt possible when he was drunk—even his eye straightened out. He'd seen it for himself in the bedroom mirror.

After a long silence Samuel asked his father again where they were going.

You'll see.

Why won't you tell me?

You'll find out soon enough.

An hour later they pulled into a parking lot on the outskirts of the city, near Louisville airport.

What's this?

His father turned off the engine. Follow my lead and try not to say too much.

Other cars were pulling up around them. Some didn't stop, but made for the entrance of a drab office building to let people out.

Is it church?

No, it's AA.

When they got inside there was a blond woman with short hair who was about Randy's age. Her skin was tan and stretched out, like the old folks Samuel had seen on the beaches in Florida.

Hi there, you two! Joining us tonight, are you?

Thanks for the warm welcome, Samuel's father said, looking over her shoulder at people moving chairs into a circle. But we just dropped by for information.

Oh? Just information?

Yes, ma'am. It's my other son who has the problems, so we just come to check it out, get some leaflets an' all.

Family members of sufferers have it pretty bad too, you know? All are welcome here.

That's awful kind, ma'am, but my boy and I got a shift at Ford. Is there any information you could give us to take home?

Well, yes there is, the woman said, peeling different sheets of paper off the table behind her. This is just to give you an idea, she said. But the real magic—the healing part—that takes place when everyone shares.

Randy nodded. Exactly what my other son might respond to.

We're here every Tuesday and Thursday, she said. There was a gold cross on a chain around her neck. It rested on the tan skin of her chest and glinted when she turned her body to shake their hands.

Back in the car, Randy handed the papers to his son. Leave those out when we get home. I've never lied to your mother, Samuel, and it's too late to start now, so when she asks where we went, it was to an AA meeting, nowhere else, you got that?

Why? Are we going someplace else?

It's not AA you need, son, it's something different…something your mother wouldn't understand.

They drove another twenty minutes and it began to get dark. When Samuel saw the giant neon sign he couldn't believe it. His father pulled into the dirt lot and parked the truck.

You're kidding, right?

That's the last thing I'm doing. There's no fun in this for me. You remember that.

This is all because I wrecked the car?

I don't give a damn about the car, Sam. Truth is, in the last six months, you been getting mean when you drink.

That's bullshit, Samuel snapped. I'm not a mean person, you know that.

You can say what you like, son, but we both know the stories about Grandma Carol's father.

The gambler?

Oh, he was more than a gambler. I don't know how many people he killed, exactly, but…

And you think I'm like him?

His father lit a cigarette. Of course not. Now let's go.

I ain't even twenty-one.

Don't worry about it.

At the door of the club they could hear thumping music from inside. Samuel's father nodded at the bouncer, a bald man with a tattoo on his neck. Randy held out some money and the bouncer took it.

Can I introduce my son, Samuel?

The bouncer nodded, but there was nothing in his face to make them feel welcome.

Just keep him off the sauce, Randy.

It was dark inside and they could feel the music vibrating through their bodies.

Samuel was nervous. He had heard about this club, and even talked to Eddie about trying to get in someday. He never imagined that his father knew a place like this existed.

You ever been to one of these establishments, Samuel?

No. Eddie said he went to one in Cincinnati, but once they took his entrance fee and money for drinks, they asked for ID and kicked him out.

His father laughed. They had him good, I reckon.

If that happened in Kentucky, said Samuel, somebody would go back and burn the place down.

In the town where your great-granddaddy grew up, that's for damn sure. It's why Kentucky has a reputation.

They found a table in a dark corner away from the other drinkers, then sat down and turned their eyes toward a bright rectangular stage at the center of the club. There were gold poles at either end with a topless girl on each. One dancer was stomping around in clear, plastic platform shoes. The other was snaking her body up and down the pole.

When a waitress appeared, Randy ordered a bottle of Budweiser for himself and a ginger ale for his son.

I ain't complaining, Samuel said, uncertain as to whether he should openly watch the dancers in his father's presence, but what are we here for, Pop? And how do you know the door guy?

I don't know him. A guy at work does. Sit tight, I'm going for a leak.

When Randy returned, the drinks had already been set down hurriedly by the waitress. Samuel's soda was in a plastic cup.

The music was now too loud to talk without shouting, so they watched the girls go through their routines. Every so often, Samuel would look at his father.

A DJ perched high up in a booth at the far end of the stage announced different girls with every new song. Each dancer was on for about ten minutes. Some men went up to the stage and slipped money into the string sides of the dancers' panties. The bills flapped in the flashing light like green tongues.

So what do you think, Samuel?

They're the hottest girls I've ever seen.

That's what I was hoping you'd say.

When the waitress came back, Randy whispered something to her. She tucked the empty tray under one arm and went off quickly.

A few moments later, a dancer in a silk top with short black hair came over to them. She had a pierced lip and tattoos on her stomach and thighs. Samuel sank back in his chair, hoping she wouldn't see his face in the darkness of the club.

Havin' a good time, fellas?

Care to join us for a little while? Samuel's father said. This is my son.

She put out her hand. Her nails were painted with black glitter.

What's his name?

When she sat down, very close to him, Samuel felt himself buckle under the weight of perfume.

Is it your first time here, sweet pea?

Samuel nodded.

Well, I don't bite—at least not before midnight.

The dancer put a hand on Samuel's knee. Did you like my dance? Did you see it?

It was amazing.

My name is Miss Odyssey.

Really?

The girl laughed.

You from Louisville? Samuel asked her politely.

Mississippi—a town you never heard of.

Buloxi?

Good guess, not too far.

Then Samuel's father got up again. Men's room, he said, pointing.

When he was out of sight, the girl leaned in so close Samuel could feel the heat of her breath when she spoke. My real name is Charlene, but I don't ever tell the customers that. It's Miss Odyssey to them.

Why did you tell me?

Because you ain't like them, she said. I can tell you're someone I could be friends with in real life.

Really? said Samuel, taking a sip of his soda. How do you know that?

Because of your cool hair. And you seem nice, alternative like me.

How long you been a dancer?

About a year.

You like it?

It pays the bills, and I get my days free, so…

Oh, you're in school?

Not yet. I have a daughter so I get to be with her. Then my momma comes over until I get home about four.

In the morning?

Oh, she's fine, fast asleep in dreamland with her bunny where every little girl ought to be.

Are guys nice to you? Samuel wanted to know. Their legs were touching now. He could feel his heart knocking like a small, mad stone.

Most of the guys here are just lonely. Or ugly. So girls don't talk to 'em outside the club. But tell me about you…you shy around all girls or just me?

I'm not shy.

I wish more guys were like that. Are you in college?

I dropped out. Wanted to work with my hands and be outside.

Well, there's plenty of jobs where you can do that.

Samuel lit a cigarette. Charlene reached over and took it from him. After a couple of drags, she gave it back.

I bet you had a high school sweetheart.

Samuel thought of Jennifer Hutchins.

Did you even talk to the ones you had crushes on? Tell me you did.

I didn't.

Shame.

What should I have said?

You can say anything if the voice is right...even hello, how are you, I'm Samuel, do you like summer or spring, your hair is pretty, do you like dogs?

Samuel laughed nervously. It's as easy as that?

You're not the only shy one, you know.

The DJ made an announcement and a girl with blond hair and cowboy boots went up onto the stage with a pink lasso. I go on after her, so you ready for your dance?

My what?

Your dad already paid for it.

What?

Don't worry, she laughed, we're not gonna do it in front of him. There's a back area.

I don't know if I can.

Charlene took Samuel's hand and led him across the club to some heavy red curtains, then into an area with private rooms. She was a short girl, but boots made her almost the same height as Samuel.

He wondered where his father could have gotten to, and what his mother would say if she knew this was happening.

The small room was dimly lit. It had fabric walls and a patterned armchair, the sort old people died in.

When Samuel was seated, Charlene smiled and took off her top. He thought her breasts were like big, soft mushrooms, but managed to stop himself from saying it.

Touch them, Samuel.

I'm okay.

But Charlene grabbed his hands and put them on her. *Relax.*

I am relaxed.

I've seen preachers in here more relaxed than you.

You're the most beautiful woman I've ever been close to.

You think I'm beautiful?

I don't think—I know.

When she smiled, Samuel was able to see how she must have

looked as a little girl. But her life between then and this moment was through a door he would never open.

She straddled him, then began to move backwards and forwards. Their faces were very close. Her perfume made Samuel feel calm and weightless, as though they were floating inside a cloud. He touched her hair and then her cheeks. Her face was warm and there was a powdery, floral scent to the skin between her neck and her breasts. Her bare legs seemed to melt against his jeans. When the lap dance was over, Charlene stood and clipped her bra back on.

I know why you're so shy with me, she said. It's because of your eye.

Samuel tried quickly to hide it by leaning forward and shaking loose some hair. But Charlene brushed the strands from his face. Don't you ever hide, Samuel, you've got too much to give to be hiding.

But it's all people can see.

No, it's all *you* can see.

She took one of his hands and rubbed it on her stomach. You feel that?

The scar?

Big one ain't it? Did you see it when I got on top of you? Be honest.

I did.

And were you disgusted by it?

Hell no.

How'd it make you feel?

It made me like you more.

And why's that?

He shrugged. I guess I felt sorry for whatever happened to you.

The dancer arched forward and touched the scar herself. It still amazes me that so much pain can lead to so much love. It's something I don't understand.

. . .

It was late when they drove home. The road was dark and for a long time they just smoked, silently, secretly going over the things that had happened.

You know what that place needs? Samuel's father said eventually. A casino.

Slot machines?

I was thinking a roulette table and some poker rooms.

We'd be there ever' day after work, Samuel said. I know I would.

Listen, I don't want you going back to that club.

Why not?

This was a one-shot deal to help you grow up a little bit. I'm still pissed at you for everythin' that's happened.

You mean the Mustang?

Again, Samuel, I don't give a hoot about the car. But the drinkin' and the drugs...lord, I never thought a son of mine would be high on drugs!

Samuel listened, but the words were softened by the spell of Charlene's perfume that lingered in his clothes and on his hands.

Charlene talked to me after the dance, Pop.

She did? About what?

I think you know.

What?

Did you tell her to say something to me? I'm not upset. I just need to know.

Say something 'bout what?

C'mon, Pop.

Samuel's father lifted his hands off the steering wheel. I just paid for it is all.

You were gone to the bathroom an awful long time.

That's because I wasn't in the bathroom, Sherlock, I was at the bar watching the Steelers get their asses handed to 'em.

So you didn't ask her to say nothing?

Why? Did she say she loved you? They all say that, Samuel.

Did you get a dance, Dad? Samuel asked, preparing himself for a strange kind of disappointment. I saw you were watching the girls.

I couldn't see a goddamn thing. I left my bifocals here in the truck, so it was all just a blur with that god-awful music. If that's what hell is like, I'm going back to church.

You didn't see the girls dancing on the pole?

I saw everything I needed to see twenty years ago.

Did you go to places like that?

Maybe once or twice. The girls would do more than just dance back then, let me tell you.

Samuel nodded, surprised at his reluctance to hear any more. He imagined his mother at home with Uncle Rusty, making holiday wreaths in the kitchen and baking gingerbread cookies that once cooled would be laid flat on a plate and dusted with cinnamon.

Don't worry, Samuel, I got all that out of my system before I married your mother. But liquor likes nothing better than to take away a man's good intentions, so stick with beer from now on, okay? Drinking like you been doin' don't make you a man, Samuel. It makes you a coward for not facing your demons head on.

What are your demons, Dad?

I ain't got too many. My parents were good people, but you can probably guess things happened in the war. And the more you try to forget it, the more it pushes back.

They didn't speak for a while, just watched the dark road with the occasional tractor-trailer rising up like a spray of red jewels.

Dad?

What is it, son.

Thanks for paying for everything with the car and not being mad, and for what you did tonight.

What did I do?

You know, for taking me to—

Where did I take you, Samuel? Think before you answer.

To an AA meeting?

That's right. And it was your mother what suggested it, so make sure you give her a big hug when we get home—once you've changed out of that shirt.

CAROL

1946

RUSTY LAY ON his back, breathing and blinking at the darkness. The windows were open and night was passing through the house. Outside, the trees were stuffed with insects flicking and rattling their shells.

Across the room, Carol sat up and saw that her son was moving around in the bed.

You alright, Rusty? Why you ain't sleeping?

Uh-huh.

You got a fever?

He shook his head. She was able to see because the room was glazed with moonlight.

How come you ain't sleeping, then?

The little boy rolled his body to look at her. We gonna die, Momma?

What kind of a question is that for a little boy to ask in the middle of the night?

Carol watched. But her son didn't move or make a sound. We ain't gonna die for a long while yet.

Bomb Momma, bomb come.

What bomb?

Bomb make people lyin' dead on floor, ain't it?

The bomb? The atomic bomb?

Yup.

We done that, Rusty, we dropped it on them. On the Japs. To stop the war. I explained all this to you.

Their heads?

What? Well I guess. I don't know exactly where it hit 'em.

Why they kill 'em?

You know why. Like the man on the radio said, it's because they wouldn't quit.

Quit what, Momma?

Fighting. But the war is over now, remember?

He moved his head from side to side, across the valley of his pillow.

It's been over for a while now, Rusty…that's why we're leaving this place.

No, Momma.

We have to. It's bin decided.

Carol got up and went barefoot to Rusty's bed in her cotton nightdress. When she sat down, the springs creaked and his body floated up to meet her arms.

What if they fall on our heads too?

Just kisses gonna fall on your head, Rusty, that's all, jus' like Bessie told you the other day.

No leave home, Momma. Stay.

We have to go. You even helped pack Momma's little green suitcase. You thought that was funny. You laughed. Mary Bright is coming too. That's Momma's little sister. Momma's little doll.

No.

It's time for you and me to see the world. You're ten years old, and I'm a grown woman.

Rusty turned to the open window, toward the coming summer he would miss with Bessie and Martha.

But world is right there, Momma. I can see it.

I mean someplace else, not just Bessie and Martha's. We been here ten years already. That's a long while, almost half my life and all of yours.

No, Momma.

We have to make it on our own. And we're going to be safe and happy in our new place, because I'm your momma and I say so.

My garden gonna die.

Martha said she'd water it. There'll be a place for you to have another garden where we're going, and if there ain't, well, we'll grow anything you want in little pots.

The world had broken into many pieces, and Carol wanted to go out and see what was left. She had desired to leave for some time, but Bessie wouldn't arrange anything until the war was over and done with.

Some of the women who visited their house left magazines behind, and Carol had spent hours looking at the pictures, taking in all she could of other women's lives in California and New York. Every morning, she hummed in the cane chair before her mirror, teasing her hair into new styles, pinning and unpinning until she felt satisfied with how she looked. The world was so much bigger than this place, she thought—and so many men and boys had already seen half of it, just by fighting in a war.

From the magazines and dramas on the wireless, it was obvious to Carol that she knew very little of life beyond Bessie and Martha's house. She had never even been to a movie theater to see the silver, flickering figures on a screen. It was just one thing on a list of things she wanted.

Carol imagined herself walking down Main Street of some town with her hair curled, wearing shoes that made a noise with each step. People who saw her would stop and stare, wondering who she was. A glamour girl from the East Coast? Some beauty from Palm Springs with her little brother who can't walk? Poor dear.

Carol practiced the things she would say in a mirror. To people she imagined meeting on a street, or in a shop as they stood on either side of a counter. None of them would know her father, or the place she had come from, or that far below the surface of their conversation, Carol was lost in a great emptiness where something should have been but wasn't.

HAROLD & MARJORIE

1946

HAROLD AND MARJORIE Bennett arrived at Martha and Bessie's crumbling plantation house in a shiny black car. They were married now and living in the big town. Harold had a job at the Kentucky Savings Bank, and their house, built during the Civil War, was made of brick and three stories tall.

In a letter to Carol, Marjorie said they had a porch that wrapped around the whole house and, best of all, a spare bedroom on the first floor with a private, indoor washroom for a live-in housekeeper and her son. Bessie and Martha had arranged the details, such as Carol's working hours and how much she would be paid for housework.

When the black car pulled up, Rusty watched the couple get out slowly. He had been slouching on the porch all morning, dividing his gaze between the green trees and a little garden he'd grown with Martha.

Marjorie often needed help standing and walking because her legs would shake uncontrollably. They told everyone it was a spine injury from a car wreck. Most days she could get up and move around, even go up and down the stairs. But when she was bad, Harold wanted someone he trusted to be there in the house.

Bessie stepped out into the sticky summer heat. I hope you brung appetites is all I'm gun'say.

Martha was in the kitchen, and Carol was inside fussing with the linen napkins, trying to fold them a way she'd seen in one of her magazines.

Once Harold had helped his wife inside, he came back out to the porch where Rusty was sitting on a green suitcase.

Well hullo there, young fella.

Rusty turned and pointed upwards. Do you got trees with webs in 'em?

The man followed the child's finger across the yard.

Well, we might have one or two like that on our street, even though it's called Oak Street. We have a lot of books in the house and a piano. Maybe you could get some lessons?

My legs don't work.

But your hands do, don't they? And your eyes look fine to me, said Harold. Books and music will take you much farther than a pair of legs.

Hmm.

Martha wrote me in a letter that you like to garden. Is that still the case?

You got whip-poor-will?

Harold straightened his silver-framed eyeglasses. I don't know about that, but we could plant one if you like.

Got to catch it first, Rusty said.

Okay, said Harold with a puzzled look. How do we do that?

Creep 'round at night, with worms hangin' I guess. Or a seed o' some kind. Or a peanut. Yuh, I think a peanut would do it.

Harold scratched his head. Well. That certainly sounds interesting. I might go back in the house and check on Mrs. Bennett. Want to join me?

Who?

My wife, Marjorie.

As it was still hard for him to walk, Rusty got down on his knees and crawled through the open door like a giant bug.

Carol was wiping plates, laying them where people would be seated, when she heard a thumping from under the table.

Rusty! Get out from under there, git! Mister Harold and Miss Marjorie are fine town folks who ain't gonna stand for your messin'.

Bessie appeared in the doorway with a pitcher of sweet tea. Thas' his spot, she said. Every child need a place o' their own, Carol, you know that.

Carol frowned. I'm a woman now, Bessie, and can safely say that he's too old for this sort of thing. One shouldn't encourage it.

But then she noticed Harold and Marjorie on the other side of the table watching her.

They smiled as Harold helped his delicate wife into a chair. Carol watched her take the napkin and lay it over her dress with such grace, she almost laughed out of nervousness. Marjorie's nails were perfectly shaped too, and her lips brushed with a vivid, glowing red. Carol kept looking at them, remembering a woman in a magazine whose mouth had been just like that, a rose about to burst open.

We have a new table in the parlor, Harold told them as he pulled out a chair for himself. It's a big one, he chuckled, and Rusty is welcome to sit under it any time he pleases.

Marjorie blinked at her husband, then turned to Carol. That is, unless you don't want him to…in which case we would follow your example in advising the child.

Carol was preparing her reply with several important words she'd picked up from the radio, when her face suddenly grew warm and she jumped up from her seat. A second later, her son appeared from under the table holding one of Carol's brown spectator shoes in his mouth.

Rusty! Rusty!

But he was already crawling into the hallway. They could hear the floorboards creak as he scrambled through the parlor and back out to the porch.

Carol flopped down in the chair and wrinkled up her face. It's just so embarrassing! she cried. The way he just does what he wants!

Her bare foot under the table, the sight of so much uneaten food, and Marjorie's lips dripping with color filled her with despair.

SAMUEL

1996

SAMUEL WOKE AND slipped out the back door while his mother, father, and Uncle Rusty were still in their beds. Sleep had been impossible for him, but Samuel knew he could rest in the afternoon when it was done. Outside, the clouds were a flat, even white, and he could smell rain coming.

Tossing in bed the night before, he'd gone over and over what might happen at the trailer park when he showed up at Eddie's door with the green suitcase in his hand. It had been several years since they'd seen one another, and just six months since Eddie's girl, Jean, had run away with their daughter—or so he'd heard.

The green suitcase had a plain cloth interior and smelled like the perfume people wore long ago. When Samuel took it from the attic, he had found inside a woman's shoe wrapped in tissue, a cloth doll, and some wooden kids blocks, crudely cut and with the paint all faded. He dumped the doll and the blocks into a box of Christmas decorations, and left the shoe somewhere prominent for his father to see. It was very old and might be worth something.

Samuel had taken his time packing the money in, imagining how it would feel when Eddie flipped the suitcase locks to look at what was inside. The case lay flat beside him on the passenger seat of his father's truck.

Since the accident several years ago, Samuel had been driving his mother's Ford Granada. If he were driving it now, people in town would recognize him in it, and wonder where he was going in the haze of dawn. But his father's truck would rumble through the streets unnoticed.

Samuel had wanted to get out of the house without waking his parents. There was nothing they could say or do to change his mind, though they might try. When it was done, he would sit them down at the kitchen counter and unpack the whole story—the long version that stretched back to when he and Eddie were in middle school, playing poker in the basement with Uncle Rusty bringing them bottles of Coca-Cola.

As he pulled onto Main Street, the truck's tired motor roared up the incline with a throaty bubbling. Samuel wished he had some coffee—the taste of it would break the dryness from that first cigarette.

As he approached a bright gas station on the edge of town, Samuel knew they would have a pot going inside, but leaving the suitcase in the truck was a bad idea. Carrying it in with him would look strange, maybe even suspicious. He made up his mind to go without. Today was special, Samuel thought, one of those times that in old age he would look on as proof he'd lived a good life.

On the floor of the truck lay a pair of his father's work gloves. The Ford logo was stitched on the wrist, and there were holes in the fingers where his father had used them for ripping out an old fence with Grandpa Joe.

Samuel drove slowly, ready to wave at any police he saw perched in their cruisers. But the streets and parking lots were deserted. The furniture shop was having a sale; a yellow poster hung in the window promising big discounts. Since the town had lost its manufacturing plant, most people now rented their beds, their couch, even the family dining table around which their lives would be decided.

The hair salon where Eddie's mother had worked for a month years ago was dark too. Inside, rows of vinyl chairs sat empty under silver helmets. Every year before Christmas, in the cold darkness of late December, Alfredia would sit in one of those chairs. As a boy, Samuel remembered peering in the window, past the tinsel and blinking lights at the girls chewing gum and teasing his mother's hair with metal combs. At home there would be presents under the tree. Holiday specials on the television. Uncle Rusty trying not to tell everybody what they were getting. A part of Samuel wanted that again, not just for himself, but for some imaginary child, and a woman he would stay up late with on Christmas Eve night, wrapping presents and rubbing them with coal dust as his parents had once done for him.

Samuel drove slowly and thought how happiness is the world distilled into something tiny—a child's sock on the stairs, the indentation of a head on a pillow, the smell of morning and the sound of boots being laced, the sight of paws tucked under the nose of a dog as it twitches from one dream to the next.

The greatest treasure of our lives, he thought, was hidden from us in plain sight.

Samuel wondered if sadness had the same power in smallness, and pictured Eddie in his trailer home holding a baby blanket or one of Jean's hairbrushes.

Outside town, away from the brick buildings and convenience stores, the clouds broke apart to reveal a hard blue.

It was Sunday morning, a gentle time when people lingered in the warmth of their beds. When Samuel was very young, he remembered rising early to dress for church. There was excitement in the house for fear of being late, and for the meal that would come after with everyone together in their best clothes. But nothing the Lord promised had come. Instead, everything was being slowly taken, piece by piece, as entire communities were disassembled, as though stripped for parts. Until something else came along that people could believe in, the churches would continue to stand like strange ornaments at the end of each block, assemblies of judgment and gossip where brittle rules punished without any hope of reward.

Samuel imagined all the trailer homes he would see, lined up like rows of pulled teeth. He imagined people's lives behind the vinyl walls. The voices of children and the sound of cartoons. Thin doors opening and closing. The smell of propane heaters. Half-empty bags of cheese puffs and overflowing ashtrays. Cereal dropping with a faint ring into bowls with faded patterns that would never fade in memory.

When a pink mist spread its fingers over uncut pasture, Samuel recognized where he was. In a moment, he would pass a narrow dirt track, a place where they'd gone four-wheeling in high school. It led to a shallow, swift river of garter snakes and snapping turtles. When the river was low you could find arrowheads. They had collected there over thousands of years because Cherokee hunters knew where animals gathered to quench their thirst.

Samuel glanced at the small green suitcase on the seat next to him. It was packed with half the money he'd won two days earlier at a riverboat casino in Indiana. He'd driven up with his father. On the way they smoked and listened to old Hank Williams and Randy's favorite, Ernest Tubb.

They stopped for burgers and frosted cups of iced tea. Randy had slicked his hair back. Wore blue jeans. Put on aftershave.

They had picked up overtime shifts at the auto plant, and in their bifold wallets were large bills for betting, a room with twin beds, and two steak dinners.

But Samuel's bed went undisturbed. His father slept from midnight to six, then opened his eyes and realized his son was still gambling. He hurried down to the casino floor and found Samuel had been holding court at a poker table. Randy stood and watched him for an hour, then wandered away in search of coffee and something to chew on.

At 8:17 a.m. it happened. Samuel won everything. At first he couldn't believe the game was over—that there were no more players. His father was dozing in a chair outside with an ashtray and a cup of coffee on the floor between his white socks and unlaced tennis shoes. The shouting woke him. He stood quickly and stared through the window at his son, still sitting at the poker table, mesmerized by the towering city of chips. There were more than he could count. And in colors he'd never dreamed of having in his possession. But Randy wasn't looking at those, and when Samuel met his father's eyes they both felt something that would always be more valuable than money, but which would never be spoken.

Randy said the gaming manager would most likely present him with a giant check, but instead they paid his winnings in cash. The casino also offered four-nights more accommodation on the house, plus meals, but Randy said they had to get back. Armed security escorted them to the truck. By mid-morning, they were on the highway back to Kentucky.

We should call your mother, tell her what's going on so she and Rusty can feel a part of it. How do you feel about stopping, Samuel?

I could probably eat something.

Randy glanced in his rearview mirror. I don't reckon there's anyone behind us, but that's a goddamn awful lot of money.

After a few more miles, Randy pulled off and found a gas station.

I'll stay in the truck, he told Samuel. You go call Mom and tell her what you done, then pick up a couple of egg and cheese biscuits, coffee, and two bottles of Mountain Dew.

Samuel found the phone mounted on the wall beside a pallet of ice melt in sacks. Men passed on their way to and from the bathroom, so he spoke quietly. There was silence on the end of the line when he told his mother, which meant Alfredia was crying. He was reluctant to say how much he'd won in case someone was listening.

After blowing her nose, she said that Uncle Rusty was gonna be tickled. And that she was proud of them both, and to please get back safe.

.   .   .

Uncle Rusty was waiting at the screen door when Randy and Samuel pulled into the driveway a couple of hours later. After everyone had held the package of money in their arms, they watched as Samuel ripped the plastic and made a neat pile on the kitchen counter. Then they drank a pot of coffee and ate slices from a ring of coffee cake.

I just keep imagining how you must've felt, Alfredia said.

When I knew I won, Mom?

It must have been the greatest feeling.

It's really Dad that won it because he taught me how to play.

Come on now, Samuel, you won that pile of greenbacks on your own. And you learned all there was to know about poker in the basement with Eddie Walker, when y'all were thick as thieves.

I'm just so proud of Samuel, his mother said. But did you ever think this might be the best time to quit?

Samuel and his father glanced at one another.

You could go out on top, Alfredia said, then went over to the sink and rinsed out her cup. Whatever you decide, just don't tell Grandma Carol because I'll never hear the end of it.

Uncle Rusty couldn't take his eyes off the money. He took a sip of black coffee from his donkey mug. What are you going to buy with it, Samuel? New Mustang?

What would you buy, Rusty?

He thought for a moment. Coca-Cola.

Alfredia returned to her seat at the counter. Maybe you'll get a case of Coca-Cola from your nephew if you ask nicely.

He don't have to ask, Mom. We'll take a drive out to Walmart later on. Maybe we'll swing by Kentucky Hobby too, Rusty, and you can pick out any model car or truck you want.

Rusty set his coffee mug in the sink and went down the stairs to his apartment without speaking.

You've done it now, Randy said, lighting a cigarette. He's gone to get ready.

. . .

In addition to collecting anything Coca-Cola, Rusty liked model cars. There were two dozen in his bedroom on a plank shelf that Samuel had painted the colors of a checkered flag. Some of the cars came on plastic stands with a name and a year.

During the day, when Samuel and his father were on the production line at the auto plant in Louisville, Rusty worked on cars in his bedroom, sometimes taking them around the local shops and businesses, where'd he go into great detail about things like engine capacity and interior options. Some of the shop owners had told Alfredia they were too busy to entertain her brother, while others gave Rusty a soda and a chair to sit in as customers went in and out.

He carried the cars in a red toolbox and wore a Pennzoil hat given to him by men in the tire shop on Main Street when they heard he was turning fifty. One of the men had walked down to the house in overalls. His hands were black with oil and engine grease, but the hat was in a clear plastic bag.

Once in Green County, Samuel took a couple of wrong turns before finding the Happy Acres trailer park where Eddie Walker had been living since his return to Kentucky, after Jean ran off with their daughter. The first home was done up with lights and solar panels. Most likely where the park supervisor lived. There was a tended garden covered with deer fencing, an American flag on a pole, and a black POW flag flying next to it.

Samuel drove along the road slowly, hoping no one would come out and ask what he wanted. He didn't know exactly which trailer Eddie was renting, but he knew his car—a white Ford Ranger flareside with tinted windows. He had bought it cheap with the idea of putting in a new transmission.

Samuel wondered if Eddie might still be asleep, or if a woman might answer his door in panties and a tee shirt. It saddened him now to think how far they had drifted since that summer in the woods when they were free.

A year after Eddie moved up to Ohio, a daughter arrived. Eddie sent Samuel a picture. But when Samuel got his number and called, Eddie explained that Jean didn't want him seeing his old friends anymore. She needed to make a new life, and part of that was making Eddie choose between his past and his future.

For a couple of years Eddie worked in a lumberyard. But when his child was two years old, the yard closed because a chain store opened off the highway and put them under. But the chain store wouldn't hire Eddie on account of his juvenile record. They said it was corporate policy. He got behind on the house payments then, and the furniture was soon repossessed, including his daughter's crib.

Eddie's trailer had corrugated iron sides and a blue tarp taped over the empty socket of one window. Eddie's white truck looked the same as it always had. The tinted glass still had bubbles in the plastic, and hanging from the rearview mirror was his middle-school graduation pennant with the year in faded gold.

Samuel put his father's truck in park, clutched the green case, and stepped outside.

He'd hoped there might be swings or a playhouse, some indication that Jean had come down—but the yard was overgrown with weeds, and there were bags of bottles and cans that Eddie was recycling for nickels and dimes.

Samuel knocked lightly on the door. Eddie? You in there, buddy?

He listened but couldn't hear anything. Then the door whipped open.

Eddie was wearing jeans and a Daffy Duck shirt. His hair had thinned, but he had a ponytail, and his unshaven skin seemed tight across the bones of his face.

Samuel!

Last time I checked.

I can't believe it's you! His eyes moved to the small suitcase in Samuel's hand. You need a place to crash?

Everyone's fine, Eddie. I just wanted to see you.

Goddamn. It's been a while!

Four years, almost.

Well don't just stand there, come on in.

The trailer carried the odor of wet clothes and stale pizza.

Want me to take my shoes off?

Eddie laughed. Still the joker I see.

I heard about Jean.

Eddie pointed to a space on the couch where Samuel could sit down. Now she's gone, I guess it don't matter that you're here. She ain't gonna know unless someone tells her or something.

But it's me, Eddie, why would she care about your old buddy?

She just wanted me to leave my old life behind. Said it never did me no good.

Is that what you want?

Don't matter what I want, Samuel. It's Jean and my little girl what counts.

Do you know where they are?

Ohio, still. She called me two weeks ago. Said I could maybe come and see Hayley.

Do you want to?

That's all I ever wanted. Hayley's been asking for me ever' day, Jean said. Askin' for her daddy. She can walk now and feed herself.

Eddie scanned the worn-out carpet. There's a photo album around here someplace. But then his eyes fell to the green suitcase Samuel had brought with him. You can stay as long as you want, Samuel, at least until Jean finds out.

Samuel tapped the handle. This ain't clothes, Eddie.

Well I guess if you was homeless, Samuel, you'd prefer living in the woods anywho. Still doin' that wilderness stuff?

Sure am. Reading 'bout different kinds of seeds right now.

What you doing for work?

Ford.

With your dad?

We drive up to Louisville together almost ever' day.

Shit, that must be nice. Randy and Alfredia. I miss them. And Uncle Rusty. Does he remember me?

Samuel's plan had been to go in and look around before giving Eddie the money. He had to be sure of something, if he really wanted to help his friend and not add to his suffering.

Eddie was now on the floor searching for the book of photos.

I swear I flick through it ever' day, Samuel. Then he looked up. Maybe it's in my bedroom. Most of the pictures are from when I took her to the park after work at County Lumber. Saturdays we'd watch cartoons and then walk around the mall. I didn't even go to bars no more. But Jean did. She told me she had to cut loose on Saturday night. She'd get all dolled up and go out with one of her girlfriends—dance a little bit, y'know. I guess it's normal.

Did she drink?

Yeah, coke too. I hate that stuff. It changes a person.

As Samuel listened, he realized that Jean sounded a lot like Eddie's mother, but he decided not to say anything.

I don't got no beer, Samuel, 'cause I'm trying to quit, but there's a can of coffee around here someplace or some RC.

Oh buddy, I'd love some coffee. I was thinking about a cup all the way here.

He watched Eddie get up and shake out some granules that had chunked together.

You got somewhere to go with the case? Eddie asked him.

I didn't want to leave it in the car is all. Can I use your bathroom?

Uh, sure. It's back there past Hayley's room.

Samuel wondered if he should take the bag, but Eddie was watching so he left it. In the daughter's bedroom was an old loveseat with dolls and teddy bears sitting up neatly. Other toys and a dolls' house were still in their boxes and pushed into corners.

The bathroom smelled like wet paper and soap. The faucets were in need of washers and there was rust around the bathtub drain. Everything dripped. Samuel pulled back the plastic curtain and tried to screw in the showerhead a little better, but he needed a pair of Channellocks to really tighten it. A rash of brown and mold coated the lower end of the shower curtain, and there was black around the tub where the sealant was rotted. Very carefully, Samuel opened the mirrored door to the medicine cabinet. He was looking for syringes, or painkillers like oxy or fentanyl. But all he found was a pack of cheap blue razors and a box of unopened tampons.

When he went back, his friend was sitting down and there was a mug of black coffee for Samuel on an old trunk covered by an American flag. Eddie was drinking water from a plastic cup and chewing ice.

I remembered how you take it. Back in Black.

Samuel laughed. Ain't that still the best song?

I can get the CD if you want. We can listen to it. I couldn't find the photo book. It's probably in my room someplace. I might have fallen asleep looking at it.

That's okay, Eddie. That AC/DC song reminds me how we used to play poker together.

Shit. You always beat me. I'm lucky it was just your dad's pennies.

You beat me too sometimes when you got lucky.

Eddie sighed. Yeah but some people have more luck than others, I guess.

Although no malice was intended, Samuel felt stung by Eddie's comment. He turned his gaze toward a photograph on the wall of a teenage girl in a tee shirt holding a baby, unsure if it was Jean or Eddie's mother.

Hey Eddie, do you remember an agreement we made years ago?

About what?

We came up with it in my basement, late at night.

With Uncle Rusty?

Uncle Rusty was asleep. It was just us.

Did I do something wrong?

We said that whoever made it first in a professional poker tour-nament would split his winnings with the other.

Eddie laughed and tipped ice into his mouth from the cup. Yeah, I remember that.

Samuel could see lines of cracked skin around his eyes. His hands too were rough and aged. They were not children anymore but Samuel could see clearly, behind the unwashed clothes and clumsy tattoos, that Eddie was still just a boy living in exile from his own life, always on the verge of being loved.

We sure used to dream big, didn't we, Samuel?

That's what being young is all about, and why it's so important you go to Ohio to see your little girl.

Eddie scratched his head. Wish I could find that book of photos.

Samuel drained his cup of coffee and stood to go.

You in a hurry? It wouldn't take a couple of minutes for me to look in the back bedroom.

Sorry, Eddie, I promised Mom I'd take her to Elizabethtown. She's making holiday wreaths and needs plastic holly, mistletoe and whatnot.

Oh, that's nice. How is your momma? Still teaching second grade at the elementary school?

Yep, and still crafting on the weekend. That's Mom. She'll never change.

Eddie looked up into the corners of his home. Wouldn't mind some decorations in here, a wreath too maybe.

I'll bring one over.

I'll put it right on the door, on the inside, so I can look at it when I'm watching television. If Jean ever comes over and sees it though, Samuel, I'll have to tell her I bought it—otherwise she'll know you were here.

Samuel stepped slowly to the thin trailer door.

Hey, you forgot your little case, Eddie told him.

That's for you.

The case?

No. What's *inside* the case, Eddie.

Is it mementos or something, from when we were kids?

We made a deal in my basement, Eddie, and I'm making good on that deal. It's half the money I just won in a professional poker tournament.

They were both looking at the green suitcase now.

But we were in middle school, Eddie said, his voice starting to shake. We were just kids runnin' our mouths.

A deal's a deal.

After a moment of silence, Eddie asked if it was a big tournament.

Yes it was.

I wish I'd been there with you.

You were, Eddie. The whole time. You earned it as much as I ever did. Maybe more.

Samuel opened the door and stepped out onto a discolored patch of grass that was littered with cigarette butts and RC cans. Eddie watched him walk over to the truck and get in.

Don't you want the suitcase back?

Use it for the trip.

What trip?

The one you're gonna take to see that little girl.

CAROL'S DADDY

1946

CAROL'S DADDY KNEW where his daughter was, and sometimes drove most of the day to get there. He would park his truck at the end of the long dirt road, then creep through the trees to stare at the crumbling house that his flesh and blood, his property by law, called home. He had figured it out three years ago from something a stranger said at the card table.

His plan was to enter one night when there was no moon. Grab her and the child—use a gun if anyone got in his way. It was his right. They belonged to him after all. Since finding out, he'd done nothing but watch the house a couple of times a month. Just knowing where she was and that he could do something at any time gave him a feeling of immense power that was hard to give up.

Swigging liquor from a square bottle, he would squat in the bushes watching lights go on and off, hearing voices, sometimes laughter, which he felt was enjoyed at his expense.

He'd usually finish the bottle in his truck, fall asleep until dawn, then begin the long journey home with the windows rolled down.

. . .

Very early one summer morning, Carol's Daddy was driving back to his own county when there was a car at the side of the road. A woman got out as he approached and flagged him down. The liquor had been steadily wearing off and his mouth was dry. The woman was waving a red rag. She was young, maybe nineteen, with brown hair and long front teeth.

It was early morning, but the sun was already burning the cut fields and drying wild grass on the hills.

Oh, thanks for stopping, mister. We got a flat tire on the back wheel. If you have a mind to help, we'd appreciate it.

We? Carol's Daddy said from inside his truck.

My daughter and me.

He strained his neck to look in the car. How old?

'Bout seven. She's in the back seat staying out of the sun.

Seven ain't no good age…can't hardly work 'em at seven.

I suppose, said the woman. I'm Mildred. Nice to meet you.

Carol's Daddy lit a cigarette and looked at the woman's round mouth, her front teeth, and the mounds beneath her shirt.

I'm Clay, he said, getting out of his vehicle. Mister Clay to you.

Ain't you gonna pull your truck off the highway, mister?

Sons of bitches can drive 'round me. Now open up the trunk and get the spare out.

The woman hesitated, but eventually understood the man was telling her to get the wheel herself. Carol's Daddy stared with amusement as she wrestled with it, then strained under the weight.

When he saw the wheel, he nodded appreciatively. That tire is brand new. You're a lucky woman. My spare is so worn the threads are showing.

The young woman dropped the wheel and rolled it a few yards to where the flat one was. Carol's Daddy just stood there smoking his cigarette.

Ain't you gonna help my momma, mister? said a small voice from inside the vehicle.

What's it to you? Carol's Daddy said. We ain't gonna do much without a jack and a wrench. That's just common sense.

After he'd plucked tools from the floor of the trunk compartment, he got to work. When the lug nuts were loose, Carol's Daddy positioned the jack underneath the flat metal part on the chassis that would take the full weight of the machine. He was sweating now, and almost completely sober.

Git you kid outta the car, he growled. How am I supposed to raise this vehicle with somebody in it?

The woman looked at the flat tire and the wrench still connected to the wheel. Before she could say anything, the little girl opened a door on the other side of Carol's Daddy, then went and stood with her mother. They watched as the car slowly rose higher and higher. The damaged wheel was soon off the ground.

Carol's Daddy unscrewed the nuts with his fingers and pulled off the wheel. His hands were dirty now and there was oil on his arms. He got the new wheel and positioned it on the axle, then put the old lug nuts back on with his fingers, screwing them in as tight as he could without the wrench.

It's mighty kind of you to do this, the woman said nervously. My husband will be so grateful.

The car was now being lowered by the winding of a lever on the jack.

How come he ain't here to change this wheel?

Oh, he ain't back from France yet, from the war. Shouldn't be too long now.

What's he doin' over there?

Fightin', the woman said, surprised by the question.

Carol's Daddy looked up at her and the young girl. You sure he's coming back? It's been awhile since the war finished up.

The child looked at her mother.

I hear, Carol's Daddy went on, that the French ladies got frilly undergarments. You ever think of that?

The woman told her daughter to get back in the car. Then she looked up and down the road. But not a single car had passed since the man had come along. Across from where they were was a field with horses. The animals watched them now.

Carol's Daddy picked up the wrench and gave it to her. I'm gonna let you do the rest, otherwise how you ever gonna learn?

The woman took the tool from the man.

Now, bend down and tighten them nuts, Mildred.

The woman moved slowly. The tool was still warm from his hands.

Make sure it's nice and tight, sweetheart. Otherwise, that wheel gonna come off down the road, and you're gonna have to pay a whole lot more for a tow.

The woman's face soon grew red from the strain. When it was finished, Carol's Daddy told her she'd done a good job, and to pick up the old wheel.

But she just looked at it, so he pointed with his cigarette.

It ain't gonna lift itself, now is it?

The girl inside the car watched from the shade of the back seat. After a few tries, the mother had it in her arms and hauled it to the trunk. When she was putting it in, Carol's Daddy came up behind and pressed his body against hers. She felt the chrome bumper push into her legs. The trunk lid was up, so the child couldn't see what was happening, and the woman must have known instinctively not to cry out because of her daughter. Carol's Daddy could feel the soft flesh of her body, hot from lifting the wheel. She tried to move sideways but he blocked her with both arms. As he began lifting her dress, the woman twisted her body around and hit Carol's Daddy in the side of the head with a piece of firewood, forgotten in the trunk since winter.

He staggered backwards a few steps, blinking his eyes, touching the place where he'd been struck. The woman was still holding the wood when he lunged with a closed fist, breaking her nose. She fell quickly, then Carol's Daddy kicked her a few times in the stomach, her eyes opening so wide with each blow he thought they might roll out of her head and under the car. The child in the back seat was screaming now, and pounding the car's windows like an insect trapped in a jar.

Carol's Daddy stood over the woman and swayed, still dazed from the blow and out of breath from kicking. He watched as the whimpering mother crawled under the vehicle. There was blood running out from her nose and mouth.

About three months later, Carol's Daddy decided it was time to fetch his daughter and grandchild back. He had a plan in his mind that involved putting them both to work in the day and having them sit with him in the evening so he could amuse himself.

He filled his gun with bullets and holstered it on his belt. He felt good about his decision. He had enjoyed the wait but now felt it was time to exercise his God-given right as a man and bring them home.

He brewed himself a cup of black coffee and drank it on the porch standing up. When her mother was alive, the girl had gone to school, so she knew a few things. But nothing useful that a woman ought to know, he thought. Still, she was something he could bring to the card table in a pinch.

Carol's Daddy rarely pictured his dead wife. She was like someone he had once met briefly a long time ago. Though in dreams, her face and sometimes her whole body hovered there before him, and he would feel afraid and ashamed. But when he drank, Carol's Daddy did not feel any fear or shame—only the impulse to pull anything apart that was not already broken or undone.

When his tin coffee cup was empty, Carol's Daddy went back inside to get his hat and some extra ammunition. He scratched his unshaven face with one hand and considered his savage reflection in the shell of each bullet. He felt that he was better than most men—stronger in every way that mattered.

As he pocketed the bullets, grinning at himself, there was a knock at the door. Carol's Daddy smiled, thinking it was another Bible salesman. He could scare 'em with his gun, he thought. Maybe even force the man to do something funny, like remove his pants, then crawl on his hands and knees off the property—or drink some vinegar like Jesus done when he was carrying his cross up the hill to be lynched.

But when Carol's Daddy opened the screen door it was not a sweating, overweight Bible salesman, but a young man in an army uniform.

Who are you? Carol's Daddy said, squinting against the morning sun. You from the power company that's putting up those things on my land?

No, sir, I'm not from the power company. I'm looking for a fella by the name of Mister Clay, the man said. Then he glanced past Carol's Daddy, at the yellow tablecloth and few articles of furniture that were in the house.

I didn't ask what you was doing, Carol's Daddy said. I asked who you was. Quit lookin' in my house.

Well, sir, I can't tell you who I am until I know if you are Mister Clay or not—this is official business I'm here on, if you must know.

That right? Well what you want with me? Carol's Daddy said, looking at the man's car, trying to figure out if he recognized it. I was on my way out as a matter o' fact, so make it quick.

You got something with your name on it, sir? the young sergeant asked. I just need to be sure you are Mister Clay.

What is it the fuck you want, boy? Can't you tell me that?

You ain't got no brothers with the same name, Mister Clay?

You dumb son of a bitch. Didn't they teach you nothing in the army? No, I ain't got no kin but me and my daughter—and her bastard child. Now tell me what you want or get out of my way.

The man swallowed. Your daughter and grandchild inside?

They don't live here at present. I was just fixin' to go fetch 'em.

The young sergeant nodded his head, then jabbed his fingers into Carol's Daddy's throat several times. Before he could do anything to save himself, his head was pulled down to meet the young sergeant's rising knee.

When he opened his eyes, he was being dragged off the porch into his own front yard. He remembered his gun then and reached for where it was holstered. But the soldier kicked the weapon out of his hand, the same way Carol's Daddy had once kicked a biscuit from his daughter's hand, then made her eat it off the floor.

I ain't done nothin'! he screeched, as the dirt went up his shirt, scraping the skin on his back. You listenin' to me?

Without speaking, the man dropped Carol's Daddy's legs, went over to his car, and opened the back door. A young woman with brown hair stepped out.

Yeah, that's him, she said. I remember the voice.

When Carol's Daddy recognized her, he padded his hands around in the dirt, searching for his weapon. Then the woman and her husband were standing over him. Carol's Daddy could see she was breathing quickly and holding a piece of firewood. He raised a hand toward her, but before he could open his mouth to speak, she brought the log down on his head with a clunk. Carol's Daddy tried to grab it but caught only air. His eyes were soon so full of blood he couldn't see anything.

Eventually the blows ceased. That's enough, the woman said breathlessly. That's enough.

Carol's Daddy could hardly move now. And his eyes felt loose in their sockets.

When a car door closed, he thought it was over, but it was just the woman getting back in.

Without speaking, the young sergeant dragged him around the back of the house, kicking open the door of the old barn and dropping him in a loose pile of straw. Carol's Daddy was doing all he could to get air in and out of his lungs. He still couldn't see and could hardly speak. The pain in his head had dropped into his chest, where an invisible hand was squeezing his heart so that it couldn't fill.

The husband drew his army knife, a V-42 stiletto, and held it at Carol's Daddy's throat. But then at the last second, he remembered what his wife had told him and backed away.

Carol's Daddy lay there all night and into the next day, just a few yards from the remains of Travis Curt, a man he had killed over ten years before, on the porch beneath his daughter's window.

ALFREDIA

1996

ON A ROUTINE visit to the ophthalmologist, Samuel and his mother were told there were new optic surgeries that could straighten his eye. Samuel had taken a personal day from the auto factory where he worked with his father, feeling the different points on truck frames with his hands to check welds made by a robot arm.

After the examination, the doctor sat with them and went over the options for corrective surgery. It was expensive, he warned them, but would be almost completely restorative to normal movement.

On the way back home, Alfredia drove while Samuel used a tissue to dab the eye that had been carefully examined after drops were put in through a syringe. In the fields around them, black cows were pulling up grass into their wide mouths.

Samuel had surprised himself and his mother by telling the doctor that if his eye was fixed, he'd still be the same person he was now, and so he'd sooner just leave it be—even though he could have used the money from his poker tournament. At the end of the appointment, Alfredia said they would think about it and thanked the doctor for showing them pictures of other people's eyes where the surgery had proved effective.

You know I've got a little bit of money too, she told her son in the car. It was supposed to be for your college, but if that's not going to happen, you're welcome to use it for this.

I am who I am, Momma.

That's fine, Samuel. I admire your decision. I'm just giving you the option is all.

Could I use that money for a car maybe?

No, you could not. It's for education or medical treatments.

About fifteen miles from home, the brown Ford Granada suddenly veered into the wrong lane. Alfredia froze, but Samuel made a grab for the wheel and steered it to the grassy shoulder, where they came to rest beside a cattle fence. Alfredia was shaking violently.

I swear I couldn't steer. The wheel just turned by itself. I could have killed you.

Samuel unclicked her seat belt and touched her hands. When she had calmed down, they got out of the car to try and see what had gone wrong. Samuel opened the hood. Stared over the dark landscape of ticking parts.

I reckon it's the steering rack, he said. Engine looks fine.

Can it be fixed, Samuel?

Fishing and cars, Mom. Two things I never had luck with.

But Dad says you're doing good at the Ford plant.

He nodded and looked around for a house where they could use a phone. But it was just acres of uncultivated pasture.

What are we gonna do, Samuel?

I could hitch a ride to the nearest gas station, call Dad.

And leave me here?

You could come.

Alfredia adjusted a button on her floral dress. You want us to hitchhike, you mean?

Just to a gas station.

Well...I don't know what your father would say.

Then an old pickup truck appeared on the horizon. They could tell it was old because either there were holes in the muffler or the motor was bad. When it came near, Samuel could see it had a converted flatbed made of thick wood, and oversized wheels and tires. The exhaust pipes had been rerouted so that black diesel fumes poured through two vertical tubes on either side of the cab whenever the driver pushed the gas pedal. The truck slowed as it came upon them, then a moment after going past, pulled to the side and came to a hard stop. The door opened and the driver got out.

Oh dear, Alfredia said. Who is this now?

The man had on black jeans and a black tee shirt with holes in it. His skin was dark, and there were tan lines halfway up his biceps. His hands were almost black with oil, and his tightly laced work boots looked a size too big.

The man came over to them slowly, not speaking, but with a half smile that revealed several missing teeth. He glanced briefly at the Granada's exposed engine and at Samuel—but his real focus was Alfredia.

I knew it was you, he said, grinning.

Alfredia smoothed the pattern on her dress and looked past the man at his vehicle.

My son and I appreciate you stopping to help, mister.

You don't remember me, do ya?

Well... Alfredia said, locking eyes with her son for a moment. Let me think for a minute.

Come on now, you're breaking my heart.

Alfredia looked the man up and down, trying not to stare directly into his face, hoping for some memory to drop into her hands and save them.

I'm sorry, Alfredia said. I've been meaning to get new glasses for a while now. Probably why I wrecked the car.

The man moved his feet quickly in place. I've been waiting for a chance to get even with you for a long time.

Alfredia looked at her son again, trying to appear more amused than afraid. What did I do this time?

I'm just hurt you don't remember me. Then he turned around and bent forward, slapping both his buttocks. Do you remember now?

Samuel felt his breath quicken. Alfredia laughed and told the man how sorry she was.

I am crushed, Missus Roberts, crushed! You were my favorite teacher! I loved you so much and you don't even remember me. My heart is broken forever!

Then Alfredia spoke in a loud, clear voice: Jason Benningfield. Second grade.

Yeesssss! the man roared. So you was just kiddin' that whole time? I knew you wouldn't forget me! Oh, Missus Roberts, you changed my life.

I did, Jason?

You tell me. I'm working a six hun'ed acre cattle farm as chief mechanic, earning more money than I thought was in the Kentucky Savings Bank.

Alfredia didn't smile or move. There was always something special about you, Jason, I knew that the first time we met.

The man's face was glowing. And now you're broken down with your son, and I get to help you. I get a chance to pay you back. How's that for karma?

You don't owe me anything, Jason. It was easy to love you.

Easy? he said, turning to Samuel. I spat in her face!

Oh, but you were just a little boy, Alfredia said.

You took me out of the classroom into the hall by the wrist and bent me over, remember that? It's why I was slapping my butt in front'a y'all! He turned to Samuel again. I didn't mean any disrespect by it...I was just trying to jog her memory so she could place me.

I'm sorry if I spanked you, Jason. I never did like to spank my students.

But don't you remember, Missus Roberts? I was bent over with my legs shaking, but you just told me to stand up again. Do you remember what happened then?

I can't say I do...

You hugged me.

I did?

You hugged me. And I still carry that feeling around. That hug. All these years later. It's still mine when I want it.

You were my little buddy, Alfredia said. I remember now.

When she said these words, the man scooped her up and swung her around.

Here's your hug back, Missus Roberts…look how big it's gotten!

They arrived home five hours later with a new rack and pin-ion, bushings, sway bar, brake pads, rotors, struts, fog lamps, tow hook, and an emergency battery charger. Alfredia's old student had towed them back to his workshop at the farm, then sent one of his coworkers into Elizabethtown for parts.

Randy was back from the auto plant and sitting at the counter drinking coffee with Uncle Rusty. He had his truck keys and was about ready to go out looking when they heard a car pull up and the engine turn off.

Randy stubbed out his cigarette and looked out the window just in time to see his wife climb out of the car with two black handprints on the back of her floral dress.

Oh Lord… he said. Oh Jesus…

CAROL

1947

AT THE SAME time every morning, Carol rose and dressed in the dark so that Rusty might sleep a little longer. She could hear the couple moving around upstairs. Harold would be shaving his face and putting on a suit of clothes for his job at the bank, with Marjorie speaking to him softly from the warm sheets.

After just over a year in the new place, Rusty still wasn't walking, but his speech had improved and he talked nonstop. He was small for his age, but patient for a child, waiting until his mother finished her morning chores before asking to be lifted from the bed or to the window so he might look out on the street where there were cars and people going by. His legs had grown, but they were still weak and withered, unable to withstand the weight of his body.

Harold and Marjorie's house was in the town. They had indoor plumbing and a toilet on each floor. Seeing movies and taking a bath at night were Carol's greatest pleasures, especially in winter when from the steaming tub she could hear people's voices outside in the cold and their footsteps echoing.

She was a good cleaner, and pretended that Harold and Marjorie were famous film stars with a house in Hollywood. Every day, she wiped out the sinks and the toilets; then each week, she polished the faucets, swept the floors, mopped, and waxed the banisters. The laundry was never-ending. Carol was used to sheets, and found it hard to maneuver the iron over Harold's shirts. She took a lot of breaks in the day, and sometimes just sat watching her son pick flowers from a patch in the backyard, where Rusty had been given permission to grow things. The bathroom that was attached to her own room, Carol cleaned on Sundays. That was her day off. She also got a long break on Tuesday and Thursday afternoons, when Marjorie went shopping or to meet ladies from the church.

For the first time in her life, Carol had a full closet of clothes—mostly dresses that Marjorie no longer wanted to wear, but they were hers to put on and take off whenever she wanted. Sometimes in the bed with her eyes closing, Carol remembered being up late on the porch with the smoke from Bessie's cigar, and the impenetrable darkness that was all around, but never closing in. In the first few weeks, memories like this made Carol want to hastily pack her things, pull Rusty out of bed, and hurry through the streets in the direction of the bus station. But always by morning, she had the strength to get through at least one more day without Bessie and Martha. Soon, those days bunched into months and her life tilted, rolling everything into the present.

One morning, Harold came downstairs as usual in his charcoal suit and slippers. He was holding an empty glass and his face was freshly shaven. Carol tried to take the glass from his hand but Harold carried it to the sink, rinsed it out, then set it to dry on the rack.

I wish you'd let me do that, she said. I don't come to the bank and start counting money, do I?

Harold laughed. Well, maybe you should, Carol. Then perhaps there wouldn't be so many mistakes.

You serious?

Harold sat on the hall bench to lace up his black oxford shoes. Take some evening classes, Carol. Finish high school, and then we'll talk about it, seriously, if it's something you want.

Oh, I don't have time for that. Marjorie still sleeping?

She got up with me, but went back to bed, poor thing.

She have a bad night, Mister Harold?

Not the best.

Harold stood and went through to the dining room, where he kept his briefcase. In the kitchen, Carol cracked fresh eggs into a pan of sizzling lard. Then she heard Rusty calling for her, and Harold appeared in the doorway wearing an apron with Christmas holly on it.

I'll finish the eggs, Carol. Go see to him, because I don't want Marjorie woken up.

Rusty was on his back with his arms in the air.

I dreamed something.

Quit hollerin', now. Miss Marjorie sleepin', and you'll get Momma in trouble.

There was a box of mice, Momma. In my dream.

Mice, Rusty?

Yuh, a whole box of 'em. And my foot was in it.

In what?

The box. My foot. Wid'em.

Carol took up one of her son's feet, still warm from being under the blanket. His nails needed cutting, and there were scrapes on his shins where a nail had caught in the night.

Is that why you were screamin' for me? Cause of them mice?

Rusty looked out the window. What day is it?

Wednesday.

Is that the same as *today*, Momma?

You know it is, Rusty, I done told you that a million times. It's always *today*.

Just as Carol was about to lift Rusty off the bed, she looked out the window and saw the big man who lived across the street. He was sitting on the porch in his overalls, drinking coffee. He had an enormous head and large hands. Carol knew he left his house the same time as Mister Harold because she heard him whistling. He worked at the paint factory in town. He whistled on his way home too. All the way down the street, then across his porch and into the house.

What you lookin' at, Momma?

Our neighbor, that whistlin' fella…he's out front having his breakfast.

You mean Big Head?

You shouldn't call people names, Rusty.

We're friends.

How can that be? You've never met him.

But I see him all the time, and when he sees me lookin' he stops whistlin' and goes like this. Rusty lifted his hand and made a funny face.

He does what now?

Rusty showed his mother again.

And what do you do?

I go like this, Rusty said, making a funny face by pulling at the sides of his mouth.

Hmm, well, I don't know if it's a good idea to make faces at people.

Why?

Well, for one, if the wind changes, your face gonna stay that way.

Rusty sat up and leaned toward the window. The man was sipping coffee on his porch.

You should go tell Big Head 'bout that, Momma…he mightn't know.

About what?

Wind changin'.

Well, stop calling him Big Head and maybe I will.

By Friday of that week, Marjorie was feeling better and told Carol she could have some extra time to herself. She decided to take Rusty to Main Street and back in his little wagon for apple pie and cream.

By the late afternoon they were nearly home.

The sun had fallen upon the streets like a golden net, and the last patches of winter snow were melting to form deep, clear pools at the end of each block. Rusty laughed passionately whenever the wagon plunged through one.

When they were almost at the house, Carol stopped walking.

Quit that, Rusty, she said. The boy looked at his hands, then bit down lightly on his thumb.

I seen what you're doing…dragging your hand in them puddles. You'll get sick thataway.

It's fun tho' ain't it?

Well, being sick ain't fun…ask Marjorie about that.

But Rusty just went on letting his arm drop over the side of the wagon into each cold, slushy pool of melting snow. Before Carol could reach down and grab her son's hand, she heard a man's voice from behind.

Let the boy have his fun, said the voice. That's what life's for.

Carol turned angrily, but the sun forced her to squint.

What you say?

All children love puddles, ma'am. The man stepped toward her and blocked the sun so she could see his face.

Oh, you're the neighbor.

Yes, ma'am. Joe's muh name.

Well, Mister Joe, puddles might be fun for a little boy, but they're a hardship for a mother when they make a child sick.

I see, Joe said. Well, maybe I could teach him how to whistle instead?

Carol laughed. And where's that gonna get him?

Oh, now listen, whistlin' will get you far in life…trust me, I know from experience.

Carol noticed his black boots because they were huge and there was paint on them. It was splattered on his overalls too, and on his hands. The big man saw her looking.

I just left work, he said. Ain't had time to clean up.

That place on the hill? You work there?

Yes'm, the paint factory. You know it?

Not really. I'm not from 'round here.

Where you from then?

The country.

Me too. Guess we're both out-of-towners.

Is your factory the one what blows that whistle ever' day?

That's right.

Carol nodded. Why is that?

It's the lunch whistle.

Well, I hate it. Makes me jump.

I guess it is pretty loud. But next time you hear it, you'll know I'm about to eat a sandwich. Sometimes it's tomato and cheese, other days it's...cheese and tomato.

You make it yourself?

Well, I live alone, so yes.

Why you in such a large house if you're alone?

Well, Joe said. In return for fixing it up for the owner in my spare time, I get to live there for a spell. I'll git something smaller eventually, in the country, along with a goat or two. Maybe a rabbit.

What's the rabbit for? Meat? You can't get no milk from it.

Friendship. Then he looked down at Rusty in the wagon. You like rabbits?

I had a dream 'bout a box o' mice. My foot was in it, mister. In the box wid'em.

Carol felt suddenly embarrassed. Rusty's a bit slow.

When no one spoke, she looked the man up and down, wondering if she could just walk away. It was starting to get cold. But when she pulled on the wagon, he said something.

Please tell Mister Harold I'm happy to fix anything he needs workin' on in the house. He don't even have to pay me. I'll do it from neighborliness. The house I'm in is about finished, so I'd appreciate something to keep my hands occupied.

Then he did something that Carol would remember until her dying day.

He stepped right past her and bent his knees so his heavy frame was almost eye level with Rusty in the wagon. He reached down and dunked his hand up to the wrist in a deep pool of melting snow. Rusty's face lit up. His hand shot from under the blanket and entered the same puddle with a splash.

Carol looked at the two hands underwater. One big and one little. She didn't know whether to laugh or slap their faces.

HEATHER

1999

AN HOUR BEFORE closing, the restaurant was already empty. Heather went from table to table, turning over clean coffee cups one by one, then laying down paper place mats. When that was done, she sat at the counter and wrapped silverware in paper napkins, fastening each bundle with a sticker. Her feet hurt, but she'd soon be in the car going home. She could take her shoes off then and drive barefoot through the darkness.

It was Halloween night and the dining room was decorated with ghosts, ghouls, and witches' hats. Alone with empty tables, Heather wondered if there were real ghosts, and if they watched people. She once found an envelope when cleaning out a cupboard in the supply closet. It was a pack of photographs from New Year's Eve 1957.

When she saw the people in those pictures, Heather knew their lives had come and gone. Those who had lived out their days in the town would now be in the cemetery with tiny, snapping American flags in the ground over where they were buried. The waitresses in the photographs had matching green dresses. The men wore dark suits or overalls—carried burning cigarettes.

Many years ago, there had been a factory nearby and the town was prosperous. Heather wondered if the people in the pictures sensed their time of abundance would pass. Or did every day seem new and unbreakable? The hardest thing about getting old, a customer once warned her, was always being shocked by the face staring back at you in the mirror.

When Marvin appeared from the kitchen, he was wearing a satin Louisville Cardinals jacket over his baggy kitchen whites. He was a tall, deliberate man with a slow but confident way of speaking. He carried several white containers in a plastic bag, most likely french fries for his children. In his other hand was a box of menthol cigarettes and a plastic lighter held together with a rubber band.

I'm taking off, Heather. I closed the kitchen and left a piece of Salisbury steak in foil for your momma.

You're a sweetheart, Marvin. I love you.

Ok, don't forget it now.

I won't, happy Halloween.

If Clyde sees it, then...

I know Marvin, I won't forget. I promise.

How she doin', anyway?

Momma? She's okay. She misses him. We all do.

The cook turned to go. Want me to flip the sign on the door?

No need, I'm right behind you.

But there were still things to do. And the sudden quiet was strange and penetrating, as though in the absence of people, Heather felt them more. She climbed onto a stool and held open the pie cabinet's plastic door with her elbow, sweeping crumbs from the clear shelves.

Heather felt she had learned a lot from being a waitress. There were regulars she knew by name. Others by face. Some of the old ladies couldn't eat without shaking and making a mess. The other waitresses made fun, but Heather knew coming to Booth's Diner was all they had left.

Some of the ladies spent hours getting ready. Pasting on makeup. Choosing what to wear. Heather guessed it was too hard being at home. The rooms once full of people were now just full of voices calling to them from far away.

Some of the old men had crushes on Heather. She knew it. It was awkward at first. They called her "Red" or "Hot Top." But since it never went beyond harmless comments about her hair, or leaving an extra dollar, she didn't have the heart to humiliate them.

One of the men who came in every day was named Hale Bennett. When he didn't show up for his usual grits two mornings in a row, Heather called the senior home and they told her he would be in the hospital from now on.

The next day she visited. Took his favorite breakfast in a cardboard box. Seeing him hooked up to machines with only a few days to go, she felt very emotional and went back the next night, and the one after that. She expected to see other people, but she was the only one.

When he passed, Heather was holding his hand. She didn't feel like a waitress anymore, but his late wife, a high school sweetheart or long dead mother—some final chance for him to die still holding the thread of his life.

It wasn't all old folks. Sometimes big, young families piled in through the double doors of Booth's on their way home from Walmart. The fathers wore camouflage clothes, had crew-cut hairstyles and balloon stomachs. Most of the grandparents smoked and were thin, with drawn in faces and missing teeth. These were folks Heather recognized as *her* people, and so she tried to give something extra, like pie or biscuits or fruit salad.

Around Thanksgiving, men would stride in with dead bucks in the beds of their trucks. A few of the staff members would go out and look.

But most of her customers were old people who drove American sedans, dressed up on Sunday, and still liked to be waited on by girls who would sit with them and ask questions about their lives.

There was supposed to be another waitress to help Heather close up that night, but it was Halloween, and both Angie and Gail had children eager to put on their costumes and be taken around.

With just fifteen minutes to go, Heather wiped down the counter and sang along to the radio. Then she heard the main door open.

What you forget? she shouted. When there was no answer, she took an elastic off her wrist to make a ponytail. Marvin?

With still no reply, Heather stepped carefully toward the entrance holding a wet dishcloth, scorning herself for not locking the door. Standing there by the soft-toy claw machine was a tall, serious looking man in gray overalls, clean-shaven but dirty, like he'd been working.

I'm so sorry, sir, but we're closed.

The man looked at his watch. Oh, I apologize. I thought I had fifteen minutes.

Well, normally you would...but it's Halloween night, Heather said, spinning the wet rag in her hand. I guess you don't have kids, huh?

Not yet. One day maybe.

Well, I'm sorry, mister, but the cook's done left already, so...

Anywhere else close by? I haven't eaten since lunch.

There's McDonald's or Long John Silver's if you like fish fry. You're not from here, huh?

No ma'am. Just passing through on my way home from work.

I knew I hadn't seen you before.

He placed his hand on the door to leave. I usually drive home from Louisville with my dad, but we're on different shifts now.

Instead of turning around and letting him go, Heather stood there and said. Don't you think I'm a little young to be called ma'am?

Sorry.

Oh, I'm just teasin', she said, wrapping the cloth around her hand. There's a burger place on Shelbyville Avenue...wait, that's closed too. How about Mexican? You like Taco Bell?

The man grimaced. Heather opened her mouth to laugh. I don't like fast food neither, but that's all there is, unless you drive to Junction City, which has a couple of bars on account of it being wet an 'all. You could get a burger there and a few beers to go with it.

I don't really drink no more, the man admitted, and I definitely don't go to the bars in Junction City.

My granddaddy never touched a drop. He always said he was the better for it. Heather noticed that one of the man's eyes was off-center. She wondered if it was made of glass and he could take it out and look at it. She felt sorry for him then and wanted to give him something.

Would you like some coffee for the road, mister? It's bin there awhile but still pretty hot.

Well, if it's not too much trouble.

I'd end up throwing it away, so you're welcome to it. Why don't you sit at the counter. Cream and sugar?

That'd be nice.

When he was comfortable on one of the orange, vinyl seats, Heather poured the thick liquid into a ceramic cup with a saucer that had Booth's written in yellow script.

I hope I'm not keeping you, miss.

Oh, it's been dead all night.

He grinned. That makes sense.

Heather stared at him earnestly. It does? Why?

Halloween.

Oh, I get it, she giggled, dead all night. Well, I'm too old for trick or treatin', in case you hadn't guessed.

But too young to be called ma'am?

You're funny. You work in Louisville?

That's right. But I live an hour south. Grayson County.

I know where that is.

I'm Samuel. What's your name?

Heather.

That name suits you.

My granddaddy said so too because of my red hair.

He the one who never drank?

Heather nodded and wanted to say more but found she couldn't. The old man had only been gone three months. Left his bed one night and went outside without anyone knowing. In the morning they found him in the deep grass of the horse meadow.

At the funeral, Heather's mother told everyone that decades ago—before he and his brothers went to fight in the war—he had played in that meadow as a boy. Then as a young man, had laid out summer picnics when courting the girl who would become his bride.

We're a sentimental family, Heather's mother had said, and that's why we're gonna suffer without him.

Later, when the funeral was almost over, her mother went pale and tried to climb inside the casket with her daddy.

As Samuel drank his coffee, Heather tidied up, humming along to a song on the radio.

You have a nice voice, Samuel said. I bet you could be on one of them talent shows on TV.

Heather took her hair out of the ponytail and looked at the man's face in the reflection of a steel shelf.

Where do you work at?

On the line at Ford. I check chassis welds, make sure the robot done 'em right.

Don't you get bored with that?

Oh, you bet.

So how do you keep going?

Well, I just imagine the car I'm checking is the one my mother's gonna buy.

She must be a special woman.

Alfredia? Oh yeah.

My momma is a good person too but she's had a rough life, and her health has gotten bad.

Where's your father?

West Texas. He left when I was four.

Well, he missed out.

And my momma had a brother who got addicted to Oxy, then killed hisself in a bathroom at the Walmart.

At least you have each other.

I'd be lost without Momma.

Where do you live, Heather?

Marion County.

That's not too close.

I know it. But I like to see different faces, and some of the people who come in here really need me—the older folks, I mean. I'm their therapist, kinda.

How's the drive home at night?

It used to be fine, Heather said, giving him more coffee to drink.

Used to be? Something happen?

I came upon a wreck, she said, realizing that if she tried to tell the story, her voice would shake.

Was it bad?

Working here with the old, you get used to people dying, but it wasn't the same. I was so frightened I could hardly breathe.

You want to talk about it?

Well, I was almost home, it was a two-lane road, and dark, I mean, so, so dark, black, Samuel, pitch black. I saw some light up ahead, like another car…but it was in my lane, so I slowed down and when I come to it, I see two cars done smashed into one another.

What you do?

I got out to help, but both the drivers had already passed.

How could you tell?

It was obvious, I didn't even go near 'em. It's like some instinct kicks in and you just know. Their eyes were open, as if they were still driving. And there was blood and bits of glass in their faces.

Oh boy. Was anyone else there?

Heather shook her head.

So, what happened then?

I had to get back in my car and drive on until I found someone, or saw a house. She dabbed her eyes with the rag and her makeup smeared. Eventually I come to a gas station. The guy was closing up, and I told him what happened, and he called the police.

What did you do then?

The police told me to stay at the gas station until they came.

Then I had to make a statement. They called my momma and she asked if they would drive me home.

Did they?

I left my car there and rode with a trooper called Jerry.

Did they say what had happened?

Only that there were open containers of alcohol in both vehicles.

Samuel leaned back on the counter stool and wrinkled his brow. Are you sure this isn't a Halloween story you made up to scare customers away?

No! she cried, hitting him on the arm with her rag. It really happened!

I'm just kiddin'. It's hard to see something like that, I bet.

I'm glad you don't drink no more...a young man like you with a good job in Louisville don't need to be drinking.

If I drink, I stick to beer.

And stale coffee.

When there was no more left in the carafe and his cup was empty, Samuel looked at his watch.

I'd better get going, Heather, I wouldn't want your husband getting the wrong idea.

She stood with the empty carafe in her hand and looked at him. I'm not currently in a relationship. Too busy for that.

Well, then, I guess that's another thing we got in common.

What's the first?

That we don't like being called ma'am.

As Samuel stood to go, he asked if he could buy a coffee cup and saucer. Heather asked why, and he said he collected them.

You seriously do? Just from diners or all restaurants?

Samuel grinned.

Heather stood with a hand on her hip bone. I'm so gullible, I'd believe anything.

I just wanted something to remind me what a nice Halloween I had this year.

Really? All I done was give you some old coffee I was gonna throw away.

He shrugged.

I guess if you come back I can ask my manager Clyde if you can just have one.

I'll pay him fifty dollars for it.

Heather blushed. Fifty dollars! she exclaimed. Then it must have been the best cup of coffee you ever had.

Samuel backed away toward the door. It wasn't so much the coffee, as something else.

What?

You know what.

Heather threw her rag at him. You're too much! she said, biting her lip. But you can walk me to my car if you want, seein' as it's Halloween.

JOE

1947

Spring came and colored the hills and meadows that lay around the town. Harold had just finished eating his supper when he heard a note drop onto the mat through the mail slot in the front door.

It was from their neighbor Joe. Harold read it, then took it to show his wife. When they had discussed the note, they called Carol from the kitchen.

How are you feeling this evening, Miss Marjorie? Carol asked. What else can I get you?

Sit down please, Carol.

Is everything alright?

Tell me, said Harold, adjusting his spectacles. What do you know about our neighbor, apart from the fact he sometimes whistles in the middle of the night for no apparent reason?

Well, said Carol. Not much. Rusty calls him Big Head.

Marjorie burst out laughing.

Harold glanced at the note in his hand. This is the man who works in the paint factory, if I'm not mistaken.

That's him, Carol said. I've heard him whistlin' at night too. I thought it would wake up little Rusty, but he sleeps through anything these days.

Harold smiled. Yes, indeed. I thought it was a nightingale at first, or one of those strange nocturnal birds Rusty has always told me about from your old house in the country. But one night I looked out and saw him pacing up and down in his bedroom, just whistling away.

I don't know why he does it, Carol said. But he could whistle for America, if there was ever such a thing.

Are you on good terms with him?

Carol looked from Harold to Marjorie, then back to Harold. Well, we've spoken a few times when Rusty and I was outside. He seems nice. Rusty likes him. What, is he dead or something?

Heavens no, said Harold, he wrote us this letter.

He gave the note to Carol and she stared at the thin piece of paper. The handwriting was oversized and round, like a child's, and there were faint thumbprints of white paint from where he'd held onto it.

Carol could recognize one or two words by their shapes—and, of course, her own name and that of her son. But the rest of it appeared nothing more than lengths of black thread, tied into pretty knots and bows.

Shall we go? Marjorie said. I think it'd be fun.

The Lord tells us to love thy neighbor, said Harold. Then he breathed in quickly. I just hope he doesn't ask for a loan.

Marjorie hit him with her napkin. So what if he does?

Carol gave the letter back to Harold.

So, you're fine with it, Carol? Friday night will be fine?

Carol shrugged. Friday's fine, I guess.

Harold tapped the piece of paper. He says to bring Rusty too. That tells me the man has integrity.

For the rest of the week, Carol tried to figure out what was going to happen on Friday night. It was true she saw and spoke to Joe regularly, but only when she was outside with Rusty, getting fresh air in the afternoons. She'd hear whistling, and then there he was. His enormous frame looming over them. Slow-blinking eyes and those paint-spattered boots.

Carol suspected that he was coming over to fix something. That had to be it. Maybe in the basement, where pipes and wires hummed and there were cool, damp boxes of things to be hung up for Christmas. But why did he want Rusty there? Maybe to play a game or show him something? Hopefully not to teach him whistling—that was all she needed.

On Friday afternoon, Marjorie told Carol to put away her mop and take a bath. Rusty was under the kitchen table with his tin race car.

I think it's nice, Marjorie said, that he's going to all this trouble—it's sweet.

What trouble? asked Carol.

Why, having us all come over for supper. I can't even imagine what a man like that would cook, maybe hamburger or bread and butter? I'm just so curious about him. For instance, why he lives alone in that big house?

Everything about him is too big, Carol said. It's like "Jack and the Beanstalk."

He can't be more than thirty, Marjorie went on, but there's something of an old man about him, don't you think?

For a long time Carol stared at the dresses in her closet. Although she could not imagine being close to a man, she did want Joe to notice her, to think she was worldly and serious. A town woman, not a country bumpkin.

When Harold came home from work, he got into his cardigan, then answered some letters at his desk. Soon it was time to go across the street. Marjorie and Carol were both in floral Sunday dresses. Marjorie had on a hat too. And white gloves.

The sound of feet on the porch announced their arrival before Harold could even knock. When the door swung open, there was Joe in a dark, double-breasted suit with a pale-yellow shirt and small-knotted tie that Carol thought made his head seem like a big brown egg, a double-yolker.

On his feet were his work boots polished to a high shine, with no trace of paint or dirt, only the faint aroma of turpentine.

Rusty felt like a rock in his mother's arms. He had already been told never, ever, to crawl under other people's furniture and had been reminded of it as they crossed the road that night.

When they got inside, Carol was surprised to see the table laid out with food that Bessie loved. There were bowls of collard greens, buttered sweet potato, johnnycake, ham hocks, and baked chicken.

The cornbread, Joe reassured them, was still in the oven fixin' to rise.

What a glorious spread, said Marjorie, clasping her hands together. And such a handsome dining room.

I don't hardly use it, Joe admitted, though it does catch the last light of day.

Perhaps you might use it when your family visits? ventured Marjorie.

Joe lowered his head. I'm afraid not, Miss Marjorie. They've never come here.

Oh, I see, well maybe one day.

Harold was still surveying the many dishes. Did you really do all this, Joe? It seems beyond the capabilities of one man.

I started last night... he said, looking around for Carol. 'Cause some things need a little time to become perfect.

My father was a lay preacher, said Harold, and years ago we took a trip to Chicago, Illinois, and got invited to a colored church for a picnic. I had one of the best meals of my life, and this reminds me of that.

Joe nodded. I appreciate you saying that, Mister Harold. Means more to me than you know.

Harold laughed a little, perplexed as to what Joe was getting at.

What do you think, Carol? asked Marjorie. Hasn't Joe prepared a nice supper?

Carol slapped Rusty's hand as he reached for a cold drumstick.

Sure, she said. But that's a lot of food for only four people and a child.

Joe blushed and moved his boots on the varnished floor.

Well, Marjorie pointed out, I think it takes a very skilled hand to prepare chicken this way.

Joe chuckled. I don't usually cook meat, Miss Marjorie, don't got the taste for it no more, since bein' in the war.

Big man like you, Joe? Harold said. I don't believe it.

It's the truth, Mister Harold. But maybe ya'll would like to sit now?

Three cushions had been strapped down with rope to the dining chair for Rusty so that he would be at table height. Carol perched him on the chair. Hush up now and fill your mouth with food.

You feelin' good, big fella? Joe called from across the table. But Rusty just looked away and stuck two fingers in his mouth.

Quit that, Carol said. Answer the man.

When she turned to apologize, Joe had gotten out of his seat and was standing over them, holding a bottle of Coca-Cola.

This is for you, he told Rusty. No one else gets one. I bought it special because you're the Coca-Cola Kid.

Rusty reached up and grabbed the bottle.

Maybe your momma can open it when you've eaten something so you don't fill up with them soda bubbles.

What do you say, Rusty?

I'm the Coca-Cola Kid.

Want to say grace, Mister Joe? Marjorie asked when he was back in his seat.

Grace? he said, rubbing his chin. Okay. I'll try, but I'm a little out of habit.

Carol squinted so she could stare at their host, but his eyes were open and he was looking at her.

Thank you, Jesus, for this meal and these people, and for the bank Mister Harold works in, and for inventing money, and paint too for that matter, and for all the people we love who is gone away forever. And for this day. And tomorrow, when it gets here.

What a nice prayer, said Marjorie. I'll have to remember that one.

During the meal, Harold and Marjorie asked Joe many questions, and he answered mostly with yesses and nos.

When Harold inquired as to whether he'd had a hard war, the big man put down his fork slowly, without making any sound.

It was not the best time. But others had it worse.

They all nodded and looked at their food.

Then Rusty asked Joe if he had a machine gun, and if so, could Rusty borrow it to shoot cans.

Ignore him, Carol snapped. He don't know nothing.

Harold pressed his lips together. He's a curious fella alright.

Well, I'll tell him, said Joe plainly, since he asked.

Rusty banged his spoon on the table with excitement.

What happen' was, on that first day of battle...I became a new-born baby rabbit.

For real?

For real, Rusty. And like all rabbits I hid from the dark shapes and the shadows all around. I just stayed in my rabbit hole as the earth was pulled apart by invisible hands.

Was you whistlin' then?

Oh I tried, said Joe, but I was a rabbit remember, so it was just fur rubbing, which don't make no sound.

What happened then?

Well, when the bad men were sleeping, I hopped out of my hiding place.

Like me and Martha! said Rusty. We seen a rabbit once too, when we was tendin' the flower patch.

Yes'uh, I believe it...well after creeping out of my burrow, I went and found each and every one of the enemy soliders, and I took all their clothes, and carried them to the river in my mouth. But being a rabbit, I dropped some on my way there.

What happened then?

Well, the bad men woke up and saw the trail of clothes and followed it, and then realized they were naked, and so jumped into the water out of shame and got carried off and we never see them again.

Did they drown, Mister Joe? Rusty asked. 'Cause they had no clothes on?

Only God knows that, Joe told him.

Harold took off his glasses, looked at the lenses, then put them back on again.

War ages a man, doesn't it, Joe?

That sure is the truth, Mister Harold. I'm thirty-one years old, but I wake up every morning with the feeling of an old man.

Carol swallowed what was in her mouth. Maybe you just need a new mattress? I saw some on sale at Hildreth's last week up in town. There was a cartoon of someone holding their back like it was hurtin' and then the man was on the bed sleepin' with not a care in the world. That could be you, Mister Joe.

Everyone looked at Carol, who continued to eat.

A woman at my bank, Harold said, tells me you met the president of the United States. She read it in the paper. Is that true?

Carol put down a cold chicken leg and touched her hair.

Joe blushed for the second time that evening. I do recall something like that.

It's because you were given the Congressional Medal of Honor? Isn't that right, Joe? For something you did in the Philippines?

Carol spoke before he could answer. The president! Well what did you say? Was he nice?

I didn't say much, to be honest. I was pretty scared. Joe caught Rusty's eye across the table. Though I did get a carrot from the White House garden, right before the president brushed my ears.

Red with excitement at Joe's words, Rusty wriggled down from the stack of cushions and disappeared under the table.

Rusty! Carol screamed. Rusty! Git up here now!

I guess I'm not the only rabbit 'round here, Joe said.

After dessert, their host made weak coffee, and everyone went and sat down in the parlor with cups and saucers. Joe told them about how he'd fixed up the house and had another two years living in it rent free, so long as he put on a back porch. The parlor had old couches from a hundred years ago that puffed out dust when they sat on them.

Who are those folks? Marjorie said, pointing with her coffee cup to a side table of framed photographs. Everyone in the pictures was Black except for Joe and the president of the United States.

Those folks there are my family, Joe explained, who raised me from when I was eight years old to when I left to make my own way in the world, mostly goin' from farm to farm as a carpenter, doin' all what Pops taught me. Then I joined the service and the war come. I don't hardly see 'em now. But it was seven years I lived with 'em in their house without the law findin' out and takin' me away.

The tea cup and saucer in Joe's hands started chattering. Guess I jus' told you my life story, he said, setting them on the floor by his feet.

I never seen so many pictures in one place, Carol said. Where'd you get the frames?

I made 'em, Joe said. From scrap pieces of wood. That older man is Pops, and the woman next to Pops is Sally, and the boys is Wesley and Marvell, my two brothers—though Marvell come back from the war without his legs on, and so he learned how to take pictures and how to print 'em. That's how I got these.

Nothing wrong with colored folks, Harold said. I've met a good many decent ones in my life.

I appreciate you saying that, Mister Harold, and not using them other words, which I could never stand, and what got me in trouble with my bunkmate on the ship.

When was the last time you saw your family? Marjorie said.

Bin a good while now. I should go out there. I'm still hopin' for the day we can eat in the same restaurant, or pray in the same church, and then they can come here.

Harold pursed his lips, as though hesitant to speak. I can sympathize with your situation, I really can, as a man who respects all colors. But if God wants it any different, Joe, he'll change it.

Marjorie turned sharply and stared at her husband until his cheeks went rosy.

Carol got up and went closer to the pictures. It's like you cut them from a magazine, she said.

Marjorie added that Pops and Sally must be mighty proud of what their adopted son has done in the world.

I think they'd be more proud if I could write and tell 'em I was married, Joe replied.

Carol whipped around.

Well, Mister Joe, Marjorie said playfully, you courtin' anyone?

The big man rearranged his body in the chair with a faint cracking of wood. As a matter of fact, Miss Marjorie, I am... kinda...in a way.

Rusty was still under the table in the other room, pretending he was a rabbit.

Marjorie turned back to her husband. That's exciting for Mister Joe, isn't it, Harold?

Indeed. Is it someone who lives in our neighborhood, perhaps?

Oh yes, Mister Harold. You know her, actually.

We do?

As a matter o'fact...she lives in your house.

For the third or fourth time that evening there was a stunned silence. Harold and Marjorie exchanged glances while Carol just stood there at the wall next to the pictures, as if in a daze—too embarrassed to know if she was flattered or horrified.

Then Joe stood up.

As a matter o'fact, he went on, shuffling his shiny boots, that's why I asked y'all here today...to see if Carol wouldn't like to get married to me.

At that exact moment Rusty crawled into the parlor on all fours. He had taken off his pants and was carrying them in his mouth. His shoes were off too and everyone stared at his bare legs, dusty and twisted, of no real use.

SALLY & POPS

1924

IT WAS MORNING time, and Sally was outside when she heard
whistling. It wasn't any kind of tune, just someone putting their
lips together and trying to make a sound. She was pinning damp
laundry to a new rope her husband and Marvell had strung up that
Sunday after church. Her mother had taught her to change it every
so often to stop the clothes from getting marks.

It was a brown house they lived in. A wood house, slightly
crooked, with animals nesting under the porch and a stove they'd
been given not long after getting married. It had come from a
tavern in Tennessee and the date 1845 stood in raised letters on
the steel door.

Sally dropped a pair of her boys' pants into the basket, then
went barefoot through the grass to the front of the house to see
who could be whistling like that. When she got to the porch, the
noise stopped, but coming up the hill she saw a blur of gray—most
likely a mule by the sound of its feet on the loose stones. When the
animal got closer, the person riding it started whistling again, and
Sally saw it was a boy—as young as the mule was old. The child
was wearing blue overalls that should have belonged to a man.

As they passed by, the boy stopped his whistling and stared at Sally.

Howdy there, ma'am!

Where you goin' on that mule, whistlin' so, child?

The boy looked up ahead, then turned to see the hill from whence he'd come.

I ain't too sure yet. *Anywhere* I reckon, he told Sally, as though it were a place he'd heard about and wanted to see.

He kept on, and after only a few yards the whistling started up, continuing until the boy was long out of sight.

A few weeks later, Sally was inside baking rolls when she heard a distant sound. She rinsed her hands in a tin bucket and waited inside the screen door. It was the whistling boy.

When the mule got close, the child didn't notice the outline of her body behind the mesh. Believing he was alone, he stopped and looked at the house where Sally lived with her husband and two boys. He could surely smell the rolls cooking inside. Sally watched as he took deep breaths, one after the other, as though trying to catch the smell of food and bury it somewhere in his body. Then he nudged the animal and kept on up the road. He could not have been more than eight years old, Sally thought. But in such a big body—people would surely have mistaken him for the age of her eldest son, Marvell, who was eleven.

When he passed by again a few days later, Sally told her husband about it over supper. He looked across the table at Wesley and Marvell.

Either you two seen this person?

They looked at one another. No, Pops, said Marvell, we ain't seen nobody like that.

Wesley was seven and small for his age, with thin ankles and large, round eyes. He possessed a heavenly voice and sang in the church choir, where he was spoiled by the old ladies in hats.

Sally spooned more vegetables onto her children's plates. I just wonder who he belong to, is all, she said. He ain't got no family on this hill, I know that.

If you're sure you've seen this whistlin' boy, best keep an eye on him, Pops warned his wife. He could be anybody, anybody at all...

Or nobody...Wesley said, copying his father's intonation, nobody at all...

Sally thought that was funny.

His older brother frowned. How can you be nobody?

Well, whoever that boy is, said Sally, he's a child. And what harm can a child do?

Pops laughed. Little boys and trouble go hand in hand.

When they finished the savory part of their meal, Sally brought over a warm fruit pie that had been cooling on a rack. They ate it with the windows open and cool air blowing through the house.

Almost two months later, the first snow came to the mountain, and with it the whistling boy. Except this time there was no mule. Just the child on foot, whistling his heart out.

Sally stopped what she was doing and went outside.

The air was sharp and the clouds were like bundled sheets. The boy was carrying something in his hand and swinging it. When he got close to the brown house, he saw Sally outside looking down at him. His face was dirty, but he smiled through it and held up a length of flint corn in one of his big hands.

This yurs, ma'am?

Wuz that you got?

The little boy looked at the item in his hand as though he didn't know the answer. On his feet were rags of cloth tied on with bits of rope.

Where's your mule, child?

How'd you know about my animal, ma'am?

Sally put her hands on her hips. Because ever' time I heard

whistlin', I seen both a mule and a boy. Now it's just a boy and his whistlin'. No mule.

The child thought this was funny. Thatta what people say, he said proudly. That I don't ever stop whistlin'...except when I'm talkin'.

Is that so?

And when I'm asleep, ma'am. Though I might be whistlin' in a dream.

Where's your animal at now?

She don't like snow...too cold underfoot.

Sally looked down at his rags. Imagined her own delicate Wesley wearing such things on his feet.

Ain't you cold standin' there?

The boy was silent for a moment, then shook his head. Can't say I am.

But Sally had two boys herself and knew how their minds worked. Before she could say anything, the boy spoke again.

I'm just glad this corn don't belong to you.

Why's that?

So I can have it for my supper.

Ain't your mamma gonna cook your supper?

The boy scratched his filthy head. She would...but she ain't here at the moment.

Where she at?

Up there, the child said, pointing.

Sally stared into the blur of clouds.

You tellin' me she done passed away?

That's right, he said. Though I suspec' she watchin' me right now from heaven, makin' sure I don't talk back, or steal nothin'... so we can be together later on.

For a few moments, Sally didn't speak.

You miss her, I'll bet.

The boy opened his mouth but no sound came out.

How about your daddy?

He's away too.

You sure is big for your age, ain't you?

The boy looked down at his body as though seeing it for the first time. Probly why I'm always hungry.

You hungry now?

Inside the house, the boy couldn't stop looking around.

It's like an oven in here! Gosh almighty, I'm burnin' up!

Don't I know it, Sally told him. It's too much furnace for one house, but we ain't got nothing else.

Oh, I ain't complainin', ma'am. I like it hot! You could set me on fire and I'd thank you for it.

Sally told him to sit down. Then she unwrapped his feet from the rags. The smell was more than she had expected, so she tossed the rags quickly into the fire.

My shoes! the boy cried. You'll burn 'em to nuthin'.

That is exactly my intention. I'm sure my boys have some old pair of shoes lying someplace. Sally knew they didn't but planned in her mind to ask at the church on Sunday. Tell them about the whistling boy and see if anyone could give her their grown children's castoffs so that he might have a few things of his own to cherish.

Then she had him stand on some warm bricks near the furnace until his feet were bone dry and she could rub them a little. Sally thought about what the boy had told her about his mother watching, and in her heart, she spoke to this dead woman the way she would want to be spoken to if it were her youngest child at the mercy of strangers.

Sally could tell when he was comfortable and warm because he stopped acting like a man and became a child again. She fixed him a warm bowl of sweet potatoes with beans.

The boy picked up the spoon she had given him. Want me to say grace first, ma'am?

He already knows you're grateful, so just go ahead and eat.

The child went at the food like a small animal. Sally busied herself so he could eat without being looked at. When the meal was over, the child sat back in his chair and grinned.

I knew whistlin' would pay off someday.

He took the piece of hard corn from his pocket and put it on the table.

Did you say your daddy was away? Sally asked him.

Yes'm.

In the mines?

No'm.

Tobacuh fields then? Sally asked. Though it's winter, so I don't know what he'd be doin'.

He ain't even in this county.

Heaven too, I suppose?

No ma'am, the other place.

Hell?

Almost. He's in jail.

I see.

You want to know what he done?

Well, I'm sure it's not my business...

You may as well know. It's not a secret.

Okay, tell me.

He stole a chicken.

That don't sound like enough to put a man in jail. Was he a nice daddy to you?

He was a big daddy, the biggest daddy I ever saw, but didn't hardly say two words. People said he was slow.

Was he?

Well... said the boy thoughtfully...he wasn't fast.

So where is it you were going when you passed my house all those times on the mule?

Oh, well now, I was jus' keeping on the road ahead, up and down the hills of this place.

Sally could see that his cheeks had turned the color of two ripe apples.

You were going by people's homes hoping to get something to eat maybe, is that it?

A few tears fell quickly, but his countenance was unchanged.

I was too afraid to ask people outright, he said, wiping his face with the sleeve of his shirt. So I just went zigg-zaggeddy all day, ever' day, hoping someone would give me a bite of somethin'.

Is that why you was whistlin'? To let folks know you were there? To bring 'em out to the porch?

No ma'am, he said. The plain truth of it is that I enjoy whistlin', and I believe I'm good at it.

Where you bin sleepin'?

Barns, cowsheds…under trees sometimes.

You ain't got a house?

I know to build a fire…but I couldn't get one going last night and almost froze. I sold the mule a while ago because I couldn't bear to watch her starve.

How's your daddy gonna find you when he gets out?

I've thought about that, and reckon my momma will tell him in a dream, like Joseph dreamed of the plagues or somesuch when he was in jail.

How you know that story?

My momma told me all them stories…but my favorite is the one where Joseph and Mary couldn't find no place for their baby to get borned? You know that one, ma'am?

Yes, I do. It's the Christmas story.

Well then, do you remember the name of Jesus's daddy?

Why of course.

Well that's how I got my name. Joe.

A few hours later, Sally's boys came home with their father in the truck he used for hauling cut lumber. Sally heard their footfalls on the porch and their excited, hungry voices in the cold air.

When they burst in and saw a child sitting there at the table, they stopped where they were and stared.

Sally put both her hands on the boy's shoulders.

This is Joe, she said.

Wesley pointed. He's, he's…barefoot.

Sally nodded. Don't I know it, son.

Pops wore an intense, serious expression as he examined the child. Then suddenly he snapped his fingers in the air.

This is the whistlin' boy!

Joe's face brightened. You've heard of me, mister?

I sure have. But all this time I thought my wife was just making you up to fool with us!

SAMUEL

1999

HE WENT TO the mall on Saturday and bought new jeans. A pair of stonewashed blue Levi's his mother hemmed quietly that evening in the front room by lamplight. He scrubbed his Reebok tennis shoes, then applied white paint from a tube to cover the scuffs that couldn't be rubbed away with hot water.

In the thin light of dusk, Samuel hosed down his father's pickup and cleaned the inside with a handheld vacuum that plugged into the cigarette lighter. Later, in bed, he lay awake going over in his mind the things they had said to one another that night in the diner. The way Heather had held the glass carafe of coffee with a slight tilt in her wrist; how she had hit him with the rag when he made a joke.

When Sunday came, Samuel ate his breakfast in silence, changing the subject when his mother asked questions about the girl he'd met at the restaurant on Halloween night. His father kept joking that she was a witch who would cast a spell on Samuel's paycheck, making it disappear every week.

When it came time to leave, Alfredia and Uncle Rusty followed Samuel to the driveway and watched him go.

Alfredia shook her head. I hope she doesn't break his heart.

I know, said Rusty. I prob'ly should have gone with'um. But that's life.

It was the first time Samuel had been out on a date since starting work at the auto plant. Although he had met women in bars and gone to hotel rooms for sex, he'd never felt good about it afterwards, dressing quietly in the dull, drowsy light of a Sunday morning, not knowing what to say as it came time for them to part.

There were others on the road that afternoon—mostly folks on their way to diners for meals after Sunday service. He passed church buses driven by old men with Stetson hats and dress shirts buttoned all the way. Small faces stared at him pensively through thick window glass, as though they were not children at all but statues of children.

After an hour of driving, he went left at the flashing red light as she'd told him to on the napkin below her phone number. He followed the road for seven miles with his window down, breathing in the deep scent of fall trees and a skunk, which lay smudged at the side of the road.

After crossing Leachman's Creek, he saw the rusted mailbox with her surname in stick-on letters. The driveway was a long, twisted dirt road with potholes, overhanging tree branches, and dust that would dull the gleam of the truck's metal.

At the end of the track was a wooden farmhouse in desperate need of repair. The gutters had separated, allowing rain to cascade down the side of the house, where the siding now peeled to reveal rot. A screen door in the front was attached by a single bottom hinge. There was a small gray pickup in the driveway that Samuel assumed belonged to Heather's mother and her silver Ford Probe. He remembered how she'd told him about her father running away when she was a child and her grandfather dying only months before.

Samuel guessed that he must have been sick awhile to have let the place fall to such ruin. As he parked and got out of the truck, the form of a woman appeared behind the mesh of the crooked screen door. She pushed through and was wearing a white tee shirt, rolled up blue jeans, and white canvas shoes with no socks. She stopped at the top of the porch steps and called out to him.

You made it then!

Her red hair had been teased out and it blazed in the afternoon sun. Samuel was struck by how a woman like that could emerge from such a place of physical decay, as though any beauty left in the old house had chosen her as its sole refuge.

Do I look okay? she asked, doing a twirl?

You look beautiful.

I do?

Like a movie star.

What kind of movie? Romance?

How about action?

Heather laughed and fluttered down the steps to meet him halfway across the front yard.

When they were close, she seemed nervous.

Is it okay if Momma meets you, Samuel? She can't come out 'cause of her oxygen tank.

Where is she at?

Inside. It's okay if you don't want to.

The living room was heavily furnished with chairs and couches, each piled with quilts and pillows for sleeping downstairs in the glow of a large television. The window blinds were all pulled down and an old air conditioner rattled as though there were small rocks being tossed around inside.

Momma likes it cold, Heather said nervously. Like ten below!

Her mother was a small, hunched woman whose body had been ravaged by ill health. She extended a claw-like hand at Samuel's approach. Her eyes were slow and watery.

Be nice to her, she croaked. *Please*, Samuel. She's all I got left.

Momma...quit it now.

The woman acknowledged her daughter's complaint by turning back to the television.

Y'all take care, and don't come back too late.

Okay, Momma.

I'll take care of her, ma'am. We'll be back before dark.

That's all I'm asking, said the woman. For my little girl to come back safe. I lost my daddy a few months back and I'm having a hard time with it, so forgive me if I seem overprotective.

No, ma'am. I understand. She's your daughter and she's precious.

Thank you, Samuel, y'all can go.

As they crossed the yard toward the truck, Samuel noticed the rear side–window of Heather's car was webbed with cracks.

What happened there? he asked, going over to it.

Oh, a rock must've bounced up. 'Bout scared me half to death.

One push, Samuel told her, and that glass is gonna fall in.

I know it, Heather said, turning her body toward the truck. I'll do something with it soon.

Samuel remembered that his father's toolbox was in the bed of the Ford. Want me to fix it?

Heather laughed. C'mon, let's go bowling. Isn't that what you said we were gonna do this afternoon?

We can still bowl. But I'm gonna take care of this for you, so it don't fall in when you're drivin' to work. I'm sure there's somethin' roun' here I can use to cover the hole.

But I ain't got no spare glass.

Samuel looked at the broken window. We're gonna have to order it...or go to a junkyard. But I don't want you cuttin' your fingers on the broken pieces.

With a rag wrapped around his hand, Samuel opened the door—but as he reached in, the window collapsed and glass fell inwards, covering half of the back seat.

Murphy's Law, he sighed, is what that is...

I wonder who Murphy was? Heather said. If there really was someone who had all that bad luck.

I know a guy like that, but his name ain't Murphy.

What is it?

Eddie Walker.

Samuel worked quickly, picking molars of glass off the seat and dropping them into a plastic bag. Then, on the carpet half under the driver's seat, Samuel glimpsed the foot of a Barbie doll. He didn't think anything of it at first. He was too busy being careful.

When all the pieces had been collected, Samuel used a pair of bullnose pliers to pull glass squares from the doorframe.

Heather watched. They're kind of beautiful don't you think?

We should keep one, Samuel said. A souvenir of our first date.

One each?

No, just one, Samuel said. This is a romance movie after all.

Heather grinned. You want soda pop or something?

That'd be nice.

When Heather was in the house fixing him a drink, Samuel went in the glove box to get the serial number of her vehicle. He was going to order the glass from the auto-parts store as a surprise. But the glove box was packed with gum wrappers and receipts for gas. When he opened the trunk, hoping to find the owner's manual, it was a mess of cans for recycling, balled-up jeans, a hairbrush, and, bundled under a blanket, a gray car seat. Samuel suddenly remembered the Barbie he had seen on the floor, and went to check that it was really there.

For a moment, he stood, holding the doll, frozen to the spot by a feeling of humiliation he could not articulate. He should have heeded the caution in his father's voice when he joked that morning over breakfast about his paycheck disappearing. It made sense to him now why such a beautiful woman had encouraged him to take her out.

Samuel peered at the bag of broken glass in his hand and felt ashamed of his new jeans, the way he had scrubbed his sneakers, washed the truck, and lain awake in bed, going over the things he might say and wondering if she would let him kiss her on the bench seat of the truck after an afternoon of bowling.

When the screen door whined, he could not bring himself to look over. But on hearing the crunch of her white shoes on the loose dirt, the sudden spite Samuel had felt, like a rope around his heart, came undone and fell slack. He felt himself hatching through the shell of an old self.

Heather had not told him about the child because she was afraid. She had been with someone in high school when she was a child herself, and the boy, like her own father, had run off.

She must have felt alone then, he thought, and seen herself as a person too miniscule for any man to cherish for more than a few moments. And now there was some little person with toys, a bed, colored socks, tubs of crayons, favorite things to eat, books with cardboard pages, and the woman that child loved most carried shame everywhere she went for those few, long minutes in the back of a car when she felt what she believed was love.

But that wasn't love, Samuel realized.

When Heather reached out to give him the soda, all he could do was stare at it in her hand.

She was no longer the girl whose fickle affections he hoped to win over. This was a woman standing before him, whose disappointment, sacrifice, and pain had been far greater than his own. He let his gaze fall upon her red hair, and he imagined it tied back as she went into labor—as though he were there in the delivery room—a ghost from the future instead of the past.

Samuel held up the doll he had taken from under the seat.

How old is your little girl?

Heather cocked her head to one side as she tried to make sense of what was happening.

It is a little girl right?

Heather tightened her lips and nodded. She did not speak or blink her eyes.

She inside?

Heather turned to look at their dilapidated home. From the second floor a curtain twitched.

What's her name?

Heather wiped her eyes with the sleeve of her dress. Linda.

Samuel stared at the grinning doll in his hands. Its hair was made from strands of orange plastic. Its eyes were happy and untroubled.

Well does she know how to bowl?

When he got home that evening, Samuel's parents were up watching *Wheel of Fortune*. Uncle Rusty was down in his apartment with the door open and his sign turned to OPEN. He was looking through his collection of Coca-Cola trucks and humming the soundtrack to the game show playing upstairs. Each vehicle had its own stand. Both the model and year it went into production were written in silver script. Sometimes Rusty would open the hood and look at the engine parts, sticking his tongue out in concentration or saying aloud words that fell randomly into his mouth.

Samuel looked in on his uncle, then went upstairs and dropped into an armchair beneath a pastel drawing of John Wayne.

His mother stopped her sewing. She was tucked snugly under her favorite quilt—one Grandma Carol had made from Alfredia's old feed-sack dresses.

So how'd the date go, sweetheart?

His father lowered the volume on the TV. She a nice girl, son?

Alfredia moved her sewing to the side table. I can tell by the look on his face he's fallen in love with her.

Samuel's father scowled. On the first date? That ain't good.

But Randy...that's exactly what happened to us.

Samuel's father reached for his cigarettes. That's true I guess.

I guess? said Alfredia. Our wedding picture was the first thing you hung up in the new house.

That's true too. And the second thing was a buck with glass eyes.

Alfredia threw a cushion. But then their attention turned back to Samuel.

I may as well tell you now, he said, that it's serious.

Serious like you're gonna get married to her? Can a mother ask that anymore?

Randy exhaled a long train of blue smoke. I'm not sure he's ready for being married. He needs to save some money first. Maybe make supervisor on the line.

Samuel picked up the remote and turned the television off.

The question Mom, isn't—am I ready to get married—the question is, are you ready to be grandparents?

MARJORIE

1950

IT TOOK A year for Carol to finally agree. He was not like any-one she had ever met. He whistled and had a big head, but he also spoke to her the way men spoke in movies to women they admired.

Carol found it harder to accept love than to give it, but she knew it was the right thing to get married when she felt like she wanted to see Joe every day and tell him things, just little things, thoughts she had.

About six months after the ceremony, Carol sat down at the parlor table to compose a letter. She was writing to her neighbor, Marjorie, who still lived across the street. Joe had been teaching Carol to write, and there were now dozens of words she read and could fashion easily into sentences. Carol wrote that she had good news and asked if they might meet on Saturday—that way Joe could be with Rusty, who still needed watching every second, even though he was a young man now, a teenager. His legs had got-ten worse, but he had learned to whistle thanks to his new father. Sometimes Carol thought she was living in a tree.

When Saturday came, it was bright and humid. After a greasy breakfast of eggs and potatoes, Joe carried Rusty outside to a wooden-framed wheelchair with a cane seat.

Carol went upstairs to change out of her housedress, which stank of fried food. In the bathroom, she regarded herself in the round mirror, searching in her expression for any trace of the girl who'd sat at the side of the road trying to get away with her small, green suitcase and doll.

Mary Bright lived in a rocking chair now. Sometimes Carol sat stroking her worn linen head, remembering her mother and sometimes even her father. She still had the feeling he'd come for her. It was a fear she had not been able to give up: that she'd wake up and he would be outside on the porch, eyes bright like an animal. Maybe he would try and shoot Joe as a way to punish her for running away from Travis Curt. This unshakeable worry kept any deep happiness with her husband just out of her reach.

At Marjorie's house, Carol held the plates as her friend cut a round lemon sponge into slices. She had chosen to wear patent leather shoes that pinched if she walked too far. The dress Carol had picked out was dark green and fell just below her knees. She had pinned her hair, but decided a hat would be too much for a Saturday indoors.

After eating a few pieces of cake and drinking hot coffee, Carol told Marjorie the news.

Oh my gosh, when?

I guess about six months from now, Carol said. Which seems like forever.

Oh, it'll fly! Marjorie gushed with a happiness that made Carol remember the pale, ashen woman in the bed so many years before at Martha and Bessie's. Carol felt clumsy then, for blurting out news that might have brought painful memories back to her friend. But Marjorie, as if sensing hesitation, heaped her delicate hands upon Carol's.

You're my best friend, Carol wanted to say. But the words were trapped, and would remain trapped forever.

. . .

Over the next few months, Carol still cleaned Harold and Marjorie's house, but soon could take only small, short steps. Joe called her the bubble that won't burst, which made Rusty want to poke his mother.

Carol wrote to Bessie and Martha. Martha penned a short letter back, saying how much they missed her and that Rusty's flower patch was still going strong after four years.

When it was decided that Marjorie and Harold would be godparents, Marjorie insisted on spending Tuesday and Thursday mornings with Carol on the porch, flicking through fabric catalogs, marking things she wanted to buy for the baby as godmother.

They wrote out long lists of names. If it was a boy, Carol thought *Henry* was good, or *Joseph* after his father.

But what if it's a girl? Marjorie wanted to know. What was your mother's name, Carol?

I only knew her as Momma. But to be honest, I've always thought *Marjorie* was pretty.

That's actually my middle name, Marjorie said. My first is Alfredia, which came from my daddy's brother, Alfred. He was killed in World War I.

How come you don't use it?

My mother preferred Marjorie before I had a say in the matter, so I guess it just stuck.

For about an hour or so each afternoon, with dinner bubbling in the oven, Rusty would settle on his parents' bed and close his eyes. Downstairs, Carol had a velvet chair in the dining room where she liked to rest too. The smell of cooking food would put her in a gentle daze, as evening moved through the house, swallowing things, one by one.

Carol would stroke her stomach, calming the child within, knowing that everything she felt, her mother must have felt too.

As always when she was alone, Carol tried to think past what she already remembered, but met only her imagination.

One evening, after a tiring day, Carol closed her eyes on the velvet chair. Rusty was asleep upstairs as usual, and the only noise was from cars, whose sweeping headlights yellowed the curtain as they passed.

When the screen door clicked and swung open, Carol woke to a still, unmoving darkness. She wondered if it were part of her dream, but then she heard whistling and a voice she knew.

Is that pie I smell?

Joe?

She listened for the weight of his boots across the varnished planks.

How come you're sitting in the dark, sweetheart?

You make a lot of paint today?

It's pink this week.

How's that?

On account of all the women in Kentucky having children.

You're kidding me.

Joe laughed and strode over, setting both his hands on Carol's shoulders. She could smell the unpleasant chemicals he used to mix color, but it was worth enduring to have him there with her, so close in that quiet room.

Is it really pink paint, Joe? You're always kidding me. I made your favorite kind of eggplant pie.

I smelled it when I come in. How's the Coca-Cola Kid?

He's upstairs sleeping. I spent half the day at Marjorie's house.

But I thought you gave up cleaning last month.

No, listen, Joe, Marjorie had to go to bed with pins and needles all over her body. So I was there trying my best to rub them away.

She okay?

Harold said on the telephone if it ain't gone by the time he come home from the bank, they gonna call in the doctor.

What kind of pain was it? Did she say?

Carol turned her body so she could look at her husband. Like a numbness, she said, a deep ache...but not like anything she's had over these last few years.

What did Rusty do while you was tending to Marjorie?

Oh, he was like a slug in heat, Joe, pulling hisself over her floor.

Well that saves you an hour of polishing, I reckon.

Except for the extra laundry it makes.

Give him a pair of my overalls.

Don't be so silly. He wouldn't even fit into one of your pockets.

He upstairs?

Yes, but don't wake him, Joe. It'd be nice for just us to sit at the table, just this once without him under it bangin' his head.

Joe went toward the door, but lingered at the edge of the room.

Carol?

Yes, Joe?

What is it you get to thinking about in here ever' night, while I'm walking home?

Why?

I'm just curious. You don't have to tell me if it's private.

Carol took a slow, long breath. Momma and my papa mostly.

Your daddy wadn't worth much, ain't that so?

No, he wadn't. But Momma made up for his badness in the years God gave her to me. You ever think o' your folks, Joe?

Oh yeah...when I'm walkin' to work, mostly.

I loved meeting Sally and Pops, and your two brothers, Joe, after the wedding last year.

They're good folks for sure, Carol, but I meant the first ones I had. The woman who died like your momma, and my daddy who stole that chicken. I don't think he was a bad person...just bad luck is all.

I know he wasn't bad, Joe. I can tell that from everything you remember about him.

I guess they just died before their luck could change. Then I got all the good luck they missed.

You think that's true?

Not just you and Rusty, but the war too. Sometimes I wonder if I'm actually dead and this is all a dream...some drawn out wish in my mind as I float faceup in the sea.

Carol listened to her husband tell her more things.

She wondered if other couples had such sudden moments of confession, when the body receded and they were just two voices, conferring in a place that was beyond judgment.

When Joe had finished speaking, Carol turned to him in the doorway.

Is it really all pink paint up there in the factory, Joe?

It was pink for a while but now it's red. It's been red for some time.

She listened to him take off his heavy boots and set them by the door, where they would sit until morning, worn and misshapen, splattered with red paint.

Then she closed her eyes. He wouldn't mind waiting a little longer for supper. He was that kind of man.

That night, Carol woke to someone banging on the front door and windows. Joe sat up calmly and pulled open the bedside drawer where he kept a loaded revolver.

Carol wanted to scream. It was happening.

Her father had come to fetch her. She could feel it. Could feel *him* and smell the stench of liquor snaking its way up the stairs. Joe put a finger to his lips for Carol not to speak. Then he took a handful of bullets from a cardboard box, dropping them into the pocket of his candy-stripe pajamas. He moved quickly for a big man, hardly making a sound.

Carol wondered if she should check on Rusty. But if he wasn't calling out, then her son was still asleep. She took quick, shallow breaths now as the banging got harder and went on for longer without a break. She bit down on the sheet so as not to scream, her body stiffening at the idea of having to go back home with her daddy.

But then she heard Joe's voice and could tell from a faint yellow spray on the curtains that the porch light had been turned on.

Joe called up to her then, said to put on a robe and come down.

Carol got out of bed and crept to the top of the stairs. Who is it?

It's Harold! Come down.

What's happened?

Harold was standing inside when she got downstairs, but when he tried to speak, his legs gave way and he flopped to the floor. Joe put the gun on a table, then scooped up their neighbor and carried him into the back parlor, where they had all once marveled at the pictures of Joe's family. Carol pointed to an upholstered chaise.

Put him there, Joe.

Harold didn't even try to lift his head, but they could see his eyes were open. He sat slumped in the chair like a puppet whose strings had been cut.

Is Marjorie sick, Harold? Should I run over there and tend to her?

Joe nodded for Carol to go, but when she reached the doorway, Harold screamed out that Marjorie was dead. The doctor had been and in the morning men would come for the body.

But she's *my* wife, he told them. And I don't have to let them take her if I don't want to.

That's right, said Joe in his deep voice. She's yours through and through.

Harold balled his hands into fists and began smacking them against his head.

They sat in the parlor all night, until it was day and cars were going up and down the street like parts in a machine.

The three of them were drinking black coffee when the truck pulled up. They heard doors, then men's voices in the street talking about a college football game. Joe laced up his paint-spattered boots and went out to speak with them.

Then Carol and Rusty moved outside to the porch, while Joe and Harold went across the street with the men to put Marjorie's body in a wooden box.

But the stairs were too narrow to get the coffin upstairs.

The two men went back outside with Joe but couldn't think what to do. The only solution was to wrap the dead woman in a sheet and carry the corpse down the stairs and out the front door. They could place her body in the coffin after it was in the truck.

Harold was too afraid he might drop her, and so it was left up to Joe, who went slow so as not to bump anything. Harold followed the white bundle on Joe's shoulder, but then an arm fell loose from the sheet. It was Marjorie's. Harold watched it swing, screaming because they had said everything they would ever say to each other. There would be no more words now, only the shadows of words blowing around in memory.

Some people from the neighborhood had gathered outside, and Carol thought they had mean, spiteful faces.

Momma? asked Rusty. Where they goin' with Miss Marjorie?

They're gonna bury her now…cause she's dead, Rusty.

Like a seed?

That's right.

Will a new Marjorie grow, Momma?

It don't work that way. You know that, Rusty.

Harold wanted to ride in the back of the truck with his wife's body, and was so grief-stricken the two men could not refuse.

Carol pictured in her mind the sewing patterns Marjorie had ordered through the mail, how the people putting them in envelopes and sticking stamps on would never know that the woman with pretty handwriting was dead, and that everything they were doing was too late and for nothing.

SAMUEL

2002

SAMUEL STOOD ON the porch of his new house smoking a Marl-boro. An old Kenworth car transporter carefully reversed up the gravel driveway with six old Jeep Wranglers from a car lot in Ten-nessee, purchased by Samuel at an online auction.

He had left his job at the auto plant, and in six months would know if his idea to build a business was something he'd come to regret. In that case, he would return to the factory and hope there was a place on the assembly line.

When Samuel saw how the driver was fixing to maneuver the rig, he waved at him to stop, then went over, crossing the upward slope of his property, all mud now after the reconstruction of a ruin that had once been his grandmother's childhood home.

Right where you are! Samuel yelled over the chugging diesel motor.

The man seemed relieved as he shut off the engine. I'd sure hate to get stuck, he told Samuel through his open window. Looks pretty slick back there.

Oh, it's all mud. I wouldn't risk it. I can tow the vehicles to where I want them with my tractor. So you can just let 'em down here, if you don't mind.

The driver had gray curly hair and a thin film of gray beard that contrasted with his dark skin. Samuel figured he had to be nearing seventy, and wondered if working was just a hobby or if he was struggling to make ends meet.

The Jeeps were all different colors. Three had broken windshields, and all but one had flat tires. When they were unloaded, Samuel took the driver into the house to give him a check and complete the paperwork. Each room smelled like paint and fresh wood from the renovation. A young pit bull belted across the couch and started licking the driver's hand.

That dog is the most intelligent animal I ever had, Samuel told the man.

The driver cupped the dog's head with his palm. I'm just happy he's friendly.

He picks up on energy, Samuel explained, handing the man a lime soda. You seem like a nice guy, so I feel at ease. The dog knows that. He treats a person based on how I feel about 'em.

That's pretty smart...like he can read your mind.

The dog was now on the back of the couch asking the driver to play by flicking his head and pretending to run away. So he don't like ever'body?

No, he don't. Especially the guy who poured the foundation for the steel barn I got going up.

The driver opened the can and took a long drink. Didn't care for him much, huh?

I never even met the guy. My wife was here when he come. First time she goes out to say hi, takes him some coffee, signs the paperwork, everything is fine...he has a crew with him. But when the cement is poured and his crew have taken off, the guy starts coming back to the house like he forgot something.

With your wife all alone? That ain't no good.

Well, the dog goes nuts.

Like he could sense something?

Exactly, and we'll never know what 'cause the guy turned around and went back to his truck.

He took off?

Right. It could have been something innocent, but that dog's got protective instincts. You live alone or you married?

The driver chuckled. You don't want to know—my daughter is full-grown with a teenage daughter who now has a baby and they all live with me and my wife. Four generations under one roof. Nobody wants to leave home anymore, seems like. Me, I was out at fourteen, workin' my ass off.

At least you can keep an eye on everyone.

I should get me one of them dogs, for when I'm outta town.

I'll be honest with ya—they don't live a long time and they have a bad reputation, but if you train 'em right, they're loyal dogs who give nothin' but love.

They both stared at the young pit bull, who was now on the floor, chewing a rubber bone.

Then the driver noticed Samuel's championship poker ring.

I see you is a card player. I fool around myself with the boys when we get the chance.

Samuel held the ring up so the driver could take a good look. I got lucky is all, won a tournament years back.

Mississippi?

Indiana. Riverboat.

You win a lot?

Fifty-seven thousand.

Jesus Lord!

I sunk the money into this here land and house. I'm trying to start a business.

It's good you quit when you did.

Oh I wanted to go to Vegas—play the big tables an' all, don't get me wrong, I considered it.

You would have been on TV. I would have seen you on TV sitting at one of them tables.

Yup. You would have. Just another hillbilly in sunglasses with a bad haircut.

The driver leaned back to laugh. Shit, he said, you're funny. But it looks like you fixed this ol' place up pretty good.

It almost killed me though. House was empty for fifty, sixty years, so we had our work cut out for us.

I can imagine, said the driver. Once the rain gets in, there ain't much you can do but start over.

I've never been so stressed out. Almost cost me my marriage.

Listen, when you're sixty-eight years old and still rentin', it don't feel too good. I once had a pile of money like you. It was from an insurance claim...but I had to get a steel plate in my head. The man pointed to his hair.

What happened?

Accident at work.

How bad?

Not too bad, except my head was in it. Now, one little blow could finish me off, or so the doc tells me.

You better drink sittin' down then.

You're right about that. It's fine if I'm careful. But if I had money? I'd do like you and get a place like this. Somewhere that's mine, somewhere way out in the boondocks where I can cause a ruckus.

Samuel remembered the phone call from Grandpa Joe, when he said they wanted to give him the property. He had been dating Heather only a few months then, but was eager to marry her. They wanted a place of their own, somewhere new, where Heather's mother could have her own little apartment.

Samuel's grandmother Carol inherited the house in 1946 when her father died, but it was half a century before she knew. Someone in Youngstown, Ohio, wanted to buy the land and lawyers had traced her through a marriage certificate.

When Alfredia found out about the house, she wanted everyone to drive out and look at where her mother had grown up. But then Grandpa Joe came on the phone and asked to speak to his grandson.

Listen, he told him. Your grandma don't want to go out to that property because it's full of bad memories. Are you old enough to understand that, Samuel? I think you are. Anyhow, your parents tell me you want to start a camping business or some such.

That's right, Samuel said. Survival and wilderness training.

Joe chuckled. When I was your age, the war was on...so we got all that for free. But let me get to the point—your Grandma Carol and I think you should have the property for something you're willing to work at.

Samuel went quiet.

You still there?

But shouldn't it be for Mom and Uncle Rusty?

Well, neither of them need it. And selling won't bring much in, with all the taxes and fees.

I never expected anything like this. I'm in shock.

Grandpa Joe laughed. You will be when you see it.

Alfredia had her hand out, ready to take the phone back, but her father was still talking.

The house been sitting empty for a long, long time. It's gonna be rotted through, trust me. I done up a house in town once and can help with the carpentry, but I'm not sure there's much we can do with this one, Samuel, except raze it.

As long as it's got four walls.

I can't promise that, but it does have fifty-eight acres, if that means anything.

Samuel lowered the phone and made a face to his parents and Uncle Rusty. Then he raised the handset back to his ear. You're kiddin' right?

Samuel! said his mother. What's goin' on? What's Grandpa sayin'?

If you want to sell it, Grandpa Joe went on, that's fine by us too. Maybe you can split the money with your folks, or use it to start your company. Your father tells me they're layin' people off left and right at the plant.

That is so.

Well then, best find somethin' else to do.

But I don't know if I can accept this, Grandpa. It's too much.

Go take a look, my boy. It really ain't nothing but a bunch of rotting wood and bad memories for your grandmother. But maybe you can turn it around. I have always believed in you, did you know that?

I appreciate it.

Your momma told me they can fix your eye and you said no. That right?

Yuh it is.

Okay, listen to me now, quickly, because your grandma just stepped outside to get the cat. I'm gonna tell you something, and it's between you and me…you understand what that means? If you do, say yes.

Yes.

Not even your parents.

Okay.

Carol's father, your great-granddaddy, his remains was found on the property somewhere, along with the remains of another man who was never identified. So I don't know what was goin' on, but it ain't worth lookin' into. You listening, Samuel?

I agree a hundred percent.

So man to man, if you see anything, bones or bloodstains or hair or clothes or anything like that, just burn it to hell, you got that?

Yes, sir.

And if you find a gun, you put it in a cloth sack with some rocks and dump it in the nearest creek. Don't fool with the damn thing, you hear me?

Loud and clear.

Now if you want my advice, drive out there with a buddy…like that Eddie character, the Cherokee. You still know him?

Sure, but…

And don't tell your momma or your grandma any of this, okay? And don't let my daughter go out there until you've looked it over. You hear me? Alfredia was always very sensitive and this sort of thing upsets her. Can I count on you, Samuel?

Yes, Grandpa.

Good, because I already put your name on the deed. You can go out there whenever you want, and no one can say nothing. It's all yours if you want it.

Samuel made a liverwurst sandwich for the driver and carried it into the living room on a paper plate with some chips and a pickle. The dog knew it was food and leapt up from its bed.

Might as well have something to eat, Samuel said, clearing a place for the driver to sit at the table. You like my filing cabinet? he asked, pointing at the piles of papers and empty soda cans. Underneath everything was a yellow tablecloth. Samuel had found it in the house when he was renovating.

That's a good table, said the driver, sitting down. Oak or mahogany?

I wish my Grandpa Joe were here, 'cause he knows ever'thing there is to know about wood. It's old-growth for sure and one of the only things I saved from the original house.

As the man ate, Samuel looked at his cell phone. He wondered if Heather and Linda were on their way home from the mall. Heather's mother had died six months before from kidney failure, and since then, Heather spent much of her free time shopping, though most of what she bought remained in the closet, unworn, with the tags still on it. They'd fought about that, mostly late at night, when Linda was asleep in her bedroom across the hall.

Samuel sat with the driver until he finished his meal. Then he signed the delivery paperwork and both men went outside to the tractor-trailer.

So, I gotta ask, said the driver, what you gonna do with all them vehicles?

I think I mentioned I'm starting my own business? Well, I got everything pinned on it right now…loans coming out of my ass to tell you the truth.

Some kind of auto repair? You a mechanic?

Samuel shook his head. Can you imagine something for me? Okay.

Power has just gone out…not only the grid, but anything with a computer, even a calculator, it's all been fried.

Fried? How come?

Samuel locked eyes with the driver. Because we've been hit by an electromagnetic pulse.

A glaze fell over the driver's face as though he were about to hear things he wouldn't understand or believe.

My business idea is to teach people how to live in the woods after some kind of natural disaster, war, or pandemic.

You got a gun range?

Maybe I will later. But what use is a gun if you've got nothing to eat? With earth, water, and sunlight, you can grow as much food as you want and live a long life. Everything we need to survive is right here free of charge if you have the know-how.

Sounds smart, the driver said. He was cleaning the mud from his boots with a brush on the bottom step of the truck. Land of milk and honey, as the Good Book says. Once his boots were clear, he got back into the cab.

How long to Tennessee?

I ain't going to Tennessee. I've got to pick something up just a few miles from here, then I have to be in North Carolina by tomorrow…where I'll get me some of that barbecue.

What you picking up nearby?

Rusted out car. Edsel, I think. The driver pointed to the shell of a green pickup at the far corner of Samuel's property. There were plants growing all around and even inside, where they had pushed up through rusted floor panels.

That a 1931 Ford?

I couldn't say, Samuel replied. But it belonged to my great-grand-daddy. He was a card player, like me. Reckon it's gonna be my retirement project.

The man scratched his head. I guess you could say delivering 'em has turned out to be mine.

With the engine turning over, Samuel dug in his pocket for some bills.

Oh, I couldn't take that, the man told him, staring at the money. You already fed me lunch.

Buy your wife some flowers so she'll let you get that dog.

I never did see such an intelligent animal, said the man, taking the money.

As the truck pulled away, Samuel inspected his motley crew of Jeep Wranglers, wondering where they had been and whose voices had once filled each cabin. A red one was missing a door, so he got into the seat. People had kissed, he thought, people had argued, and songs had been played over and over through the speakers—emboldening dreams that by now would have come true or gone forever. He would never meet those people, but he felt their lives crossing into his like wind through trees.

At six o'clock, the dog jumped off the couch and roused Samuel from his slumber. He locked the animal in its cage and looked out the window to see Heather walking down the driveway. She was wearing his vintage Iron Maiden concert tee shirt and red-tinted sunglasses. Then he saw Linda standing in a mud puddle at the end of the long drive. She had on shiny rain boots and a sweater with the tags flapping.

Her biological father lived in Sacramento. Without Heather knowing, Samuel had been in touch with him to try and get paperwork signed so he could legally adopt Linda. But in order to do it, her father wanted money, so Samuel gave up on the idea.

When he got outside, Linda was staring at the Jeeps across the muddy slope.

Which one do you want? he asked.

The red one, Dad.

Do they even run, Samuel?

I doubt it. But figured we'd try 'em out together. He held up the keys in one big bunch. Though first we're going to have to figure out which is which.

Linda rushed forward. I'll do it!

But Heather wanted them to change out of their mall clothes first. Inside, the dog was whining at the sound of their voices.

After some coffee and something to eat, they all went out to inspect the vehicles.

You really think we can make money from this? Heather asked. She had given up her job at Booth's Diner but still drove up there to see the people from time to time.

Eventually, once they're running and painted all the same color with our company logo on 'em...and we got the website going... maybe some advertising. Then we can go after corporate contracts and set up those experience weekends I was telling you about. That's where there's real money, especially during Derby season.

Heather climbed into the driver's seat of a blue Wrangler and put her hands on the steering wheel. You think we can do all that? I'm worried it's not gonna work out.

We'll be fine, but we ought to save as much as we can until things are up and running.

Quit shopping, you mean?

Well, Samuel said, feeling them move toward another argument. I guess we're okay, for now.

But Heather was red with shame. I can take all that stuff back anytime. You just say the word. That's why I leave the tags on. You see all the tags, right?

Then suddenly, near the old green pickup, something moved.

Heather, look, Samuel whispered.

A family of deer had wandered over the tree line and were ripping up weeds near the rusted truck.

A few years ago, I would've gone for my rifle.

Linda pulled on his wrist. But you wouldn't now, right Papa?

No, I don't reckon I would.

RUSTY & JOE

1951

ONE DAY, JOE came home more tired than usual. His supper of squash and green bean stew was ready in the pot, but he had to sit down for a while first. Rusty was asleep in the upholstered chair in the dining room, the place where his mother usually sat in the evenings. His bare legs were dirty from where he'd dragged them across the floor.

Joe sat looking at his son's body.

Then Carol appeared and in a hushed tone said, I didn't dare help him back upstairs for his nap, Joe, not in my condition.

Carol was now so large that even getting plates in and out of low cupboards was impossible. Within weeks there'd be a new baby in the house.

Joe remained in the chair, his gaze fixed on the sleeping boy.

Rusty could drag himself around the house with some effort, but to go outside the doctor said he'd always need a wheelchair. Carol had given him a little bell because he still needed help in the bathroom, getting on and off the seat.

There's something I got to do before we eat, Joe said. I've been thinking about it, and planning it for awhile and there's just no reason to put it off no more. Carol watched him get up and leave the room. Then she heard the creak of the basement door and Joe's feet on the wooden steps.

Rusty blinked and sat up.

Is Daddy in the basement, Momma?

Hmm-hm. I guess there's something down there he wants, Rusty.

A moment later they heard his ascending thuds, then Joe appeared holding a red bicycle with làrge training wheels Joe had taken from another bike.

Rusty's eyes widened into saucers. But Carol was annoyed.

That bicycle is no use to the baby, Joe. And Rusty can't even sit on a thing like that.

This here bicycle is a tool, Carol, it's not a toy.

How long's it been in the basement? Where did it come from?

The hardware store. Where I buy all my tools.

A tool? Carol asked, thinking it cruel to dangle such a pretty thing in front of a child who couldn't ride it. How can a bicycle be a tool?

Joe put the red machine down, then went and lifted Rusty from the upholstered armchair.

What are you doing, Joe? He can't ride that.

It hurts me to say it, but we've been crazy to let our son carry on in this condition for so long.

It was nothing for Joe to lift Rusty up, even at sixteen years old, and when lowered onto the wide saddle Rusty instinctively put his hands on the grips. Joe took some ribbon from his pocket and began tying the boy's bare feet to the pedals.

Now just hold on, Rusty, he said. This won't take but a minute. The frame will hold you up if you don't lean over too much.

Carol was livid. What in tarnation are you doing to the boy? I think you should stop this right now.

Joe ceased tying the ribbon and faced his wife. I will if you want me to. But have I ever done anything to hurt you, Carol? Tell me, have I?

But, Joe...

Have I ever made you feel afraid by words or deeds?

No, you never have…but…

And have I ever done anything to this boy, who I cherish as my son?

No, you ain't…

Then just wait and see what I'm gonna do, please. 'Cause I been plannin' this operation for some time now.

Carol stood with her arms crossed. She wanted to shout at her husband but knew she couldn't. It was one of the biggest challenges of marriage, she had learned, staying quiet when everything your husband did was just plain wrong.

Once Rusty's feet were secure on the pedals, Joe carried the entire machine with Rusty still on it out to the front sidewalk. Then he took the porch broom and tied it to the bicycle's frame, underneath the seat.

A FOR SALE sign hung on the front door of Harold and Marjorie's old house. It had been empty for three months now. Harold was in Lexington after putting in for a transfer to another branch of the bank.

Joe! Carol said. What you fixin' to do out here in the dark? Let the boy come in and have his supper.

Not until we've done our walking for the day. Right, Rusty?

The child was making engine sounds with his mouth. Carry me 'gain!

I ain't gonna carry you no more, son. A baby is what you carry… not a big little fella like you.

Gripping the broom handle, Joe moved forward slowly. The bicycle's pedals squeaked, turning Rusty's flimsy legs in slow circles. They had only gone a few inches when the boy screamed in pain.

Joe! Carol shouted. Stop it, you're hurtin' him!

But Joe took three more steps forward. Rusty cried out as his crooked legs revolved with the pedals.

Joe! You're gonna kill him!

We're just gonna go a few more yards, Carol, then tomorrow, we'll go farther.

Carol rushed down the steps and grabbed the broom handle.

Joe, you're gonna crack his bones!

But Joe went forward again, pushing the bicycle as he went. Carol was forced to walk with them.

His bones are fine, Carol. I took a day off last month and went to Frankfort on the bus. I met with a new kind of doctor that I've been writin' to about Rusty.

What are you talking about?

It's his muscles, Carol. They're weak as string.

Why didn't you tell me?

Because I didn't want to get your hopes up. He told me that Rusty could go live at a hospital for children like him—where they would put his legs in braces to get the muscles woken up.

Rusty leave home?

I know. Never in a million years, I said. So I just figured we keep the boy where he belongs and do it ourselves as best we can.

Joe went forward a couple more steps and Rusty yelped in pain.

Carol was in despair. Where are these letters, Joe? I want to see 'em.

After half a block, Rusty screamed out for Joe to stop. They went to the end of the street. Then Joe untied the ribbons and carried Rusty back to the house. Carol wheeled the bicycle.

You did well today, Joe said. I'm proud of you.

But Rusty was crying and red in the face.

He wouldn't even eat his dinner, nor look at Joe, or even say goodnight to him. Later, the couple stood and listened at the door as he cried bitterly into his pillow, as if trying to cast out some new and ungovernable pain.

Every night for many weeks, Carol watched in horror from the front window. But she did not try to stop her husband again. Fairly soon, everyone who lived on the street knew to expect the sound of a child screaming for five minutes around suppertime.

Someone said they'd heard Rusty three blocks away on Beech Street and run over to see what was going on. Some neighbors flicked back the curtain and shook their heads in condemnation of such a brutal father, forcing his crippled child to use a toy meant for normal children.

But a year later, those same neighbors couldn't believe it when Rusty and Joe jogged by their windows with baseball mitts on their hands—and Carol, just a few yards behind with their daughter, Alfredia, in a baby carriage trimmed with the lace Marjorie had sewn in those happy, final weeks of her life.

UNCLE RUSTY

2003

SAMUEL AND UNCLE Rusty spent the day driving to different box stores in town, trying to find the things they needed for Grandma Carol and Grandpa Joe's anniversary party. Samuel had printed out some ideas for decorations from the internet, and Rusty wanted to be in charge of finding everything. He had been talking about the party nonstop, especially when it came to balloons, as Rusty knew how to blow them up and tie the ends, which he called *belly buttons*.

After hours of staring at colored boxes and spools of ribbon, they got hungry and went to a fast-food restaurant. Rusty slid into a booth while Samuel ordered at the counter. After a few minutes, he came over with a plastic tray of things for them to eat.

Over fifty years they been married, Rusty. Can you imagine that?

Rusty picked up a mozzarella stick and looked at it. I don't need to remember, Samuel, 'cause I was there.

You were a teenager then, Rusty. What was it like?

Fine.

But what were *you* like? Did y'ever get in trouble?

Yup. Got in trouble and spanked for it too.

From Grandpa Joe?

No, Momma did it. Daddy watched with his hands up like this. Alfredia was cryin' real hard.

What'd you do that was so bad?

I peed on the wheel of the mailman's truck.

How old were you?

Pretty old.

Can you remember how old, Rusty?

Yes I can.

Why'd you do it?

There was dust on it. I wanted to clean it but didn't have no rag.

What did the mailman say?

Why'd you piss on my wheel, boy? My sister told Momma and she spanked me.

Did it hurt?

Rusty grinned. Felt pretty good I'd say.

Samuel dipped his sandwich into a little basin of ketchup. Rusty watched.

That's what you did at Ford, Samuel. Dipping them cars in special paint so they don't rust none, am I right?

That was Dad's job, Rusty. I used to check the welds.

Welds?

That's right.

On the cars?

Trucks, mostly.

Ford trucks, Rusty said with a chuckle. I worked on a few of those m'self.

When they were finished eating, both men went slowly back to the car. Rusty was having knee problems and walked with a cane.

I think we've got enough stuff now, don't you, Uncle? We should think about getting home.

But when they were halfway back to town, Rusty remembered the balloons.

Samuel lay both hands on the steering wheel. Christ. Balloons. How did we forget that?

We need balloons, Samuel.

Hmm.

It ain't a party without balloons.

That's exactly what Linda told me the other day, Samuel said, turning the car around. I was wonderin' where she got it.

On the way back to Walmart, Samuel lit a cigarette and went over the plan for the party.

Mom and Dad are gonna drive you out to Grandma and Grandpa's house early tomorrow, pick up Grandma Carol, and bring her back here to town so she can visit the hairdresser. Now, you're gonna stay with Grandpa Joe at their house, and I'm gonna pick you both up in the early afternoon and bring you over here for the party at four. I gotta leave early 'cause my house is kinda far away now. Heather and Linda are gonna come separate from me.

Okay, Rusty said. But it ain't a party without balloons.

Samuel lowered his window and blew smoke out. What you gonna do tomorrow with your dad, Rusty? While you're waiting for me to pick y'all up?

Watch TV.

I thought Grandpa Joe didn't like TV?

He lets me watch what I want.

Hospital shows, Rusty? Doctors doing surgery. You still like that?

Oh yeah, just like Bessie done for all them ladies.

Bessie?

Mama's friend.

Ok. Well, just remember, Rusty, don't tell Grandpa Joe about the surprise party.

Can I tell him we got balloons blowed up?

No, definitely not. It's a *surprise* party. When I show up in the afternoon, I'll just say I'm taking you both out to eat.

Where we goin' eat?

We ain't going out to eat, Rusty. It's an anniversary party.

But Daddy don't like to leave the farm.

Ain't that the truth.

That house is where I grew up with Alfredia after living in the town.

You and Mom lived in town?

By the courthouse. It's where Joe rolled me on my bicycle to fix my legs. I hated ever' minute of that, Samuel. Ever' minute.

I thought you and Alfredia always lived in the country.

No. We lived in town. Then we lived in the country and I worked at the lunch counter while Alfredia was in school. Then I went bald.

What lunch counter?

At the drugstore while Alfredia was in school. I got bald serving too many boiled eggs I reckon.

Oh yeah, Mom said something about that. The old pharmacy. Druthers'?

I was rich then, Samuel. I had so much Coca-Cola I could have filled a swimming pool and jumped in.

The next day, Samuel was up early at the kitchen table with a cup of coffee. Linda appeared in her Cinderella nightgown.

Hey, Daddy. Mommy still asleep?

That's right. You ready for the anniversary party today? Want some juice?

She wiped her eyes without answering, so Samuel got up and poured some into a plastic cup with fish on it.

I need to do the recycling before I leave, want to help me?

But I'm not dressed.

Drink your juice, then go put some old clothes on, okay, sweetheart?

Is Momma gonna help?

She still sleeping. Momma had a toothache last night and didn't get to bed until late.

The truth was they had been arguing. For some time now, Heather had been crying in the evenings. When Samuel asked what was wrong, she wouldn't tell him. Then last night she confessed to feeling trapped.

When the cans were crushed and the bottles bagged, Samuel said he'd help Linda with her chores so they were out of the way. They passed the new shed and steel barn, recently converted into a suite of guest rooms, and were soon traipsing through long, wet grass to the end of the property. They passed Samuel's great-grandfather's green truck, then arrived at the chicken coop. Samuel had got the idea after discovering a mesh fence half-buried at the tree line. Now they had ten chickens. Brown and white birds. Linda liked to sit and watch them peck the ground. One of her chores was to fetch the eggs every morning and wash away the muck and feathers.

The training course for the repaired and painted Jeeps was just under a quarter mile from the house. Samuel had been worried about the noise and smell of diesel when he had a full schedule of clients learning how to drive off-road. But the problem now was drainage. When it rained the area was more water than dirt.

So, how's school going?

I hate it.

Why?

It's boring.

I hear you. But it's really friends what make it bearable.

Linda shrugged. There's a girl, Maggie, but she already has a best friend.

That's tough. Ain't no getting around that.

I liked my old school better.

Well it figures, as most of your life you knew those people.

Linda nodded and adjusted a button on her denim overalls.

I promise it'll get better, Linda. And we ain't gonna move again, so when you enter the middle school, it's gonna be open season on friend making.

It will?

Trust me.

Did you like middle school, Daddy?

It's where I got my eye injury.

Linda thought for a moment. Do you think that'll happen to me too, seeing as we're related now?

Not if you wear the safety glasses in shop class and don't fool around like I did.

How'd it happen?

My best friend, Eddie. He flung a nail.

Mom said he's in jail.

Yeah, but they might let him out early.

What's jail like, Daddy?

Samuel took the basket of eggs and hoisted Linda up onto his shoulders. It's like elementary school I reckon, hard to make good friends and the food sucks.

Linda laughed. Then jail stinks.

What are you going to wear for the anniversary party this afternoon?

I don't know.

You've got a while to think about it because I have to go pick up Rusty and Grandpa Joe, then take them over to my mom and dad's house.

Will there be balloons, Daddy?

If Uncle Rusty blew them up last night like he said he would.

Samuel stood now at the very edge of their property, then turned so they were facing the house, a small white square in the distance.

That's my room, Linda said, where all my toys live.

When Samuel arrived at his grandparents' house in the early afternoon to pick up Rusty and Grandpa Joe, Rusty was sitting out on the porch by himself, rocking back and forth in the chair with a sheet of paper in his hand.

When Samuel got out of the car, his uncle stood up.

They done took him, Samuel.

Took who, buddy?

My daddy.

What are you talking about, Rusty?

He went upstairs to lie down and that was it.

Grandpa Joe is sick?

He's dead.

Samuel rushed into the house and took the stairs two at a time. He could hear Rusty out on the porch calling him back.

His grandparents' bedroom looked the same as it always did, except that the bed was messed up and there were muddy boot marks all over the floor.

Samuel flew down the stairs to where his uncle was back in the chair, rocking.

Where is he, Rusty?

Heaven, I reckon…by now.

Was he taken to the hospital?

Nope.

So, you went upstairs and he was sick?

No, he wadn't sick…he was dead, Samuel.

How did you know?

Because I seen it on TV. He was cold and his eyes was both open. His teeth were showing too. Like this…

Samuel knelt down before his uncle. Rusty, you have to tell me: Where is Grandpa Joe?

I called the home on Route 23, 'cause I remember their number from the sign. I told them, you can come get him. And they said who is this? And I said, Rusty. And I'm calling to say he's ready to go. But they wanted his name, so I said, Joe, and they showed up a while later in a big car, like he was going to the Gran' Ol' Opry.

Which funeral home, Rusty?

His uncle handed him the piece of paper. This what they give me.

Samuel snatched it and began to read.

Police come too, Uncle Rusty said. And a police doctor called Ronny. He was Black like Grandpa Pops, so I told him that he and Daddy was maybe related, cousins or something.

Samuel continued to read without looking up. What did the doctor say, Rusty?

He tol' me that all mankind was related if you go back far enough.

No, Rusty, whud he say about Grandpa Joe?

That his heart got too old to go on thumpin'. Doctor Ronny let me listen with his steth-o-scope like I seen on TV. But I didn't hear nothing neither. So we both figured he was gone.

Samuel felt suddenly short of breath and dropped into one of the porch chairs like a stone.

Why didn't you call us, Rusty?

I didn't want Alfredia to see her daddy like that.

What do you mean?

She's always bin the sensitive one.

I just can't believe it, Rusty. We have to call Mom and Dad.

Or we could jus' tell 'um at the party, Samuel. 'Cause I already blowed up the balloons.

CAROL

1954

WHENEVER ELVIS PRESLEY came on the radio with "Blue Moon of Kentucky," Carol couldn't stop herself from singing. She'd turn up the radio with Joe at the wheel and their two children in the back seat. They usually went out driving on Sundays in their blue Ford Customline if the weather wasn't too bad. Sometimes, while Carol was tying her scarf in the hall mirror, Joe would be out in the drive-way with the hood up, telling Rusty how each part made the car run.

The deeper they went into the country, the more dusty and uneven the roads became. And every time they hit a pothole, Rusty would throw his arms across his little sister, Alfredia. They had been best friends since the day she was born.

You're the protector, Joe had told him. As big brother, it's your duty to love Alfredia and to never leave her side.

He was nineteen years old now and often mistaken for her father.

Carol listened to her children laughing in the back seat. Rusty made faces and never got tired. He would do anything Alfredia asked of him a hundred times or more.

Carol thought a lot in those days about her mother. A woman who had not lived to the age Carol was now. If only she could have seen her little girl, riding through the countryside in a blue motor car with gray seats and white piping, her husband's large hands on the curved spine of the wheel and their two children bouncing around in the back like popcorn.

One Sunday they got lost and went up a dirt road.

Carol had not worried about ever seeing her father again, nor Travis Curt. Not since the night that Marjorie died. And so she told Joe to follow the country road and see where it went.

Feels like trespassing, he said after they'd rolled down it a little way. But before he could turn the car around, they spotted a small house at the end of the track.

Joe stopped the car.

Keep going, Carol told him. We could ask directions. Find out where we are.

Rusty leaned forward between the front seats. I know where we are.

You do? asked his mother.

We're right here.

Joe laughed as the car stopped and he stepped out of the vehicle. He studied the house for a moment, then got back in the car and drove right up to the front porch. The automobile windows were open, and they could feel their bodies warm in the sunshine that came splashing through the trees.

It's empty, Joe said, spitting tobacco juice on the ground. Every Sunday afternoon he liked to chew.

How you know that, honey?

Those vines, he said, pointing. See how they're growing over the front door and windows? No one has been in or out of that house at least since last winter.

How long's it been empty then?

Less than a year is my guess, as the roof is in pretty good shape. Want to get out and take a look?

What if there's a man inside waiting to kill us? Carol asked, winking at Rusty and Alfredia.

She meant it as a joke, but her husband hardened at the remark.

You think I'd let that happen, Carol?

She hadn't meant to upset him but could see the muscles in his jaw clenching.

Stay here with the kids, he told her.

Carol sighed. Joe! But it was how he got if she mentioned anything that might bring violence into the family.

They watched as he crept up to a window and cupped his hands on the glass.

Carol played with the tips of her white gloves. Can we come out now? Is it safe, General?

Then Alfredia shouted, Daddy! When he turned it was the Joe they knew.

When they had walked around the property a few times, Joe told the children to go explore—but to stay away from anything that could be a well.

With his legs straight, Rusty had tried attending school. Joe talked the elementary school into starting the seventeen-year-old in the six-year-old class. But by the middle of second grade, the teachers said there was nothing more they could do for him. He did enjoy being with the children, who made him chase them around pretending to be a monster. The school board psychiatrist believed Rusty was destined to always be six years old. Carol wept when they said he would need taking care of his whole life.

Joe was normally quiet when the doctors told them things, but this time he spoke up. He might have the mind of a six-year-old child, Doc…but he's the cleverest one you'd ever meet, I swear.

I believe it, said the doctor. He'll become capable of many wonderful things, but living alone or having relationships with women will not be one of them.

In the car on the way home from the meeting, Joe had stroked his wife's arm.

He'll always be innocent, Carol, look at it that way.

I know, but what if something happens to us?

We should think about that, he said gravely. Maybe I can ask Henry at work if he'd take our kids in. He is my best friend, after all.

But Henry is colored, Joe.

Her husband turned to look at her.

I don't mean that, Joe. But you and Henry can't even work in the same part of the plant. It's not allowed. By law.

Well goddamn the law to hell, he said, and it was the only time in her life that Carol heard him curse.

There were flowers growing wild all around the abandoned house, and daffodils dotted the front yard like yellow bells. They reminded Carol of a patch of ground where her mother used to take her. That was one of her strongest memories. Sometimes her mother took a yellow tablecloth and put it down for them to sit on.

So many beautiful trees. It's peaceful out here, ain't it Joe?

It should be, we're about twenty miles from the nearest place to buy eggs or milk.

But if we had a cow and some chickens, we could make our own, don't you think?

Well, the old place needs work, but the roof is good. That's one thing. And the air is nice...for whistlin', I mean. He put his lips together and whittled out a tune. A second later, they heard the same song from not too far away, just a bit slower and off-key.

That boy looks up to you so much, Joe.

He does?

When you're sore at him, it's like his whole world is crashing down.

Well, then, it's lucky I'm not sore at him much.

Carol reached out and put her palm against a tree.

Seeing you and Rusty makes me realize what I never had.

Because you're a woman?

No, Joe, because I never had a good daddy like you.

Joe came and put his arm around Carol's neck. I loved you the first time I heard your voice through an open window.

Was I singing, Joe?

No, you were yelling at Rusty.

Carol batted his arm and they kept walking. Who do you think lived in the house? she asked.

Old timers is my guess.

I wonder if it was a happy home...or mean one.

Joe surveyed the house. Happy I reckon. Just a feeling I get.

They walked around the property several more times, following the thread of their children's voices.

A few months later, Joe came home very late one night. Rusty and Alfredia had eaten, bathed, and were watching a small television in the sitting room. Joe ate his supper in silence. Then, with the children in bed, he took Carol out to the porch. It was cool and they could hear insects in the trees, scratching and whistling in the last few weeks of their lives.

I need to tell you something.

Oh God, what is it?

Well...I don't know how to say this exactly.

Just say it, please. Whatever it is.

Carol...I lost my job.

Okay, that's fine. I thought it was gonna be something worse.

What could be worse?

Well, my daddy could've come by, or Harold shot himself, or you fell in love with a gal in the lunchroom, or Sally and Pops was sick...

Joe grinned and touched his hair. Well, that's fine then, I thought you were gonna be upset.

I am upset, in a way. I just don't understand how you could have lost your job when you're a supervisor.

It didn't make no difference.

When did this happen?

Last week.

Last week! And you didn't say nothing to me? Joseph! I'm your wife. In sickness and in health, remember?

Joe looked across the street, up into a bright room where Harold and Marjorie had shared what remained of their lives together. A new family lived there now.

It's just that I've never been fired before, Carol. Guess I'm ashamed is what you might say.

Well, you don't have to be ashamed with me. I'm your wife, Joe, and I'd love you no matter what. You should have told me.

I didn't want you to worry is all. I wanted to tell you when I had a plan.

You gonna work at that new lumberyard where Henry went?

I already tried that. It ain't gonna happen.

Why?

It's complicated, Carol. I even spent a couple of days going over to the next county, but there's hardly anything…what with people flooding in from the country, sick of mining.

Did you spill paint on the boss's shoes or something? You're a supervisor, Joe. They can't just fire you. What happened?

Joe looked at his old boots, still splattered with paint from his last day. I lost my temper.

But that's not like you.

I should've walked off, like I always done.

Like you always done? Was it about Henry gettin' fired last month?

Carol waited for him to speak, but all he did was swallow, as though forcing the words deeper into his body.

You don't have to tell me what happened…I can probably figure it out.

They baited me, Carol, I just know it. The whole thing was planned.

The police come?

Bossman said if I left with no trouble and never come back, they would forget the whole thing.

You been working there a long time, Joe.

I know. Since I left the service.

It don't count for anything that you're a war hero?

Not to men like this. Makes it worse actually.

I can't believe you didn't tell me any of this when it happened.

I didn't want you to think I was like your daddy.

Carol's wet cheeks caught light from a passing car.

Don't cry, sweetheart, I didn't get to the good part yet. That I found a job. It's a part of the plan I wanted to tell you about.

But Carol couldn't stop herself, as though the tears had been there a long time, just waiting for the right time to be shed.

I'm going to mix chemicals on a tobacco farm and help around the place.

Carol blew her nose into a small kerchief from her pocket and imagined her husband balanced over giant vats of smoke and bubbling. But isn't that dangerous?

Well, so long as I don't drink the stuff. I'm also gonna tend hogs and get the cows milked. It's a big old place. Kind of like where Pops worked as a carpenter.

Well, where is it?

You ain't gonna believe this next part…it's owned by the people my daddy stole the chicken from.

Carol stopped crying and looked at her husband.

Say that again?

When I came home from the war and got settled here in town with my woodworking tools, this house was a ruin then, did you know that?

Yes, you told me. But I want to know about this farm.

Hold on, sweetheart, this bit is important.

But just get to the point, Joe, please…

I will, I will…now, when I started working at the paint factory, I got me some money and I went and bought a bunch of chickens, 'cause that one stolen chicken would've had babies over the years and—

Joe!

Okay, okay…well. I took 'em over to the farm in a truck I borrowed. The old man my father had taken the bird from was dead. He'd passed in thirty-one, during the Depression, and it was his daughter and her husband running the place. They wouldn't take the chickens at first, but I insisted. I wanted to right my first daddy's wrong…for my own mind…so his soul could rest. Anyway, they made me stay for dinner and told me something that made me very happy. Do you know what it was?

No, but I have a feeling you're gonna tell me.

That their daddy told the sheriff that he didn't care about no single bird, but the sheriff was running for a political office and wanted to get as many people in jail as he could so folks would vote for him. When I heard that, I cried with anger and relief both. I told them that he never had no mean intentions and they believed me.

Well is it far from here? The farm? We gonna have to move?

Here's the other reason why I waited so long to tell you I was fired.

Oh no, what?

Remember that house we saw many Sundays past, the old place that was empty? When we chased the kids around the house a hun'ed times?

The house with the yellow flowers? And the beautiful trees?

We bought it. It's only seven miles from Pearl and Victor's farm, so I'll be home for lunch ever'day if that suits you.

Carol threw her arms around her husband's neck.

Hold on now, I'll be making much less money, I should tell you that…but we can sell the TV and the car—get an old truck if you don't mind.

I don't care about any of that, Joe.

Our time in this house is about up anyway, since I put the back porch on.

Carol looked down the street at the dark row of houses already receding.

They would tell Rusty and Alfredia in the morning.

Then start packing things into boxes.

Joe would take the car back to the dealership with its snapping flags and salesmen with perfect teeth. He would explain that he could no longer make the payments and hand over the keys.

Joe and Carol sat beside each other on the porch until the early hours of the morning, whispering details they remembered about the house, or ideas that came into their heads about how to decorate or where to put things so it would feel like theirs.

And although she was no longer afraid of being made to go back, Carol realized that her father would never find them in this new place. Not with Joe's surname on the mailbox and away from any neighbors who knew anything about her. Her nightly dreams then would be curious, harmless stories made up from scraps of feeling, the heart's leftovers.

Carol imagined her daddy, twisted with anger, tramping through the empty rooms of their soon-to-be old house where there was nothing but cool darkness and memories he could not open. She could hear his boots on the stairs, his hard-wheezing breath, and the low growl of his words as he searched for the only person alive who had once, long ago, been willing to love him.

EDDIE

2007

WITH HOURS TO spare, Samuel stopped for a large breakfast. When his plate arrived, both eggs had torn over the grated pota-toes, making them glisten. Everything tasted salty and hot. The diner was just off the highway, a small red house with a tall sign that lit up at night, not far from Eddyville and close to the prison. Samuel ate quietly, shuffling his knife and fork with care. There was nobody else in the restaurant, but the silence seemed precious, like a lake so undisturbed that it becomes invisible.

After eating, Samuel paid the tab, then went outside and smoked a cigarette with one foot up on a tire. It was time, and so he drove the three miles to the parking lot as the prison's recorded phone instructions had directed. In a bag on the passenger seat were a few things Eddie—in a letter—had asked Samuel to pick up. They included a pair of sunglasses and a wig of long blond hair, which would have been amusing to Samuel when they were young but now seemed part of something hopeless and tiring.

When Samuel saw the prison building rise up in the distance, he felt ripples of fear. It was a vast stone fortress encircled with barbed wire. In the parking lot were two or three other cars: people wanting to be let inside for visits, or perhaps, like him, waiting for someone they knew to come out.

A minivan parked nearest to the gate was full of balloons, and their bright heads pressed against the glass. Two women, about twenty years apart, were fussing with a homemade sign that said WELCOME HOME GRANDPA.

That made Samuel think of his own grandfather, whose body they had committed to earth almost five years before. Joe had died on his wedding anniversary, but for the men carving his stone, not even Carol knew his birth year, which differed on all his documents. Those who had known him as a boy were not only dead but forgotten—except in name. Samuel had been given his grandfather's war medals, and he remembered the feeling of them in his hand at the service, like sharp, impenetrable flowers.

He lit a cigarette and opened his window to release the curling smoke. The cool smell of morning brought back another memory, the time when he and Eddie were boys, just a few years older than Linda, trudging up the hill to middle school, sharing a biscuit, telling each other stories—not of things they had done but things they would commit to as men. They had been happy because anything was possible, as though the future were something laid out, like a feast, just waiting for them to arrive.

After half an hour, other cars began to arrive, and soon people made their way toward the prison entrance. Some of the visitors were children and they ran ahead, skipping and shouting things.

The penitentiary was famous in Kentucky because it was more than a hundred years old and built to resemble an English castle. When people began to thread the turnstiles, Samuel noticed a familiar figure appear from a door on the other side of the tall fence. He was walking toward the gate where people were going in. He had on a large khaki shirt, khaki pants, and white sneakers—all prison issue. His hair was very short, and he was thin in a way that made him appear unwell.

Samuel went around to the front of the car as he got closer, then put his arms out. But Eddie just stood before him, grinning.

Once inside the vehicle and driving away, they talked excitedly, mostly about things on the surface of the present, such as the weather or the price of cigarettes or flat-screen televisions—as if no time had passed, except it had been ten years.

After a few miles, Eddie began rooting in the bag for the blond wig and sunglasses.

Something you need to tell me, Eddie?

There's a lot I need to tell you. Many years' worth. And not all of it good. But you'll see why I need this, Samuel...very shortly.

Let me guess. You're gonna rob a bank as Pamela Anderson?

The old Eddie would have laughed at that, but this new person kept his eyes fixed on the bag as though guarding its purpose. There's one more favor I have to ask of you, Samuel. It's okay if you don't want to do it...but I'm gonna ask.

I ain't making out with you in that wig, Samuel blurted out, with almost immediate regret.

Take me to Louisville.

Louisville? I thought you were gonna stay with me.

I am, but there's something I've gotta do first. It won't take long, I promise, and it can't wait.

Samuel looked at the wig in Eddie's hands. In his mind, he could hear Alfredia's voice telling him not to go. Can you at least tell me why?

Not yet, no.

Samuel tapped his fingers on the steering wheel. Is it against the law?

It might be.

Jesus, Eddie, you just got out.

Well I ain't gonna kill anyone else, if that's what you're worried about.

Samuel nodded, unnerved not by the mystery of his intention, but by this new tone in his friend's voice. They didn't speak for a while. Samuel hoped the tension would come apart with no words to hold it in place, but it was like a knot they would have to untie.

Finally they saw the sign to Louisville. Neither of them spoke, but Eddie reached into the bag and touched the things there. Three miles later, with the turnoff coming up, Samuel checked his mirror, then swung the car across two empty lanes toward the exit ramp.

I know I'm going to regret this, but what part of Louisville are we going to?

When Eddie didn't answer Samuel turned and saw the reply in his eyes and on the surface of his cheeks.

I thought you said she had a restraining order.

Jean filed a restraining order, but my daughter is old enough now to make her own decisions. I've been in jail most of her life, Samuel. She don't even know what I look like.

I know, buddy, I understand. I'm a father myself. But maybe I could email her for you first? Don't you want to enjoy freedom just a little bit?

You can drop me at the city limits if you want. I won't mind. I can walk. Ain't no law against walking around. All I want is a glimpse of her, Samuel. That's all…just five seconds to see how she's grown.

Samuel kept driving, the way his father did sometimes when he was afraid to speak his mind.

The prison was now many miles behind them.

When Eddie closed his eyes and tilted with sleep, Samuel pictured him back in the cell. A home that was not a home. A place of darkness and artificial light. Lying still in the early hours of some morning going over his plan—going over this very moment—casting into the future with the hope of reeling in some detail that would not be washed away by sleep.

When an hour had passed, Eddie woke up and reached for the box of cigarettes.

Kind of weird you ended up in a place called Eddyville, Samuel said, passing him a lighter.

I know...they teased me about it inside. Said there wouldn't be a prison if not for me.

Did you make any friends?

Duane.

What was he in for?

Murder. Same as me...but he got four years left.

I've thought about you ever' day since they locked you up, Eddie. Wonderin' what they was giving you to eat, if you got to go outside and see the day, you know, breathe it in...

I went further than that, actually, to all the places I ever saw, and all the folks that have been part of my life. In prison, Samuel, a man is dead to the world. So I wandered about my own life like a spirit, going down all the paths that led me to that bit of mattress in my cell. Eventually I come to the realization that I was meant to be in jail.

Shut up, Eddie.

He laughed. I'm serious. There weren't no other choice because in order to survive and to protect others, I have always had to break the law.

Samuel tried to imagine Eddie in his cell, diving into the rooms of his past, holding his breath for as long as he could sustain the memory. Then surfacing to the tide of his cellmate's breath, the faint aroma of bleach from the gleaming metal of the toilet bowl, muffled sounds from another part of the prison.

I appreciated your letters, Samuel. I really did. I would read one sentence a day so that each would last a couple of weeks.

If I'd known that...I would've written more.

Eddie turned away, to the window where he was faintly sketched. Samuel thought he might be crying again, so he kept his eyes on a grain silo up ahead in the distance.

But then Eddie asked about Heather and their daughter, Linda.

We almost got a divorce a few years ago. I was too focused on the business, and she felt like she was losing herself, having moved away from her childhood home and given up waitressin' at Booth's after we were married.

So what happened?

We saw a therapist.

I believe in that, Samuel. We had one in the prison. I saw him once or twice myself.

Well, we both spoke our minds in her office, and things got worse, but then Heather started going to school and we weren't together every second of the day. Things got really good then, and they've been fine ever since.

You're about the same as I remember, Samuel. I love it.

Thanks, buddy.

I suppose you want to hear about the case. What really happened.

Samuel took a deep breath. He only knew what he'd read in the newspaper and seen on the television. The exact details were something he expected to hear someday, directly from Eddie.

If you want to talk about it, sure.

Well, I don't regret what I done, but I'm sorry it had to be that way. I truly am.

I figured you wouldn't regret anything because you're so bullheaded.

Tell me you wouldn't have done the same thing, Samuel, to protect Heather and Linda?

To be honest, I don't know if I would have had the nerve to go through with it. But there's stuff I don't know, right?

Eddie nodded. Oh hell yeah, and that's why in my heart I know I done right.

You didn't mention that to the judge though?

Eddie drew another cigarette from the open box on the dashboard. Actually, I told everyone straight up from the get-go. And she was okay in the end. Downgraded the charge from murder to first-degree manslaughter durin' the plea deal, so at least I got a sentence I could see the end of.

I didn't know that.

The lawyer was good too…he told the jury I didn't mean to kill the man…that I was just trying to protect my girls from a violent criminal, which was true, and that things got out of control.

Samuel nodded. That's what my folks believe, and what I told Heather.

Eddie ran his fingers along the grained vinyl dashboard. He pulled hard on the cigarette and held in the smoke.

But you know, between us, I meant to kill him from the outset. Jesus, Eddie.

Samuel reached into a cooler on the back seat. He slipped out a can, then handed it to his childhood friend. After several deep gulps, Eddie went on with the story.

He was dealing meth, I bet you didn't read that in the papers. But the judge knew, my lawyer made sure of it. He had a lab and everything.

And you were worried he was gonna get Jean involved, is that it?

Eddie was silent, but Samuel could see the muscles and tendons working in his jaw as though he were gnashing his teeth.

No, that wasn't what done it. It was something else.

Samuel pulled in behind a tractor-trailer and set the cruise control so he could concentrate on the conversation.

His temper? I read that he had been charged with felony assault even before he took up with Jean.

That's all true, but it was the way he looked at my daughter. That's what started it. I was in the habit of seeing Hayley on Sundays and giving Jean some of the money from the poker winnings you give me. He was usually out, but one time he was getting high on the porch when I brought Hayley back from Peter Pan Pizza, I saw his eyes and they were crawling all over her. When I got home to Kentucky, I was so mad I took a hammer and broke up the sink in my bathroom. Then Jean called me crying a couple of weeks later. Said there were marks on Hayley's body. Black and blue marks on her arms like she got shaked. And a cigarette burn. Jean said she was too scared to tell the police. When I heard that, Samuel, I knew I was gonna spend part of my life in the penitentiary.

You should have come to me, Eddie. My dad would have helped us figure something out.

Yeah, it could have worked that way, you're right. I didn't think it through. And what if he'd got to me first? Where would Jean and Hayley be then if I was killed?

So, you went over there...

I thought it was gonna feel good, to kill somebody like that... but for a time after I felt sick, not in a way where I was sorry...just sick, physically sick, like throwing up. Then after I got caught, I spent years angry at him for making me do it. Then my cellmate at the time got me to thinking 'bout what makes a person who they are. And I wanted to know how he became like that.

I didn't know about the marks on Hayley's body. We all thought you were just jealous.

There was some of that...but what I done was for them, not for me.

You always were loyal, Eddie. Even when people let you down.

Yeah, I'm like a dumbass dog, I guess.

I wouldn't say that...

Really? Thanks, Samuel.

Because you can train a dog...

Jesus, you're still an asshole.

I love you too.

But you know, I just hope she doesn't hate me, is all.

Who?

Hayley. I hope she doesn't think I ruined her life. I just want to see her. Make sure she's okay. It's all I could think about in the pen...*sometimes too hot the eye of heaven shines.*

What's that?

Professor Louie from the local college came to teach us in the prison. First we'd watch a movie. Then we'd read a few pages photocopied from the real book. Most guys did it for the free potato chips and soda, but I kinda liked it. Whenever one of us asked a question, it made the teacher so happy, even if it was stupid. *Hamlet* and *Prometheus* were my favorite stories because I could relate to their situations. Prometheus suffered because he trusted people who betrayed him, and Hamlet was fucked up

233

because of his mother and her new boyfriend. Sound familiar? Ever'thing moves in cycles, is what we was taught, not just in books but in life too. I believe I broke that cycle for Hayley by what I done. When I told the professor that, he didn't know what to say. But Hamlet killed people, I told him, *bad* people, and he's the hero of the book, so go figure.

I'm just glad you're out of there, Eddie.

If only I hadn't got laid off from the lumberyard all them years ago. I think Jean would have left me eventually, but with a job I mighta' got custody of Hayley. How far we from Louisville now?

Do you even know where Hayley lives?

Duane found out for me.

Your friend in the prison?

His girl Starr got the address.

At the city limits they stopped at a drive-through restaurant and bought hamburgers to eat in the car. Eddie made a point of putting his wig on the backseat so as not to get barbecue sauce on it.

So how's Heather doing in college?

She's applying to graduate school now.

What's that about? Teacher's college?

No, it's where you go to become a doctor. Heather wants to work with old people who are dying.

That's a real job?

Sure is.

There's so much about the world I just don't know, Samuel.

They finished their meals and put the bags of wrappers and sauce containers on the floor of the back seat.

So, are we gonna do this, Samuel?

It's prob'ly gonna get us in trouble, you know that?

It'll be worth it.

No it won't, but show me the address.

Eddie had it memorized. The street was about twenty minutes across the city, through downtown and a mile or two on the highway.

Eddie pulled the wig over his crew cut and slid the sunglasses on. Then he flipped down his visor to look at himself in the mirror.

We're just a couple who pulled over to talk about our relationship, Eddie said. That's the story.

There's no way we're a couple.

We have to be, in case a cop shows up, we can pretend to be making out.

Jesus, Eddie, no way.

Do it for Hayley.

It's not that...

What then?

I never did like blondes.

Eddie flipped up the visor. Still the joker.

Once on the street, Samuel followed numbers on the mailboxes. The street was shaped like a horseshoe, and the houses were small, pushed together like teeth crammed into a mouth. Some had porches with tiny yards, while others had been paved over to park old cars and motorcycles in varying states of decay.

There it is, Eddie, that green house up ahead.

Jesus, there's someone outside, stop the car, Samuel.

I can't stop in the middle of the street, we'll be seen.

Eddie leaned over onto Samuel, straining to see as they crawled past a teenage girl sitting on a porch swing with her feet up on the railing. She had spiky hair and was wearing a long-sleeve Marilyn Manson shirt.

Jesus Christ, that's her! Eddie screamed, grabbing the wheel and jerking the car into an empty spot just ahead of the little house. Eddie jumped into the back seat to get a closer look. Eddie's daughter was tall and lean, with a high forehead like her father. She was drawing on her arm with a marker.

The last time I held her in my arms, she was going on five. Now she's sixteen.

That's crazy, Eddie. Let's search for her on social media when we get back to the house. Linda can help. Ready to go?

But we just got here.

I'm worried we'll be seen—

That's what the wig is for, Samuel. How do I open the window back here, it's too tinted.

Don't open that window, Eddie. You jumpin' around is bad enough.

Oh she's amazing. Goddamn it! I wonder if Jean is inside. Probably watching TV. She loved TV. *Friends*. Is that still on?

Just then, Eddie's teenage daughter got up and walked out to the sidewalk. She had some small bills in her hand and was counting them as she crossed the street.

Jesus of Nazareth, she's coming this way! Eddie said, leaping back into the front seat so quickly his wig snagged and was tugged off. She's gonna walk right past the car, Samuel.

Then get down for Christsakes!

But Eddie was pushing something on the door.

Stop it, Eddie! Put the window up!

Oh my God, look at her sneakers! They're black Converse!

The girl was staring at the money in her hands as though she intended to buy something from a convenience store on the corner.

Hey, girl! Eddie shouted as she passed.

Burning with shame, Samuel crouched as low as he could in the seat. Eddie's daughter stopped and turned, but after a moment just kept walking. Eddie opened the window a few more inches.

Nice shoes, goth girl!

She spun sharply around this time. Get outta here, losers!

But you're cool! Eddie shouted from his crouched position on the floor.

Samuel was now in a full panic. He started the engine, but Eddie reached over and flipped the key.

The girl stood her ground on the sidewalk. You better get outta here. My daddy kills assholes like you.

Samuel turned the ignition key again and threw the shifter in drive. As he peeled away, nudging a parked car, Eddie jumped back into the rear seat and pressed his face against the glass. When they got to a red light at the end of the block, Eddie scrambled back up front. Samuel turned to curse out his friend, but was startled by an expression he had seen only once before, on the riverboat in Indiana, moments after winning the big game, when he noticed his father watching him.

ALFREDIA

1958

WHEN ALFREDIA TURNED seven, she got a new pair of shoes and couldn't stop sniffing the leather. Carol baked a cake with the years written in red. Rusty whistled the song instead of singing it, then watched as Alfredia blew out seven small fires in two breaths.

That's it, said Joe, one puff for each lung. Now you get two wishes.

They sat on the porch and ate slices of cake with milk poured on to soften it. Alfredia was thinking about her wishes. One of them was to start school. That way she'd be able to show off her new shoes. She was already a year late in going. In late spring her parents had received a letter from the county, explaining that formal schooling begins no later than six, and that Alfredia had been automatically enrolled for the fall at such and such elementary school in town. And so Carol had spent a good part of that summer sewing so that Alfredia would have a different dress to wear every day, in a style that was modern and not frilly. Joe had been bringing empty feed sacks home from the farm. Carol had learned to trace out a pattern, then cut and sew the pieces to make dresses. The cattle feed companies had learned what mothers were doing decades ago and begun printing patterns on the sackcloth. Mostly it was flowers, but sometimes there were rabbits or stars or cherries or buckets of green apples.

Alfredia loved all the clothes her momma made and couldn't wait to show them off at school. With her feed-sack dresses and her birthday shoes, she was ready to meet her classmates.

There were many other things that made Alfredia feel proud. She could milk any cow. She had been knocked down by a mama goat and gotten back up. Without crying. She could make soap from pig fat. And she'd once caught a chicken with her bare hands—though when her daddy cut its neck she wept bitterly.

Alfredia wondered if other children's parents owned such a pretty house as theirs. Or did some of them come from the shacks they passed on the way to town. She knew she was the first in her family to be born in a hospital and to have lived in a house in the center of town with people and cars going past all day and all night. It had been a brick house, with a staircase that went on forever and ever. Rusty told her there was a big table they used to play under, but Alfredia couldn't remember that.

For Alfredia's seventh birthday, Rusty let her sit on his bed in the tiny room he occupied at the back of the house. It was more a large closet than a room, but he loved it. On every surface there was something red with the name Coca-Cola written on it. He had been collecting bottles, cans, signs, and paper advertisements since he could remember. Anything branded that he found—even a piece of torn paper, came home in his pocket and went up the next day.

At the end of summer, a week before school started, Joe drove into town to buy his daughter notebooks and pencils for her first day. Alfredia had to stay home with her mother and try on dresses, but Rusty was allowed to ride along with his dad.

After choosing things from a list, they had lunch on chrome, vinyl-topped stools at Druthers', the biggest, newest pharmacy in the county. Rusty had his own way of eating egg salad, which made people stare at them. But he didn't mind that, for above his head was an advertisement with the two most important words in the world.

C'mon, said Joe. Eat your sandwich, Rusty...or we'll be here all day.

Then a man wearing a white hat and apron came over to them. I'm Dale Druthers, he said. The waitress is on her break so I came to ask if you need anything else.

Joe smiled and shook his head.

The man focused on Rusty. Did you enjoy your sandwich?

It was okay, Rusty said, not looking up from his plate. Say, mister...can I keep this pop once I finished?

The man looked at the glass soda bottle in Rusty's hand.

Well, sure...if you want.

Joe took some coins from the pocket of his overalls. Appreciate that, he said. My son collects anything with Coca-Cola printed on it. Anything at all.

Well that's neat, said the man. Then he paused, and a look of intense fear took over his face.

You okay? Joe asked.

Your voice, said the man, swallowing. Do I know you?

I don't think so. But we sure enjoyed our lunch, mister.

You're not on the radio?

The radio? No, sir, I'm not. Just plain old Joe, that's me.

The man put his palms and elbows on the counter and sank down. I could have sworn we've met. Your voice...I can't place it, but—

I ain't even from these parts, Joe admitted. You must have me confused with somebody else.

Probably right, the man said, straightening himself up with a long sigh. He counted the coins Joe had put down with his eyes, then slid them into his palm. I'll be right back with your change, big guy.

Joe thanked him again for letting Rusty keep the pop bottle.

The man was gone for some time. When he came back, he was no longer wearing his apron or paper hat. He looked solemn, as though he was about to deliver some bad news. Then he set all the money Joe had given him back on the counter.

I do know you, the man said. And I know where from. Your money is no good here.

Joe stood quickly, towering over the manager by almost a foot. But when he spoke, his voice was soft and slightly shaken. I sure hope we ain't done nothing to offend anyone.

Rusty was oblivious to any tension, cradling the Coca-Cola bottle in his arms like an infant.

Rusty, I want you to give the bottle back…

No, no… the man said. It's not the bottle. It's nothing like that. Would you mind sitting down for a second?

The other people at the lunch counter had stopped talking and were chewing their food in silence. Joe sat back down. The man could not take his eyes off him.

Does the name Leyte mean anything to you?

Joe felt his chest tighten and everything around him, the shelves of medicine, the cabinets of pie, even light tumbling from high windows, seemed to go out of focus, as though reality was stretching or coming apart entirely.

Well, said Joe, catching his breath. I never thought I'd hear that name again.

So, you remember it then?

Yes, Joe said, his large hands shaking. But…if you'll excuse me, we have to get on…

I knew it was you, said the man, throwing his hands over Joe's hands to prevent him from leaving. Now shoppers had stopped to see what Dr. Druthers was doing.

I'm sorry, said Joe, but I don' know you from Adam.

That's because when we met I couldn't speak and I couldn't open my eyes neither. My face would have been all blood and sand. But I knew it was you when I heard your voice.

Joe looked at Rusty, who was half sitting and half standing, still clutching the Coca-Cola bottle.

I went down on the beach, the man said, taking a napkin to wipe his eyes. I don't know how long I was lying there, but when I couldn't feel pain anymore, I knew as a medic, and I made my peace with God...then you come along and start jabbering on about chickens and feed and God knows what. And when there was nothing left to say, in the middle of a battle, with bullets flying ever'which way—you started whistlin'.

When it was all over, in those first months off the ship and home again, Joe did a lot of crying himself. In his bed, in the bath, on the floor in a heap—even as he worked fixing up the old house. It was sometimes hard to focus on the nail he was putting in. The sound of birds in trees, the slap of a paintbrush, dogs barking down the street, a sudden breath of afternoon light through the side window. Anything was liable to set him off. Everyone he thought was dead had come back and was living in the house with him. Not only the men he knew, but the men he'd brought down.

The only thing that kept them at arm's length was whistling.

They would follow him up the hill to work, stare from inside the bubbles of paint, wander through every cavern of his sleep. But whistling was like a wall they couldn't see over or get past. Sometimes Joe woke in the middle of the night and could feel them breathing on him, in the darkness. That was when he'd had to whistle the loudest.

The awkward silence was broken when a girl skipped through the door from the kitchen.

This is my child, the man said. Hazel Druthers. He steadied his young daughter by cupping both of her shoulders, but she ducked under and rushed back through the kitchen door.

Sometimes at night, Dale said, I still hear you talking to me, Joe...still...to this day. Ain't that something?

Sure it ain't your wife reminding you to take out the garbage?

He had meant it as a joke, but Dale didn't laugh. No, it's your voice I hear, Joe, when I'm lying in my bed next to my wife in some dream, back on the beach, more afraid than I ever thought possible.

. . .

At dusk, they ate sandwiches on the porch and Joe told Carol and Alfredia the whole story. Around them insects were winding up, preparing themselves for the coming darkness.

Before we left, he wanted to know if there was anything he could do for us. I said no, we was fine, but he insisted. Told me to come home and talk to you about it.

But there is something he can do for us...don't you see? Carol said, motioning with her napkin toward Rusty. Let's talk later when everyone's in bed.

Do you mean me? Alfredia said.

No, Carol whispered. I mean your brother. Now go and check all your school things are in order, give your daddy and I some peace.

When the first day finally came, Alfredia woke at dawn and tried on all the various things her mother had made. With every feed-sack dress arranged on her bed, Alfredia chose the one with daisies. It would match her shoes, she thought, *perfectly*.

Her older brother was going to ride with her on the school bus to town.

At Carol's suggestion, Joe had returned to see Dale at the pharmacy and asked him to give Rusty a job.

You can pay him in Coca-Cola if you want to, Joe had said, but he's twenty-three years old, and his mother and I think it'll do him good to be out of the house. He can ride the bus each day with his sister if the school board allows it.

Okay, Dale said. That's fine. Now, he's special, your boy, ain't he?

Yes, he is. I know he looks mean when you see him from a distance, but he's a gentle creature with the mind of a first grader. Trust me when I tell you he wouldn't hurt a fly.

. . .

When her first day of school was over, Alfredia hurried nervously to the drugstore where she found Rusty sitting on a crate outside the back door. He was still wearing his paper hat and white apron.

You have to come on the bus, she said. Like Momma told us. Did you enjoy your first day of working, Rusty?

No.

You gonna come back tomorrow?

I have to if I want free Coca-Cola.

Well I wish we could switch places, Alfredia sighed.

Don't you like school?

Lunch was okay, I guess.

What did they feed you?

Meatloaf. But if I could stay home tomorrow, I would.

Me too, said Rusty, as his sister pulled him up off the crate.

They didn't talk on the ride home. It was dusty and loud with the diesel engine. Other children were leaning over the seats, shouting things at each other. On the floor, someone had dropped an uneaten bologna sandwich and it had been trampled.

Joe and Carol were waiting at the top of their dirt driveway when the bus came.

That's an awful sour look on your face, Carol said as Alfredia came down the bus steps holding the satchel with all her new school things.

Joe took the bag and ruffled her hair. Your momma and I can't wait to hear what happened. You hungry?

But Alfredia just stood there, fixed to the spot. When the bus was far away she opened her mouth.

I had no idea we were poor!

Carol looked at her husband. What does she mean by that?

Joe scratched his head.

Alfredia was tired from the journey. Her throat was dry and her legs were itchy under the dress. For your information, she scowled, I was the only person in my class wearing a dress made from a cattle-feed sack!

Well, what was they wearing? asked Carol.

Woolworth's.

What's that? asked Joe.

Carol folded her arms. Store-bought clothes.

Joe picked Alfredia up and put her on his shoulders. But you don't feel poor, do you? I mean, we always have enough to eat, wood to burn, and a house that's owned outright.

No, but we *are* poor, Daddy, that's clear to me now. Like—we use soap made from pig fat. No one has done that for a hun'ed years.

So we're poor... Joe said, mulling it over.

We ain't poor, Carol snapped. We're jus' country is all.

Joe's face brightened. That's exactly what we are, just like the music Rusty plays on his radio, he said, looking around for his son, who was still sitting on the bus, halfway to the next stop.

BESSIE & MARTHA

2008

I'M SURPRISED YOU didn't want to keep it, Heather said. With only the floor rusted out.

They were at the kitchen table, Samuel's wife standing behind their daughter as she bent over the last of her summer homework. Books were spread out on the yellow tablecloth. They were from the school library and had been touched by many hands over the years.

The engine was bad too, Samuel told his wife. Completely seized up. I'm happy it's gone.

But it was your great-granddaddy's truck.

I know, but there was something about it...

Like what?

I don't know. It gave me the creeps. Eddie felt it too.

Linda glanced up. Cool, like *Christine*.

Who? asked her father.

That's a movie she wasn't supposed to see, Heather explained, because it's rated R...but Kristy and Kelly had it playing at a Halloween sleepover. Don't ask me why.

Halloween is my favorite holiday, Linda. Did you know that?

How come?

Because it's the night I met your momma.

Linda let her face drop. I know, I know, you've told me the story a hun'ed times about you trying to buy the coffee mug for a million dollars.

Fine. But do you want to hear something really spooky?

The girls nodded.

Well, I never told y'all this before, but in the glove box of my great-granddaddy's truck, I found hun'ed-year-ol' poker dice and bullets.

That's not scary, Linda said. It's boring.

Well there was somethin' else.

A ruby? Linda asked. Then, lowering her voice, A bloody hand?

It was an address he must have written down.

Linda sighed. We need to watch a horror movie, like right now, Dad, because you have no idea.

Whose address was it? Heather wanted to know.

Beats me. It's a town a few hours along the parkway.

Is there a person's name?

No, sweetheart, just an address. I was thinking of driving there on Saturday...just for something to do.

Don't we have clients coming in?

Just a group of three for off-road driving. But Eddie can see to it. Might have been where my great-granddaddy did his card playing. A secret gambling den.

Linda looked up from her schoolwork. I'd be down for a road trip. Before school begins.

Samuel looked at Heather for the final word. It was something he had learned to do and that she appreciated.

Fine, she said. Fine, but that *was* sixty years ago, Samuel. Probably just a parking lot now. Don't be disappointed if it's not Caesars.

Maybe it's a Walmart, said Linda. If it is can I show you the Xbox I want for my twelfth birthday? Can I?

Heather pointed to the open book on the table. If you finish your homework, we might consider it.

. . .

The next day Heather packed a cooler with turkey sandwiches, bottles of water, cheese, apples, chips, ranch dip, and cans of Mountain Dew. It was a long drive, and Samuel wondered how it must have been for his great-grandfather in the old truck. The roads would surely have been dirt back then, he told his wife and daughter.

Halfway, they stopped at a fast-food restaurant to use the restroom. Samuel bought Heather a milkshake to go with their sandwiches in the cooler. Linda wanted a Happy Meal but was too embarrassed to order it. A couple of old men stared as Heather indulged her daughter's wish. But when she turned and smiled in her usual way, one of the men stuck out his tongue.

When they were back in the truck, Heather said, This town gives me the creeps.

I know, said Linda. They didn't even put a toy in my Happy Meal. Samuel turned the car off. I can go back in.

Let's just keep driving, Heather said, passing Samuel a sandwich from the cooler. We ain't but halfway yet.

When they started getting close a few hours later, the town was more built up than they had imagined, with dollar stores and car washes. But Main Street was run down, with stripped 1970s cars abandoned in alleys and whole buildings rotted and grown over with weeds. There was no Walmart, just a few specialty shops, a bank, a Goodwill, a Laundromat, and a women's dress shop on West Main Street with glittering prom dresses on 1950s mannequins.

Once they left the center of town, there were no more closed-down buildings, just a lumberyard, and a new gas station with a hot dog restaurant and locked cages of propane tanks in the front.

Then the landscape changed again, to empty paved lots and patches of field that were littered with old couches and abandoned household appliances.

I think that's it up there, Heather said. She had been reading numbers on mailboxes, though many of the buildings had already been pulled down.

It's...an office, Samuel said. After all that.

But as they got nearer, Linda noticed mesh over the windows.

I think it's a jail, Dad.

Samuel pulled into the parking lot and they saw a long sign on the roof.

Linda read it aloud, Kentucky Women's Health Center. I guess it's some kind of hospital.

My great-granddaddy died in about 1950, they reckon, so whatever was here is long gone.

Heather leaned over and whispered to her husband that it was an abortion clinic.

Then Linda spotted something else a hundred yards back in some shallow woods. It was the ruin of a large plantation house that had been fenced off with barbed wire.

That must be it, Samuel said. That must be the place where he was headed. Good job, Linda, I'd have missed that.

They drove across the concrete lot and parked against the tall fence. The once palatial home was broken down, caving in on itself, with weeds and small trees reaching what remained of the second floor.

Samuel put an arm around his wife. There would have been woods all around back then, I reckon. To think, my great-granddaddy might have stood where we are now.

But what's that other place? Linda said, pointing back to the clinic.

Never you mind, said her mother.

Samuel wanted to get out and walk along the fence, but an older man and woman had entered the parking lot and were hurrying toward them. They were carrying signs and looked to be in a panic. They approached the driver's side of the vehicle to where Samuel had his window open.

Oh Lord, Heather said. Be careful, Sam.

Howdy, folks.

It's a sin you know, said the small, thick woman. She was wearing a white knit sweater and khaki shorts that went down to her knees.

The worst sin! added the man. The worst sin there is in fact.

Samuel pointed to the ruin beyond the fence. See that big ol' place?

The man and the woman both looked.

My great-granddaddy used to live there, I reckon...

That your house? asked the man.

No sir, but it's where my ancestors might have lived.

You gonna live there? asked the woman. In the shadow of this abomination?

Samuel laughed. No, ma'am. I just wanted my family to see it.

Oh, the woman said, flushing with embarrassment, you're not here to see doctor death then?

Samuel could feel Heather's eyes on him, and Linda listening intently, trying to figure everything out.

Not today, ma'am.

His comment took the woman by surprise. Legal murder is nothing to joke about, young man.

Is that what your sign says? Samuel asked.

The woman held it up to reveal a man's head with horns and a goatee painted on.

This here's the devil, said the woman. Harold Bennett. Take a good look at public enemy number one.

Take a *good* look... said the man. That there's the evil banker who funds this freak house of murder.

But don't you worry, said the woman, her voice rattling. He'll burn in hell!

Heather touched her husband's leg. Let's go.

Well, Samuel said, nodding at the man. Good luck, I guess.

Thank you, son. And if you ever want to join us, Christ could always use more foot soldiers.

The woman took a few steps to the side and glared through the tinted window at Linda.

Hell is real! she hollered. Repent your sins, beg God to forgive your sins before it's too late.

As if on cue, the man raised the sign above his head with both hands and began pumping. It read, GOD HATES AMERICA RIGHT NOW!

Then they both pumped their signs and Samuel slowly pulled out of the lot, back onto Pine Ridge Road.

That was weird, Heather said.

Is it true? Linda asked. That God hates America right now?

That depends, sweetheart, Heather said, on what kind of God you believe in.

Well, what kind do you believe in, Momma?

You know that already sweetheart, my God doesn't hate anybody, he's just love—pure love.

Those people were crazy! Linda said. What were they so angry about?

It's complicated, Samuel said, looking for a place to pull over and get out for a cigarette. But it's your body, Linda, don't you ever forget that.

Heather poked his leg. She's too young for this.

No, I'm not! Linda snapped. I'm almost twelve.

Linda, honey, Samuel said. Please don't speak to your mother like that because it hurts her feelings, even if she don't say so.

Okay, I'm sorry, but I'm not young anymore. I wish she could see that.

I do see it, Heather said. You're a young woman.

Which is why, her father went on, you're gonna learn all about what goes on in that clinic in school. Then you can come to me and your mother with any questions.

Can't you just tell me now?

Well, are you old enough to drive?

No.

It's the same with other things.

But what did she mean about sins? Do you believe in sin?

There ain't no sin but hurtin' people on purpose, Samuel said.

Were those people in the parking lot sinners, Dad?

No, they were just assholes standing up for what they believe in. Samuel!

Linda laughed and leaned forward between the front seats. But why do people do mean things in the first place?

'Cause they're afraid of somethin' or ashamed? Samuel said. I don't really know to be honest.

Everyone gets afraid, Heather said. But God is there for us in those times. It's why we pray.

If you believe in God, Samuel said, which I don't.

So, you think all these trees and clouds, rivers and creeks, and oceans, Samuel, and stars, you think they just grew out of nothing?

That's exactly what I think.

Heather leaned over and kissed his cheek. Well then, I've got a lot of praying to do if we're all gonna be together in heaven someday.

On their way home, even with food left in the cooler, they stopped at a place to eat fried catfish. The name of the restaurant was written in big letters on the sloping roof. Instead of fish, Linda ordered side dishes of mac 'n' cheese, hushpuppies, and stewed apples.

For the last hour of driving, the road was very dark.

Linda had fallen asleep, and the ice in the cooler had melted to water. They could hear things sloshing around as they went around curves.

I'm sorry I've been so snippy lately, Heather said.

You mean that stuff about God and religion?

No, in general.

It's normal sometimes, I reckon, in a marriage. But I appreciate you saying something. I felt like I was doing something wrong. You worried about starting graduate school?

No, I love school. But it's going to be harder for me next year, Samuel. Much harder.

How come?

Because I'm pregnant.

CAROL

2010

SOME YEARS AFTER her husband's death, it became obvious to the family that Grandma Carol could no longer live alone. But she still refused to even visit her grandson in the house he had spent almost a year renovating—much less consider moving there to live in the small apartment they had originally designed for Heather's mother.

But one Sunday at Randy and Alfredia's house, Samuel asked his grandmother to look at some pictures on his iPad. There were photographs of Heather, Linda, and Little Joe. Then he swiped to reveal a porch, a front hallway, a kitchen, and a small dining room. He kept swiping until she had seen every room of the house. Grandma Carol had to admit she didn't recognize anything, and likened her old house to a hotel—nothing at all like the place she'd run away from at the age Linda was now.

I basically tore it down, Samuel said, then built it up new. I can't tell you how much lumber had to be delivered. It's really a new house, I swear. For three months it was me and five guys sawing and hammering. Every wall is new, even the staircase we had to replace.

. . .

A month later, Alfredia convinced her mother to visit Samuel, Heather, and the kids. For the first hour after she arrived, Carol sat in the car. You go on now, she told Alfredia. Let me settle myself a moment.

The family watched from the front window. Linda soon got bored and went upstairs to where Heather was giving Little Joe a bath.

She's tryin' to make peace, Randy told his son. That's what she's doin'.

It breaks my heart, Alfredia said, that after all this time, she's still torn up about whatever happened here with her daddy.

It's lucky Samuel didn't find him during the renovation, if you know what I mean...under the floorboards or something.

Alfredia gave her husband a strong look. This is where our grandchildren live, Randy. Please don't put ideas in people's heads.

I was only kidding.

I know you were, she said, her voice softening. You have a good heart.

Eventually, Grandma Carol waved her arm out the car window.

She was mostly silent as Samuel and Randy helped her move through each room with her walker. But in some places she wanted to stop and have a good look around.

It was all dark wood before, Samuel explained, but I used a light wood this time, like they do in Sweden and Norway.

Samuel even took her outside to show her the accommodation block where his clients stayed, and where Eddie Walker lived with his fiancé, Gretchen, and their rat terrier, Beale.

Eddie is our head groundskeeper, Grandma. He makes sure the Jeeps are clean and running right and that all the hammocks are slung for when we sleep outside. We're hoping to buy the adjoining forty-five acres and expand the business.

Finally she spoke. There was a barn here, Samuel. Before you made all this. Sometimes I'd sleep in that barn.

It was all rotted, Grandma. I had to pull it down.

She circled the lower part of her jaw, as though winding up to speak. I used to hide in it. It was full of green bottles and even a couple of animals at one time. But he killed 'em out of spite, or they escaped. A grin spread across her face and she gripped her grandson's arm. Just like I did, Samuel. Though I had to leave my dog behind. Did you know I had a dog? His name was Rusty.

That's your son, Grandma. Rusty is your son. He's in the house taking a nap.

No, Rusty was my dog. Oh, how I loved him.

I'm just amazed you remember the barn was here, Samuel said, because we changed the direction of the house.

I know by the trees, she told him. They're the same beautiful trees. Just older and wiser. Her entire body was shaking now.

Are you cold, Grandma? Shall we go back inside, get some hot tea? Linda and Joe Junior want to see you.

But the old woman was fixed to the spot.

Is there anything else you'd like to see? Chicken coop maybe?

Samuel, she said, we've had our differences, but I want you to know something.

What's that, Grandma?

That you've brought something back to this place that hasn't bin here for a very long time.

Our family?

No, not quite, Grandma Carol went on, holding Samuel's arm for support. I mean the thing that *makes* family, not blood, but the certainty that you're never gonna be lonesome—that all the joy and all the sufferin' we get in life is somethin' that will always be shared.

He thought of his two children and his wife, inside the house at that very moment, moving through the bright rooms, buzzing with the day's thoughts.

I mean it, Samuel, whatever badness was here, you've crushed it out of existence. If only my mother hadn't met my father and fallen for him.

But then you wouldn't have been born, Samuel said. None of us would.

Grandma Carol turned her walker back toward the house. I guess that's true. There's only one thing missing now.

What's that, Grandma?

She stopped and raised a small, quivering hand to her ear. The sound of someone whistlin'.

Linda was waiting for them on the porch steps with her great-grandmother's special cushion. She had gotten it from the car without anyone having to ask.

Then Heather appeared with a ring of coffee cake and hot tea on a tray.

Alfredia poked her husband. I taught her how to make that.

I know, I was there remember?

When Little Joe was dried off from the bath, he came outside too. He waddled over the porch planks to Grandma Carol in his diaper, holding some yellow flowers Linda had given him.

You picked those for me, Joe? Grandma Carol said, her voice so old and thin it had to stretch over any sentiment.

Fower, he said. *Fower.*

Then Linda brought over a whole can of the flowers and set them on the table near where Grandma Carol was seated.

You know who Linda reminds me of? Grandma Carol said when Alfredia came out to sit with them. My own dear mother.

Linda blushed. I do?

That's right, Grandma Carol said. My mother looked like you and walked like you and picked the same kind of yellow flowers as you from the same patch, way out in them woods. The old woman laughed gently. You might be her come back to me after all these years. Imagine that.

This is Linda, Momma, Alfredia said loudly. Your great-granddaughter, she's fifteen now.

Grandma Carol looked up irritably. I know who she is, Alfredia! I'm just saying that she's *like* my mother.

With a great effort she turned and looked out past the meadow, to the woods beyond. Joe and me used to wonder where we go once our time is up. Some people say heaven, and some say hell, but I don't think we leave. My Joe is still here. I can feel him sometimes.

I know, Alfredia said. I hear his voice telling me ever'thing will be okay. Even now, as a grown woman.

Grandma Carol closed her eyes. I guess we'll just have to wait our turn on the wheel to get him again.

After they'd eaten, the sound of greasy plates being washed in the kitchen filled the air like something precious, a sort of unintended music.

The curtain of night was falling. Fireflies winked in the dusk over fields of gold and green. The woods were still and silent. Already dark.

I love it here, Grandma, Samuel said, putting his arm around Heather. I'm so grateful to you for letting us have it.

It was your grandpa you should thank, she said. He convinced me it was a good idea. One thing I do regret, she said, is that I wasn't sweeter to him.

Oh, now, Momma, Alfredia said. You loved Daddy. He knew that. We all saw it.

I did love him for sure...not at first, but years after we were married I loved him as much as one person can love another. You just don't realize when you're young that ever'thing is going to be taken away from you, and you'll be back where you started...except you understand it for the first time.

After a long sleep in the guest bedroom, Rusty was sitting quietly on the porch drinking hot coffee with cream. He was an old man now with heart problems that couldn't be cured. He had given his Coca-Cola collection to Linda and planned to give his model cars to Little Joe when he was old enough to work on them himself.

When it was near time to leave, Grandma Carol surprised everyone by announcing to Samuel and Heather that if the offer was still on the table, she wanted to sell her house and move in with them. Linda jumped up from her chair, knocking a mug off the porch. When Grandma Carol heard it shatter, she shivered. But everyone else was laughing, even Linda, who had felt shame the moment it happened.

A few months later, Linda was helping her father fold laundry in the utility room when she saw something at the back of the cupboard. She reached in and pulled out a yellow tablecloth.

I love this, it's so pretty.

I think so too, Samuel said. I found it right here in the house. Where your grandmother's bedroom is now.

As Samuel folded towels, still hot from the dryer, Linda took the yellow tablecloth and went downstairs to Grandma Carol's part of the house, which had a sitting room, a bedroom, a toilet, and even a shower she could enter into with her walker. Linda was the only person in the house who didn't have to knock.

Carol had been sleeping in a chair. When she opened her eyes, there was a teenage girl she recognized standing over her. At first, she wondered if the vision was real or if her memories were now leaking out into the world around her.

Look what I found upstairs. It's the same color as the flowers you like.

Carol reached out to touch the yellow fabric, but Linda placed it in her lap.

It's yours now, Grandma.

No child. It's yours. It has always been yours. Don't forget it this time.

Okay, Grandma, but let's keep it here to brighten things up a bit.

It pained her to move, but Carol nodded obediently.

Later that night, she lay in the bed with her eyes wide open. She could hear a television somewhere in the house. Faint bursts of laughter. But there were other voices too.

At dawn, a low mist unfurled over the eastern part of the county. Carol sat up and blinked several times because there were figures at her window. She couldn't say who because her sight was bad, but she knew they were there and she did not feel afraid.

She closed her eyes and lay back down. The figures remained. She reached out a hand and felt the coarse yellow fabric beside her bed, like a map she could read from touch.

Then, without putting on slippers or reaching for her walker, Carol drew the yellow tablecloth around her shoulders and shuffled into the dark hall of the sleeping house.

She slipped out easily through the back door, still in her nightgown, still with the bright cloth, and went barefoot over the packed mud and wet grass until she reached the tree line where roots came up and then churned back underground, as if chaining the forest from below. Carol turned for one final look at the house. But it was not hers anymore, only a place she had visited.

Without her walker it was painful and slow. But Carol knew she would not be going back the same way she had come. When she reached the ground where the wildflowers grew, the old woman took off the cloth and spread it flat over the damp earth.

Then, she lay down and closed her eyes, waiting for the figures she had felt standing at her window to come now in some faint, flickering form and claim her. It no longer mattered if it was Momma, or Bessie, her beloved Joe, or even her father, because the end is just the end of memory. Everything else remains, waiting to be lived again.

ACKNOWLEDGEMENTS

I would like to thank my family and friends, along with my literary agent, Susanna Lea. I also wish to recognize the editorial brilliance of Joshua Bodwell, whose devotion to this book and to its characters was inexhaustible. And to Beth Blachman, who elevates copyediting to an artform. Also worthy of praise are Brooke Koven and Tammy Ackerman, whose talent for design not only enhances the reading experience but turns books into beautiful objects.

The cover is an image from the imagination of Amy Friend, a revered artist I am lucky enough to share an epoch with.

While the research for this book took place on porches, long drives, in fields, in locker rooms, and around dinner tables as family stories were shared, there was some historical research required. Therefore, I wish to recognize a book that stood out, and that I believe is a vital work of scholarship for anyone interested in the history of the United States: *When Abortion Was a Crime: Women, Medicine, and Law in the United States, 1867-1973* written by Leslie J. Reagan, published by University of California Press (1998).

The title of this book is a line from the children's work *Sylvester and the Magic Pebble* by William Steig.

Old Man Walker's advice to Carol about what she gives being returned to her and what she takes being taken from her has its roots in modern religious texts, but in this case was directly inspired by a line in the 2006 Western film *Seraphim Falls*: "That which is yours will always return to you. That which you take will always be taken from you."

A concept from one of my favorite books, *Four Quartets* by T. S. Eliot, inspired Grandma Carol's line in the final chapter: "You just don't realize when you're young that ever'thing is going to be taken away from you, and you'll be back where you started…except you understand it for the first time…"

ABOUT THE AUTHOR

Simon Van Booy is the author of ten highly acclaimed books including *The Illusion of Separateness*, a national bestseller, and *Love Begins in Winter*, which won the Frank O'Connor International Short Story Award. He is also the editor of three philosophy books and has written for the *New York Times*, the *Financial Times*, the *Guardian*, the *Times*, *Poets & Writers*, NPR, and the BBC. His books have been translated into many languages.

Raised in rural Wales and the countryside around Oxford, Van Booy was a promising rugby player who moved to Kentucky at eighteen, after being offered a scholarship to play American football at Campbellsville University. He lived in Kentucky for several years and has maintained strong links with people in the state for almost three decades.

A NOTE ON THE TYPE

Night Came with Many Stars has been set in Janson. Named for the Dutch printer and punch cutter Anton Janson (1620–1687), the typeface design was later attributed to the Transylvanian Protestant pastor and schoolmaster Miklós Kis (1650–1702). The old-style typeface has a crisp, high-contrast serif design that makes it eminently readable.

Book Design by Brooke Koven
Composition by Tammy Ackerman